SECRETS AT NIGHTFALL

AMANDA BONILLA

Secrets at Nightfall
Copyright © 2022 by Amanda Bonilla
Ebook ISBN: 9781641972178
KDP Print ISBN: 9798832161358
IS Print ISBN: 9781641972215

NYLA Publishing
121 W. 27th St., Suite 1201, NY 10001, New York.
http://www.nyliterary.com

For all of the readers. Thank you for not giving up on me—or Darian.

[1]

I'd been changed. Throughout my marrow. Right in the pit of my soul. The problem? I couldn't remember who—or what—had affected that change. I mean, I used to be a cold-hearted bitch who didn't need anyone or anything. But that was before . . . what? Xander and Raif and Asher? Before the supernatural world had opened its big arms to welcome me? Before I'd learned to quit closing myself off from everyone and everything? Before . . . *something*. And that inexplicable *something* had me up every night thinking, wondering, guessing.

"What's the matter with you? You look as though you're going to be sick."

I glanced over at Misha and took note of the Fae's curled lip and furrowed brow. Supernaturals could be so uptight. "Worried I'm going to yak all over your fancy rug?"

"Of course not." He fixed me with a stern eye. "You're not going to, are you?"

I swallowed a snort. When Xander—along with Raif and Asher—had pulled up anchor and left for their homeland to deal with Xander's traitorous SOB of a cousin, Saben and the coup he'd planned, the Shaede King had set me up with a temporary

1

handler. Misha shared the Shaede King's haughty attitude as well as Raif's stern, dry personality. I'd never openly admit it, but I liked him.

I cut him a look. True, something wasn't right with me. Hadn't been for a while. But the unease I felt wasn't going to make me lose my lunch. What I felt wasn't physical in nature. Not exactly. It was emotional. Spiritual.

I was tired of worrying about it. Tired of trying to unravel the mystery of a feeling that had no definition. Tired of attempting to fill a fathomless emotional hole that seemed to grow larger by the day. I had bigger problems to worry about than a little unease. Like, for starters, the fact that someone had put a *million-dollar* price tag on my head.

What can I say, I'm a popular girl.

I tossed a polished turquoise stone and Misha snatched it out of the air. The more I worked with him, the more I learned about the Fae. He turned the touchstone over in his palm and his lids drooped almost imperceptibly. Fae relics gave me the creeps. Their magic had a unique vibration frequency that I swore I could feel in my teeth. I didn't know what the stone could do or what it was used for and I didn't want to know. It was nothing more than proof of death for me. It equaled a paycheck, that's all.

Misha glanced my way. "I take it everything went smoothly?"

If by "smoothly," he meant, had the bastard met the pointy end of my dagger? "Yep. Easy-peasy."

"Good."

He tucked the touchstone into a black velvet pouch and crossed to the large safe at the far end of his study. He cast a tentative glance my way from over his shoulder before he dialed the combination and I rolled my eyes. So mistrustful.

"My money . . .?" I let the question hang. I swore getting a dime out of him was like pulling teeth. I sometimes wondered if Misha wasn't Fae after all. He hoarded wealth like a dragon.

"Already wired to your account." He tucked the pouch into the safe and closed it before giving the dial a spin and turning to face me.

My brows shot up and he smirked. "Really? That's so unlike you."

He gave a noncommittal shrug. "I knew you'd get the job done."

His confidence in me almost melted my Grinchy heart. "Damn straight."

I'd been working myself to the bone for the past several months. Not only to keep my mind off the gaping wound in my soul, but because I needed some serious cash. Ever since someone had blown my building to shreds nearly a year ago, I was in the market for somewhere permanent to hang my hat. Not that I didn't appreciate having a place to stay at Xander's, but the tension between Anya and me didn't seem to be letting up. In fact, she'd yet to speak a word to me since the day I'd moved in. Didn't exactly make for the healthiest living environment. For either of us. Which was why I wasn't staying there anymore.

Plus, I wanted my own space. I did better on my own. Thought clearer. And if there was anything I was desperate for right now, it was clarity.

"What else do you have?" Like a shark, I needed to keep swimming. Otherwise, I'd suffocate. The emptiness would eat me alive. "And I don't want anything that doesn't provide a decent paycheck."

Misha studied me with his inscrutable stare that reminded me so much of Raif. "I don't have anything at the moment," he said. "It seems no one needs killing."

"Bullshit." Someone always needed to be held accountable for something. It was just how the world worked. "You're holding out on me." I'd suspected for a while that Xander had given Misha very specific instructions to keep an eye on me as well as keep me out of trouble. True, trouble always had a way of finding me, but that was hardly my fault. Well, most of the time anyway.

Misha smirked. "I'm not. You know these dry spells come along. There's nothing I can do about it."

I snorted.

"You act as though you'd like for me to go out and find someone for you to stab."

I hiked a shoulder. Why not?

That trouble I suspected Misha was trying to keep me out of would inevitably find me if I had any idle time on my hands. The wily Fae had done his best to distract my attention from looking for the asshole that had put a million-dollar price on my head, as well as look for the mysterious guy who'd saved me from almost checking out for good a couple months ago when an ambitious assassin had tried to collect on that million dollar bounty. I couldn't remember a damn thing about him. Not his face, his height, his build, nothing. But I remembered his energy signature. So much power. The memory of it tingled over my skin and I shivered.

"No." Misha strode across the room toward me and pointed an accusing finger as though he'd read my mind. Hell, maybe he had. "You promised to leave it alone. At least until Raif returns."

I offered up my most dramatic eye roll. "Whatever." I *might* have let Misha think I could be patient and lay low until I had a little backup. Misha's trust issues were worse than mine and until Raif and Xander were back in Seattle, he'd warned me to keep my head down and my nose clean.

So far, so good. But my patience was running out. And now that I had nothing to occupy my time, my track record for staying out of trouble was sure to tank.

Misha pulled his cell from his pocket and dialed. I fixed him with a caustic eye. "Who are you calling?"

"My realtor."

I let out a chuff of laughter. "You're kidding, right?"

"Not even a little bit. I'll keep you occupied if it kills me." He looked me up and down. "And I suspect it just might."

Smart ass.

"All right." I needed to get a place nailed down, after all. "But I hope your realtor has the patience of a saint. I haven't worked my ass off for a year to throw down my hard-earned money on just anything."

"Oh, believe me, Darian, I know." Misha let out a long-suffering sigh. As if he'd be any less particular. The Fae's house in Capitol Hill was just as pristine, snooty, and uptight as he was.

His realtor must have answered, because Misha turned his back to me and strode from the room. Not sure what in the hell he thought he needed to discuss in private, but whatever. I took a seat on the couch that I'd spent more than a few nights camped out on and fell back against the rest. God, I was tired. I really had been putting in the overtime and it was starting to weigh on me. My eyes drifted shut and my body relaxed as sleep threatened to take me. In my mind, a pair of haunting hazel eyes stared back at me. A zing of sensation rushed through my bloodstream and I jerked upright, my eyes flying open. I took several deep breaths as I tried to calm my racing heart.

I rubbed at my sternum to try and banish the ache that settled there. "Jesus." The word left my lips in a rush of breath. I was so tired I apparently didn't need to be entirely asleep to fall into a dream.

Misha came back into the room and gave me a suspicious glance. "She'll be here in ten minutes," he said. "You're starting in Capitol Hill."

Who needed Xander around when I had Misha to make all of my decisions for me? "I can't afford anything in Capitol Hill."

"Nonsense." Misha gave a dismissive wave of his hand. "I know you received an insurance settlement from the damage done to your previous residence. And don't forget who's been writing your paychecks these past months, Darian."

Well, he had a point there. "Yeah well, I wasn't planning on emptying my bank account on a place." I mean, come on. I needed to keep some Honey Nut Cheerios money in my pocket.

"At least start in Capitol Hill," he suggested. "You can slum it afterward if you don't find something that suits your needs."

A hot retort sat at the tip of my tongue. My stomping grounds in Belltown weren't "slumming it" by any stretch of the imagination. Yeah, Capitol Hill had the largest concentration of supernatural residents, but maybe I was looking for a little peace and quiet away from my own kind.

"I'll look," I grumbled. "But I'm not making any promises."

"Good." I could tell by Misha's tone that I was about to be dismissed which was fine by me. "And Darian, can you at least try to be personable?"

Ugh. "Fine." It showed how much I liked Misha that I'd humor him. "But I don't have to enjoy it."

"As is your prerogative." He pursed his lips which was as good as a smile.

Dry as a saltine.

———

Misha's realtor, Eleanor, was Fae—or at least part Fae. Elegant, sophisticated, perfectly coiffed, and friendly. And I was pretty sure she'd sell her own offspring for the right price. Misha must have told her I had money to spare because she didn't waste any time showing me the most expensive properties first. Old, enormous houses like Xander's that had been a part of Capitol Hill since Seattle's early days. Totally not my style.

"Do you have anything more warehouse-y?" I asked.

Eleanor looked at me like I'd lost my mind. "Excuse me, dear. What?"

"You know . . ." Did I have to spell it out for her? "More industrial. Like an old abandoned warehouse or something? I don't want a million rooms. Just one, big open space."

Something like my studio in Belltown that was now blown to bits.

I'm pretty sure Eleanor's head was about to explode. We'd been at it all day and I'd shot down each and every place she tried to push on me. Why did everyone want me to be so damned fancy? I just needed four walls, a roof, and a bed. She plastered a pleasant expression on her face and swiped through pictures on her phone. "How about this?" She held out her ungodly large smartphone for my inspection. "It's positively abysmal."

I took the phone from her. The building was actually pretty perfect. About the same size as my previous one and right on the water which was definitely a step up. It was also within walking distance of Xander's place which I'm sure he'd be smugly pleased with.

"Neighbors?"

Eleanor took the phone back and checked the listing. "Not many. A seafood restaurant to the north and a few gift shops to the south. The building is zoned commercial, but I believe it was dual use at one point, so there might be a few hoops you'll have to jump through with planning and zoning if you want to turn the loft space into a residence. But the dual use may be grandfathered. I can do the leg work for a small additional fee."

As though that would deter me. Jumping through hoops was one of my favorite forms of exercise. "Let's go check it out."

She looked around as though trying to find a good excuse not to.

"A sale's a sale, right?"

A sigh escaped from between her perfectly penciled-in lips. "All right. But I'm warning you, it's atrocious."

Abysmal . . . atrocious . . . . She could lob the insulting descriptions all day and I'd just keep smacking them away. "Right up my alley." I flashed the sweetest, widest smile I could muster. No doubt Misha was going to make me pay for this.

I knew before we walked into the building that I'd buy it. A wrought-iron staircase led from the basic first story that boasted an office, reception area, and a bathroom, to the second story loft that housed two separate office spaces. I'd knock the wall out and open it up so the bedroom looked out onto the first floor. No one can sneak up on you when they don't have any place to hide. Security was my number one concern. With the street on one side, the water on the other, and flanked by the restaurant and shops, I was confident I could monitor comings and goings of any suspicious characters. Namely, contractors trying to collect on that million-dollar bounty.

"I'll take it."

"Darian, be reasonable." Eleanor smoothed a hand over her trendy silver-gray hair that some girls spent big bucks to replicate. "The remodel costs alone will drain your bank account. The place isn't even close to inhabitable."

Okay, so there were a few broken windows and the plumbing, electrical, and probably the foundation would have to be checked out, but I was confident I could get the place up and running to my standards for a hell of a lot cheaper than Eleanor thought.

"I want it."

"Misha won't—"

"Misha has no say." Seriously? Since when did I need permission from him to buy a damn building? I swore, he acted more like Xander every day. "This is *my* money. *My* choice. And I *want* this building."

"To live in." Eleanor leveled her disbelieving gaze.

"Yes." I rolled my eyes. "To live in."

Her lips puckered. "I'll get the paperwork started. My guess is, it'll be at least a year before you're able to move in, though." That last comment seemed to give her a bit of perverse satisfaction. "You'll need to get everything up to code. If you want something now . . . I have some turnkey homes that would suit your unusual taste."

Unusual? I let out a snort. Eleanor was bursting with compliments. And a year my ass. I'd bust out the walls and throw a cot down in the loft as soon as the ink was dry. "This is what I want. I'll give you a nice tip if you rush through that paperwork."

Eleanor checked her watch. "I'll give you a call in a couple of days."

"Perfect." A little of the tension that pulled at my muscles loosened. It would be nice to have my own space again. "Talk to you then."

I didn't have the patience for anymore small talk, so I became one with the afternoon light and made a quick—not to mention invisible—retreat.

[2]

After a day of tedious house shopping, nothing took the edge off like ridding the world of one more miserable slime ball. I was more than happy to take the last-minute gig from Misha without my usual diligent research prior to agreeing to the job. Misha knew my code and he'd never ask me to kill anyone who didn't one hundred percent deserve it. My step faltered as something tickled at the back of my brain. A memory. Or the ghost of a memory. I couldn't quite put my finger on it. As though Misha wasn't the first handler I'd ever asked to acknowledge my strict code of ethics and agree to adhere to it.

My head began to throb.

Then again, I'd never really had a handler before Misha, preferring to work freelance. Was that true, though? Again, something scratched at the back of my mind with an annoying persistence. What in the hell was wrong with me? For the past several months, I'd felt like I was losing my mind. Crazy headaches, memory problems . . . . If I hadn't known better, I would've thought old age and dementia were finally hitting me.

I shook off the strange feeling of déjà vu and continued down the sidewalk. Thanks to the bounty on my head, I'd been keeping a low profile lately. That wasn't about to stop me from working, though. I had to be more careful, that's all. Pay better attention. Be more in tune with my surroundings. Honestly, it was good for me to have to stay on my toes. I'd gotten a little too comfortable over the past couple of years thanks to Raif, Xander, and my own damned ego. So yeah, I was totally okay with keeping my eyes open and watching my own back.

It's not like anyone else was going to do it for me.

Tonight's job wouldn't be difficult by any stretch of the imagination. I was used to taking down supernatural baddies and my mark, though anything but mundane, sat pretty low on the supernatural food chain. I knew he was a shifter, though Misha didn't indicate exactly what kind. He only told me the guy wasn't a threat to anyone other than humans. Particularly, children. The asshole was a predator in every sense of the word and after tonight, he wouldn't hunt anyone or anything ever again. I'd make sure of that.

I glanced down at my phone and the picture of the mark that Misha had texted me. Guys like him fell under my blade when they managed to piss off the wrong person. In the shifter's case, he'd gone after a politician's daughter. A politician with enough knowledge of the esoteric supernatural world, and influence to know who to call when he wanted someone wiped from the face of the earth.

According to Misha's intel, my mark would be in the vicinity of Pike Place Market for the rest of the night. The market was one of my favorite Seattle landmarks, a place I frequented often, especially when all I wanted was to feel a little more human and a lot more mundane. I hated to think that opportunistic assholes like the shifter wandered around my favorite haunt looking for young girls to victimize. It made me even more eager to put the son of a bitch down for good and do my part to make this city a safer place. Let's see how he liked being the prey for a change.

I wandered the market, temporarily dazzled by the hustle and bustle, like I was every time I came here. So many colors and sounds, the press of bodies, locals and tourists, the sheer vibrancy of it all. I passed by one of the flower vendors and my hand jutted out almost involuntarily to brush against the satin soft petals of tulips, roses, and gladiolas. I breathed in the floral sweetness and my lids grew heavy as a sensation of bliss wafted over me. I couldn't count how many times over the decades I'd lost myself here. Pike Place Market was as close to a church as anywhere I'd ever been since becoming a member of the supernatural community. And the congregation of beings gathered here was as close to a religion as I'd ever had. I loved it here.

A tingle of supernatural energy raced along my flesh and I paused. I recognized the signature as a dual-natured creature which meant my mark was more than likely close. Of course, he wasn't the only shifter in the city, but I was willing to bet I was on the money. Misha said he wasn't a typical shifter—whatever the hell that meant—and this energy signature was just off enough to make me think I was on the right track.

My focus snapped to attention. I dialed in my senses—sight, sound, smell—and tuned out the distraction of the vendors, and shoppers, and wares on display. I turned to my left and headed in the direction from where I'd felt the ripple of energy. I took one last glance at my cell and the picture staring back at me before tucking it in my back pocket. An early autumn breeze fluffed the tails of my black duster behind me and I melted into shadow as I made sure to stay upwind of the shifter as I tracked him.

I was as good as invisible. He wouldn't know what hit him.

I followed the shifter from the market to the less crowded streets by the wharf. He was a creature of heightened senses as well. He couldn't see me and thanks to the direction of the breeze he wouldn't catch my scent easily. But something had to have tickled his instincts to prompt him to give up his own hunt for the night. I had a feeling he was intentionally drawing me away from the more heavily populated areas, perhaps anticipating a fight.

Guys like him rarely had a single enemy. He'd likely amassed a crowd of adversaries over the years. He was cautious and rightly so. His life was about to be forfeit.

I stepped from shadow into my corporeal form. The daggers sheathed at my hips—a gift from Xander—hummed with anticipation of impending violence. Fae weapons were nothing to laugh at and my daggers thirsted for blood. Blades made for an assassin. Sharp, perfectly balanced, relentless in battle. The damned things were practically sentient, and they answered to only two people: me and Xander. They scared the shit out of me, but with the current state of my life, I felt a hell of a lot better having them sheathed at my sides rather than safely tucked away in their box. Plus, they got the job done.

I let the shadows swallow my feet to silence the sound of my boots as they struck the pavement. The shifter's steps faltered as he bristled and threw a guarded glance over his shoulder. He'd caught sight of me, but it didn't matter. What I'd wanted was a good look at his face and I'd gotten what I needed. He was the one I was after and it was time to get down to business.

He didn't seem too bothered by my presence. At least, he didn't give anything away. He kept his pace nice and easy, his posture casual. If he was worried about me, he didn't want me to know it. Then again, maybe he didn't consider a Shaede much of a threat. His mistake. He'd see how threatening I could be soon enough.

While I bolstered my own ego in preparation for what I was about to do, I let my focus turn inward. That was my mistake.

Chaos erupted in a cacophony of gunfire and frantic screams. Bodies scattered from the sidewalks as a dark blue BMW sped by on the street, the barrel of an AK-47 shoved through a crack in the blacked-out windows. I dove and rolled to avoid the spray of bullets but not fast enough. Pain exploded through my upper arm and I sucked in a breath as the hot slug ripped through skin and muscle before exiting near my elbow. The tissue began to heal as soon as the damage had been done, but the close call was enough to rattle me. A gunshot wound wasn't going to kill me, but if their aim got any better, any substantial damage and blood loss would slow me down enough for someone to attempt to get the job done.

Son of a bitch. A girl couldn't even work without having to deal with greedy assholes trying to kill her. The assassin game, man. I really needed to rethink my career.

The attempted drive-by managed to spook my mark. There was no way in hell I was letting him get away, though. He cast another furtive glance over his shoulder before he turned to run. I pulled one of the daggers from its sheath at my hip and flipped it so I held the blade in my hand. The weapon would never fail me in battle, and I had faith it would hit its mark as I pulled my arm back before letting the dagger fly.

The squeal of tires let me know the machine gun wielding cowards weren't through with me, but I kept my eye on my mark as I watched the blade sink to the hilt at the nape of the shifter's neck, severing his spine. He dropped to the ground, and I rushed to pull the dagger from his neck, opening the wound further. I dug my toes into my boots as I propelled myself forward and shed my corporeal form to join the night air. I'd like to see those bastards try to shoot a shadow.

I raced on a wind current as a car door slammed. And then another. And another. I guess I should have been flattered to know a small army had come out tonight to attempt to take me out, but right now, all it did was piss me off. I hated when my careful plans were curtailed. And someone was going to pay for it.

A cool million was enough to bring a host of low-life pieces of crap from their respective holes. And all of them wanted to see me good and dead.

I was outnumbered and armed only with close combat weapons. I never used guns, too impersonal. But it obviously wasn't an issue for the assholes trying to turn me into Swiss cheese. I gave a sad shake of my head. Absolutely no finesse.

A second squeal of tires drew my attention. My concentration faltered and the shadows released me, sending me into my corporeal form with a jarring lurch. Deafening shots rang out once again, as the bullets bit into the pavement around me. I ducked and covered my head with my arms, a knee-jerk reaction. The bullets wouldn't necessarily kill me, but a shot through the skull would put me down for more than just a moment. Just because I was self-destructive didn't mean I was a masochist.

One on one—even two or three on one—and I could've held my own in a fight. The number of bodies converging on me now was closer to ten and there was no way I was going to get the upper hand with those odds. A single bullet wound, I could manage. A few hundred was another story. Round after round of gunfire rang out and the warmth of shadows settled over my skin as I prepared to leave my corporeal form behind and get the fuck out of there. A strange spark of energy sizzled in the air around me and the world went silent. Still. And it stopped me dead in my tracks. Not because I'd been subjected to the strange power that seemed to suck the very oxygen from the air, but because I'd definitely felt this energy signature before.

A sense of familiarity danced over my flesh and brought chills to the surface of my skin as I felt a wicked headache coming on.

Greeeaaat.

Bullets froze in midair. My breath caught in my chest as the weight of powerful magic pressed down on me. Nearly a dozen assassins were rendered immobile in a split second and even the sounds of the resulting chaos went silent. My head whipped around, frantic to get my eyes on this new, unseen potential threat. At this point, I had to assume another assassin had entered the fray. One who had no problem taking out the competition. Icy cold snaked from the ring around my thumb, over my wrist, and up my left arm. My breath fogged the air and I shivered. A spike of pain shot through my head and my teeth gnashed as I dropped to one knee and cradled my splitting skull in my right palm. A gunshot to the head would have been less painful.

Not another assassin. This was someone—something—else.

Jesus. I needed to get out of here. Now.

Unlike the assholes trying to kill me, I was unaffected by the strange magic that froze everything around me. Shadows enveloped my corporeal form, cloaking me in invisible warmth. I took one last furtive glance around, only to find no sign of whoever wielded the mysterious magic. Too bad. I would've liked to have gotten my eyes on the individual who'd now saved me twice from whoever wanted me dead. And as much as I wanted to know exactly who could wield that sort of power, part of me was scared shitless.

I had a feeling I was in way over my head with this one.

———

UNDER THE COVER OF SHADOW, I RACED BACK TO MISHA'S HOUSE. The bone breaking pain ebbed with every mile I put in my wake and the cold chill of magic no longer rippled over me. I was shaken up as fuck, though, and couldn't quell the razor-winged butterflies that swirled in my stomach. I needed to figure out who in the hell wanted me gone, and fast.

I wasn't ready to check out quite yet.

Misha wasn't home when I got to the house and that annoyed me almost as much as the shit that had gone down to nearly botch tonight's job. It's not like I expected him to be sitting around waiting for me, but damn it, it would've been nice not to show up to an empty house. I paced the confines of his living room as I continued to stew. My agitation grew with each passing minute.

Unknown variables didn't sit well with me and whoever—or whatever—had frozen those assassins and their bullets in their tracks was definitely a big, dangerous question mark. All I needed was one more complication in the current clusterfuck that was my life.

The front door opened and closed, and I whipped around, my hands wrapped around the hilts of my daggers, ready to draw them if need be. I couldn't help but be a little skittish and it took all the willpower in my stores not to draw the enchanted weapons to stab first and ask questions later. Misha gave me one of his trademark long-suffering sighs coupled with an exasperated stare. He tossed his keys into a bowl on a table in the foyer and strolled through the living room, past me, toward the kitchen.

"I swear to the gods, Darian, you are the most melodramatic creature I've ever met." I couldn't argue that one. But considering what had happened, I felt like my reaction was warranted. "Did something go wrong tonight?" Misha reached for a wineglass from the cupboard and bent down to retrieve a bottle from the tiny refrigerator tucked into the kitchen's island bar. "Don't worry about it. You'll have another shot at him, I'm sure."

"The shifter is dead." I didn't know what annoyed me more: the crazy powerful magic I couldn't identify, or that Misha thought I hadn't gotten the job done. "But not before a small army of overzealous mercs tried to fill me with lead."

Misha straightened and looked me over. The level of disinterest in his expression sure warmed my heart. "You're not dead." Have I mentioned Misha had *amazing* powers of observation? "Or covered in bullet wounds."

"Yeah, because something fucking freaky happened the second shit started getting real."

Misha cocked a haughty brow. "Freaky?" He popped the cork on the bottle of luminescent golden liquid—faerie wine—and poured it into the glass before taking a long sip from the lip and settling into one of the high-backed barstools at the island. "Darian, you do realize we're supernatural creatures. *Freaky*, as you call it, is commonplace."

"Oh yeah?" I was about to blow his mind. "So you know of a creature that can literally freeze time and space?"

Misha paused mid sip and fixed me with a serious stare. The cool steel of his irises gleamed almost silver in the low light. I'd never seen him cloaked in a glamour. He was much too arrogant —or unafraid—to be anything other than his true self in my presence.

Like all Fae he was ethereal. Eternally youthful. Willowy and graceful. And beautiful in the way a lithe jungle cat might appear in the moment before it pounces on its prey to rip it to shreds. "Go on . . . ."

Well, at least now I had his attention. My head still throbbed with another of the relentless headaches that plagued me, and I motioned to his glass. "How about pouring me one of those?" I typically tried to avoid the faerie wine, but it was the only thing that tempered the marching band in my brain. If ever I needed a drink, it was tonight.

Misha gave me a dubious look but poured me a glass anyway. "It must have been quite a night."

I took a sip of the shimmering liquid and sighed as its warmth rushed through me. "I'm not exactly sure how many mercs were on the street, but I know it was at least a dozen. It started with a drive-by style shooting, right out their car windows. No finesse. They weren't professionals. Maybe ambitious bangers, but they had the firepower. I managed to bury my dagger in the shifter's neck before the assholes got out of their cars and came at me. It totally caught me off guard. I mean, that shit only happens in the *Godfather*, right?"

Misha sipped from his glass while rolling his hand in a "get on with it" motion.

"I'm getting ready to join with the shadows and get my ass out of there when this incredible energy settled over me. Everything froze." I leveled my gaze on Misha. "*Every-thing*. The bullets, the assholes shooting at me, the sounds, anyone within a two-hundred-yard radius. It was like some surreal suspended anima-tion. But the weirdest part? It didn't affect me. At all. It was like I was immune."

Misha regarded me with an unnerving amount of undivided attention. I didn't like it one bit. "And you never saw who wielded this particular magic?"

"Nope." And that really pissed me off. "Whoever the hell it was, they stayed hidden."

A space of silence passed. I leaned my hip against the kitchen counter while Misha sipped his damn wine and contemplated whatever it was cold, emotionless creatures like him contemplated.

"Interesting."

That was it? I was pretty sure my eyes bugged out of my head as I stared at him. *Interesting?* I mean, seriously? I took a healthy drink from my glass before leaning forward for emphasis. "That's all you've got?"

"For now." His insufferable calm managed to get on my last damn nerve. "I need to make a few calls, ask some questions. But I think it would be best if you laid low for a while."

"You're kidding. Right?" All I'd been doing for months was laying low. I couldn't get any fucking lower.

He graced me with the type of sigh reserved for impudent children. "For a day or two, Darian. Not a decade. I'm sure it won't kill you."

I fixed him with a sour expression. "Don't be so sure." I was tired of playing it safe, looking over my shoulder, and watching my back. One thing was certain: tonight's little display only revved up my desire to find out who wanted me dead.

I'd double, triple my efforts. Whatever it took.

I was going to get my autonomy back if it was the last thing I did.

"I can make it worth your while. All you have to do is walk away."

It was my own stupid fault for letting myself be seen. In and out, that had been the plan, but my curiosity had gotten the better of me. I'd never been hired to kill a woman before . . . . Okay, that wasn't true. I'd been hired to kill women before. This was simply the first time I'd taken the job.

Cindy McPherson sounded like the sort of name attached to a former cheerleader. Eternally upbeat, with a never-faltering smile and sun-kissed good looks that drew the eye of everyone who knew her. My mark was definitely stunning, though her usually blond hair was now dyed nearly black, and her equally dark eyeliner did a lot to mask her appearance. It certainly made her look a hell of a lot more unapproachable. She'd almost fooled me.

Almost.

Maybe the disguise had drawn me in. Or maybe it was her usual cheerleader façade that masked the ugliness underneath. Either way, I couldn't help but wonder why a woman who seemingly had everything going for her would live a double life, manipulating and exploiting other young women, condemning them to a drug addled fate while they were *passed around by disgusting millionaires looking for a little distraction while in Seattle on business.*

I wouldn't have even considered Cindy McPherson a "madam." That title was too good for her.

"I've got money. Lots of it. I can pay you more than whatever it was you were paid to kill me."

She was smart, I'd give her that. But her confidence far outweighed her fear as she offered her proposition. The Petshop Boys', West End Girls filtered through the upstairs office from the nightclub space below, and I focused on the music for a fleeting moment, as though thinking about her offer.

"You can kill me if you want," she made a show of giving a uncon-cerned shrug as she crossed the office to look through the privacy glass at the dancefloor below, "but someone is just going to move in and take my place. It won't change anything."

Cindy wasn't wrong. The guy who'd hired me wasn't exactly squeaky clean and I surmised he was more interested in taking over Cindy's high-end clientele once she was out of the way. I could take them both out if I wanted to, but criminals were like cockroaches in Seattle. Smash one, and three more show up the next day.

"Maybe not." I honestly had no idea why I even indulged her.

"Men don't want women thriving in their arenas. Whether they wear expensive suits or chef's coats, or hell, drive a bus. I mean, you'd think things would be different now. Aren't we supposed to be liberated and all that?" She let out a derisive snort. "We're not. It might as well be the 1800s."

I wanted to tell Cindy that comparing women's rights in 1984 to the 1800s was a little ridiculous, having lived through it and all, but to be honest, we really hadn't come that far as a gender. Score another point for the cheerleader. She had me again.

"What are you getting?" My reluctance to chat her up had her nervous. A bead of sweat formed at her forehead and she casually swiped it away with a long graceful finger tipped with a perfectly manicured nail.

"Five thousand?" When I didn't respond she let out a disbelieving chuff of laughter and leaned closer. "Ten?" I remained quiet and she began to pace. "Jesus." She let out a breath. "I guess I should be flattered they think I'm worth more than ten dead. I must really be a threat to their livelihoods."

I had no idea who "they" were, but I assumed my client must have represented a group that wanted Cindy out of the way. I'd look into it later. Until then, I had a job to do.

"Sorry, Cindy." I almost was, too. I reached for the dagger sheathed at my side. "It's the end of the road for you."

———

I WOKE IN THE MORNING WITH MEMORIES STILL SWIRLING IN MY head. It seemed like a lifetime ago, fragmented, inserted like seat filler in my mind. The memory wasn't false, just . . . distant. I hadn't recalled many recent memories—nothing that happened over the past ten or so years—in the past several months and it ate at me. Why? Did supernatural creatures need to worry about things like memory loss?

My phone buzzed, giving me a welcome distraction from my worries. I scooped it up and swiped my finger across the screen, grateful to have something else to focus on.

"Darian, it's Eleanor. I'm afraid there's a problem with the building."

I didn't miss the obvious glee in Eleanor's tone. After the night I'd had, I definitely wasn't equipped to deal with silly issues like real estate hiccups. I'd barely slept. Tossed and turned and paced the confines of Misha's guestroom as I went over the events at Pike Place Market over and over again in my head. I'd eventually passed out on the couch, too exhausted to continue to stew over what was already over and done with. I let out a slow sigh and locked my jaw down before I said something to Eleanor that I might regret. Her too chipper tone made it obvious that she thought she'd be able to convince me into spending more on a better place. But I'd learned over the course of my existence that "problems" could easily be circumvented. I wasn't walking away from that building. No way, no how.

"Oh yeah?" I replied in a nice, equally chipper tone. "What's the problem?"

"The owner has decided he doesn't want to sell." Seriously, her enthusiasm was a little over the top. "He said he'd consider a long-term lease, but since I know you're not interested in leasing, I told him—"

"Hold up." If there was one thing I hated, it was people making assumptions—and decisions—on my behalf. "Get this guy on the phone and tell him I'm open to negotiation." The more I thought about the building, the more I fell in love with it. I wasn't going to walk away.

"A lease would—"

"Tell him I'll pay twenty-five percent over what he's asking. If he still won't bite, tell him we can discuss a lease." Eleanor let out a defeated sigh. If I ended up leasing the space, she'd be out a hefty commission. Dollar signs were likely flying past her eyes. "Don't worry," I added. "You'll get something for your trouble."

"I'll call you back in a half hour." The disappointment in her tone was palpable as she let out a huff of breath.

"Sounds good." I ended the call and tossed the phone down beside me on the couch.

I looked up to find Misha studying me. He always seemed to keep one eye on me as though wary I might turn on him without warning. Suspicious SOB. "Trouble?"

The issues with the building were barely an annoyance in comparison to my definition of trouble. I gave a dismissive wave of my hand. "You know your realtor is a little high strung, right?"

Misha chuckled. "Does this mean you're going to be sleeping in my guest room for a while longer?"

His tone was light, but I could tell I'd overstayed my welcome. In fact, he'd never actually invited me to stay in the first place. I'd sort of set up camp under the radar. One night on his couch became two, and so on, and after that, I'd commandeered the guest room. I just couldn't handle living in Xander's house while he, Asher, and Raif weren't there. They were the only reason I ever went there in the first place.

I used to like solitude. Now, it seemed I went out of my way to find company. Anything was better than sitting around, thinking about the gnawing ache in my soul that slowly ate me alive.

"No." I snorted. "Do you really think I want to stay here another second, let alone another night?"

Misha cocked a brow. I didn't think he was buying my tough-girl routine. "What do you plan to do? Jab him with the pointy end of your dagger until he has no choice but to sell to you?"

Supernatural hearing. What a pain in the ass. Not that I cared that Misha had overheard my conversation with Eleanor. It just took the excitement out of telling him myself. "If it comes down to it," I said with a shrug. I *wanted* that building.

A smile played at the corner of Misha's mouth. "I'm sure you'll charm him into submission with nothing more than your sweet countenance and equally disarming wit."

I let the backhanded compliment slide. Misha didn't find me sweet or disarming. "Whatever gets it done," I replied. "I'm not taking no for an answer." I gave him a pointed look. The stubborn owner of the building wasn't the only person I refused to let shut me down. "In the meantime, I want you to find another job for me. As soon as possible."

Misha pursed his lips. "You're insufferably stubborn, do you know that?"

"I've been told." Misha wanted me to continue to lay low, especially after last night's drive-by-slash-magic-show. But if I was going to pay an extra twenty-five percent on top of my offer for the building, I was going to need an influx of cash. "I don't think Eleanor appreciates it, either."

"Please," Misha scoffed. "She lives for these types of negotiations. I wouldn't put it past her to use a little muscle herself in order to get the sale."

The thought of prim, petite Eleanor putting the smackdown on anyone coaxed a grin to my lips. Though, she had Fae blood . . . and they weren't exactly a passive lot. Supernatural creatures were inherently violent. Living among humans didn't do much to tame that wild spirit.

"You're deflecting." I wasn't going to let him change the subject. "Are you going to find a job for me or not?"

Misha let out a sigh and handed over a folded piece of paper. "Despite having specifically told you to stay out of the public eye, so to speak, I had a feeling you'd pull something like this on me. And since I find you ridiculously uncontrollable, I suppose giving you something to do will keep you out of bigger trouble."

I looked at the name and address on the slip of paper along with the dollar amount I'd be paid once the job was done. Misha was usually much more detailed, supplying me with background info on the mark, photos, etc. Talk about sketchy as fuck.

"This is it?" There was something familiar about the way this was going down. As if I'd gone out on a similar job much the same way. A dull ache settled at the base of my skull and I forced my jaw to relax. Supernatural creatures weren't supposed to succumb to things like Alzheimer's, but I swore there were days when I felt like I was losing my damned mind. "No pictures? No proof of death? Special instructions? Precautions to take? Just storm the castle, slit his throat and beat feet out of there?"

"More or less," Misha replied. "The client isn't particular. Just wants the job done."

"What did he do?" Some assassins weren't as scrupulous when it came to the jobs they worked. Misha knew that. Which was one of the reasons the lack of details made me nervous.

Misha's gaze hardened. "Killed someone."

"Who?"

Misha's expression became guarded. He was definitely hiding something. "An innocent."

An easy, not to mention convenient explanation. My jaw squared and I fought once again to unclench it. "And I'm just supposed to take the client's—and your—word for it?"

Misha pushed himself away from the desk he'd been leaning on. "Are you questioning my honor?"

"Not your honor," I replied. "Just your interpretation of the truth." As a general rule, Fae couldn't lie. But it didn't mean they didn't have ways of practicing duplicity when they wanted.

"You're a bigger fool than I first thought if you believe I'm interested in inviting your—or Alexander Peck's—wrath. I know what you will and will not do, Darian."

A twinge of guilt pulled at my chest. I'd started to consider Misha a friend, sort of. I didn't want to think that he was setting me up. Maybe I needed to consider taming my suspicious nature.

Someday. Until then, I wasn't doing shit until I knew for sure the job was legit. I opened my mouth to tell Misha just that when my cell rang. I checked the caller ID, Eleanor, and instead fixed him with what I hoped was an intimidating death stare. "All right." I'd do recon on my own. Later. "I'll do it." With business concluded for now, I swiped my finger across the screen and brought the cell to my ear. "I hope you have good news for me, Eleanor."

"Well, he didn't outright decline your offer, but he didn't roll over and agree to sell, either. He's agreed to a meeting to discuss terms if you're available. Tonight. Midnight."

Midnight? What the hell was this guy, a vampire? I guess I didn't answer fast enough because Eleanor spoke up, "I know, it's an outrageous time for a meeting. But he insisted it was the only time he had free and said we could take it or leave it."

Sounded like I was about to meet my match in the stubborn department. "Midnight it is, then." Whatever his tactics, they weren't going to work. I refused to quit until I lived in that building. "Where are we meeting?"

"At the property," Eleanor replied. "I'd suggest asking Misha to come along but I suspect you have no problem taking care of yourself."

I let out a soft snort. "Back at ya, Eleanor."

She laughed. I'd like to think we'd bonded over our little girl power moment. At least enough for her to back me on this deal and see it through. "I guess it's set, then. I'll draw up the paperwork just in case."

I liked her optimism. "Sounds like a plan. See ya then."

I ended the call and didn't bother filling Misha in. He'd heard everything already anyway. "When does the job need to be done by?" It would be nice to know the parameters I had to work within.

"By the end of the week," Misha said.

Good. Plenty of time for a little digging. "See you on Friday, then." I brushed past him and left without another word.

I had an entire day to kill until I met with the guy I planned to persuade into selling me the building. If anything, he'd offer up an interesting challenge which was fine by me because I could definitely use a distraction.

———

ELEANOR LOOKED PRETTY PEEVED WHEN I SHOWED UP AT THE building. I doubted that midnight real estate deals were her cup of tea and she was probably ready to add a hefty inconvenience fee to whatever deal we managed to strike tonight. While we waited for the building's mysterious owner to make an appearance, I walked the confines of the space, more convinced than ever that I needed to live here. My spine tingled as the presence of another supernatural creature brushed my senses. I stiffened, but kept my attention on the building and not the creature approaching us.

"Sorry to keep you waiting, Eleanor. Thank you for meeting with me."

I whipped around at the rumble of a deep masculine voice. Supernatural energy vibrated over every inch of his six-foot-plus frame as he leveled his intense blue gaze on me. I should have figured the owner of the building wouldn't be human. Not that it mattered. Familiarity sparked in his expression, and I wracked my brain as I tried to recall where I might have previously met him. A dull throb settled at the back of my skull and I swallowed down a groan. I was getting pretty damned sick of the persistent, not to mention annoying, headaches.

"Darian Charles." He inclined his head slightly as he addressed me, which made me think he might be some sort of nobility. Each faction had their kings, leaders, whatever. It served to reason from the way he carried himself that he was someone who was used to being either feared or respected. Probably both.

"Do I know you?" Congeniality wasn't one of my strong suits.

One corner of his mouth quirked in a half smile. "You saved my life once."

Okay . . . . That certainly didn't ring a bell. I wasn't generally in the business of saving lives. The guy was striking. Handsome and commanding. Not the sort of face you forget. Intuition tingled over my skin and down my spine. Another assassin? Shit. I wasn't going to take any chances. Time to call it a night.

"Let's go, Eleanor." No way was I going to wait around for this SOB to try and plunge a dagger into my throat. "We're done here."

"Come on, now. You don't remember me?" Mister tall, dark, and mysterious gave a chuckle. "Of course, the last time we met I was quite a bit furrier and wearing a silver collar."

I stopped dead in my tracks and slowly turned to face him. The dull throb in my cranium graduated to a steady thrum and I fought the urge to massage my temples. Eleanor looked from him to me and back again, her delicate brow furrowed as she tried to catch up. My eyes narrowed as I studied him.

There was definitely something familiar about his intense gaze, but I rested my hands on the pommels of my daggers just to be safe.

"Steve?"

That wasn't his real name, of course. His real name was . . . Cameron, or Carson, or something like that, but I couldn't remember how I knew that, or who had told me. Something was seriously wrong with me. Maybe I needed an MRI. At any rate, I was pretty sure I was looking at the highest-ranking Werewolf in the Pacific Northwest.

He pursed his lips as though it took an act of sheer will to humor me. "Camden," he replied. "Camden Walsh."

Bond. James Bond. I bit back the urge to say the words out loud, but damn was he ever rocking the vibe. The name rang with familiarity—I wished I could remember who'd told me that. "Right. Camden. I remember." *Sort of.* He didn't need to know that, though. A couple of years ago, that lying, cheating, kidnapping piece of shit Lorik and I had been tasked with delivering Camden —who'd been in his wolf form at the time—to the temple of Mithras. I'd managed to secure Camden's freedom, though the details of just how I'd done it were a little hazy. We'd shared a common enemy which sort of made us friends, I guess. "How've you been?"

His expression turned serious and my stomach knotted. "I've been better. We have a problem, it seems."

Just one? In my experience, problems tended to pile up. "So, wait a sec." I needed to focus on something other than the headache currently ripping through my skull. "This isn't about the building? And what do you mean, 'we?'"

"We'll discuss the building later," Camden said. "You saved my life. I owe you a debt. If you have a problem, I have a problem. *We* have a problem."

Well, shit. His words sent a jolt of anxiety through my blood-stream. Eleanor cleared her throat and took a step forward. "As that particular business between you doesn't concern me, can we discuss the issues with the building first?"

Camden gave me a sidelong glance and my jaw flexed. "He doesn't own the building." God damn it. I'd totally been played.

"No," he agreed. "I don't. But I've been authorized to represent the owner." He turned to Eleanor. "The building is Darian's if she wants to lease it. The owner wants twelve dollars a year in payment, no strings attached."

Twelve dollars a *year*? What the actual fuck? There had to be not just a string attached but a giant bungee cord. I was still trying to wrap my head around what Camden had just said as Eleanor gave an indignant huff and opened her mouth to speak, no doubt seeing any hope of a commission wither and die.

"For your trouble . . . ." Camden cut Eleanor off before she could complain. "And for drawing up the contracts, you'll be paid the commission you would've gotten for the sale. Now that the business with the building is settled, can we get down to the real business of the night?"

Eleanor's expression went from indignant to Cheshire-Cat-pleased in a nanosecond. "Seriously? Twelve dollars a year?" My voice echoed in the empty space. "I'm not a charity case. And no strings attached, my ass. What in the hell is going on here?"

"Darian," Eleanor said from the corner of her mouth. "Don't look a gift horse in the mouth."

Of course, she didn't want me to question anything. She was getting her big fat chunk of the commission pie no matter what I'd be required to pay.

"Consider it a mutually beneficial arrangement," Camden said. "You get the building for a steal, the owner takes a loss and gets a tax ride-off. It's a win-win situation."

Yeah. No way was I going to buy that. My gaze narrowed on the Werewolf. "You're going to have to do better than that."

He let out an exasperated sigh as though he'd been coached to expect me to be less than cooperative. Interesting. "You're going to have to trust me, Darian. For the sake of argument, we'll call the owner of this place your benefactor. And as your benefactor, he has your best interests at heart. If he didn't, I wouldn't be here right now."

I didn't trust easily. Or at all. It must have been apparent in my expression because Camden closed the space between us and lowered his voice to a murmur.

"I was told there would be things you might not remember. But you were instrumental in securing my freedom from Mithras and as such, you've earned my loyalty."

The words resonated with power. I assumed it wasn't a small thing to have the most influential Alpha Werewolf in the land tell you he was loyal to you.

"Believe me when I say I want only what benefits you. You can trust me. And likewise, trust the one who sent me to you and be patient that all will be revealed in good time."

Easier said than done. I had the patience of a toddler. But something in his words struck a chord. He knew I'd been having trouble with my memory. How? I could have walked away and washed my hands of the entire situation but that would've been foolish. For starters, I wanted this building, and I was willing to take the risk. And secondly, the identity of my so-called "benefactor" had piqued my curiosity. I would have pegged Xander for the role, but Camden's knowledge of my current condition—aka, black hole of lost memories—ruled the Shaede King out. I'd be stupid not to play along and see where it all went.

My gaze never left the stoic Werewolf. "All right. Draw up the papers, Eleanor." I swore to god I heard a cash register chime as her smile grew impossibly wide. I hoped my decision to see where this went didn't end up biting me in the ass. I lowered my voice an octave and wrapped my hands around the grips of my daggers. "Now, tell me what in the hell is going on."

[4]

Eleanor didn't waste any time excusing herself for the night. She'd come out ahead on the deal and she didn't have two shits to give about my history with Camden or anything else. I couldn't look at him without thinking of the cute, fluffy Werewolf I'd nicknamed "Steve" and whose fur I'd ruffled, much to the shocked indignation of . . . someone. A sharp pain shot through my skull and I sucked in a breath. Goddamn it, I was seriously falling apart.

"Are you all right?"

Camden canted his head to one side, lending him a feral edge, as he studied me. I could certainly see the animal nature in his predatory gaze and unwavering attention. I didn't have any experience with werewolves aside from our lone encounter—the memory of which was hazy at best—and I wasn't sure what to expect. Like all supernatural creatures, I assumed he possessed heightened senses. Could he smell my anxiety? My worry that there was something seriously wrong with me? Or the hope that somehow, he knew why I felt this way and might miraculously be able to help me?

"Headache." There wasn't really any point in lying about it.

Camden nodded as though he understood. "We have a lot to cover, but if you're not feeling up to it—"

"No." The sooner we got down to business, the better.

"You know there's a price on your head?"

Well, I'd wanted him to get right down to business. "Considering I've been dodging bullets and daggers for the past several months, you could say I got the message loud and clear."

"And I understand your previous residence was blown to oblivion as well?"

Wow. Someone had the inside track on my life. Not gonna lie, it made me a little twitchy. "No offense, but you seem a little too informed for my comfort level."

Camden hiked his shoulder, unconcerned. "I'm the Alpha. It's my job to be informed."

Sounded a hell of a lot like something Xander had once said to me. Could the Shaede King be the one feeding my supposed new ally some of this information? He was certainly high-handed enough to do so. Maybe I'd underestimated Xander's ability to gather intel on me.

"Yeah. Which is why I'm taking over this gem." I waved my hand to encompass the warehouse space.

"From what I understand," he said, "you've made a host of enemies over the past several years." His smile grew. Mischievous. "I'm afraid you've added another illustrious name to your list."

I met his unwavering gaze. The suspense might just kill me before anything else did. I liked to think I had the inside track on the assassin world. That I'd been unable to discern who had it out for me was a thorn in my side. I didn't like that the Alpha wolf seemed to know what I'd been unsuccessful in learning. "Funny," I replied, desert dry. "I've been trying to figure it out for the past year. I'd been sure it was the left-over acolytes of Mithras, wanting to avenge their fallen god." A flash of cold encircled my left thumb and wove up my arm. I twisted the ring that encircled the digit, as mystified by it now as I had been every day for the past several months. Camden seemed to be in the know. Maybe he could help me piece together that puzzle as well.

"The cult of Mithras is dormant, for now. But don't worry, Darian. I'm sure we'll both have to deal with him again. Someday."

I guess I really shouldn't have been surprised. "Funny, I thought when I'd killed him, it had ended any chance of having to deal with him again."

He graced me with an indulgent smile. "Do you really think it's possible to kill a god?"

"You separate anything's head from its shoulders, it's going to die."

At least, that's what I'd convinced myself. Then again, there'd been a time I'd thought I was unkillable. A myth perpetrated by that lying son of a bitch, Azriel.

So many details about that night at the temple of Mithras seemed to be missing from my memory, however. Maybe I wasn't remembering any of it the way it had actually happened.

"I watched him die." At least, I thought I had.

"You watched his *body* die."

Huh. I'd never thought about it that way.

"That's a story for another time, though." Camden's expression became serious once again. "We'll deal with the god when the time comes. Your immediate threat is much more dangerous."

More dangerous than an unkillable god? Lovely. "And that is . . .?"

"The Arx."

Whenever I thought I'd learned everything there was to know about the supernatural world, someone—or something—threw me a curve ball to teach me otherwise. Would I ever come to a point when nothing surprised me? "Who?"

"Not who," Camden said. "What."

"Okay." I let out a breath. "What, exactly, is the Arx?"

"The Arx," Camden replied with a derisive snort, "is the esoteric name given to the Human Purist Society. A seemingly secret faction of humans with too much knowledge of the supernatural world. They've tasked themselves with policing us, so to speak, and in many cases, eradicating us, to ensure we don't become the dominate beings on the planet."

Dominate beings? I held back a snort of my own. "Why do they call themselves the Arx?" Seemed a little redundant to go by two separate names.

"They are the Citadel." Camden's tone mocked the grandeur in the word. "The unknown fortress that protects the mundane. They can't very well go around referring to themselves as the Human Purist Society around those of them not in the know," he continued as though I should have already surmised as much. "The connotation reeks of prejudice."

He wasn't wrong. And from the sound of it, prejudice was definitely their thing. "Okay, so what does this Arx have to do with me?"

Camden's brow furrowed. "The Arx believes that you're a threat to humanity. That's all I can tell you right now."

Annoyance burned in my chest and I drummed my fingers against my thigh and the dagger sheathed there. It hummed in anticipation, sensing my agitation. "I don't like secrets," I said pointedly. "And I don't play games." I wasn't so quick to trust. If Camden wanted mine, he was going to have to pony up some info.

"He said you'd be difficult," Camden said on a sigh. "You'll get your answers, Darian. I promise you that. But it won't be tonight."

He? Who in the hell was *he?* Every word out of the Werewolf's mouth only built mystery and suspicion in my mind, not to mention anger. "I don't work with people I can't trust." And until I got some answers, I couldn't trust Camden. "So tell your boss, or whoever the hell he is, thanks for the offer on the lease, but I think maybe I'm going to go ahead and pass." God, Eleanor was going to *kill* me. I just didn't think it was a good idea to get entwined with some unknown mastermind that might be lulling me into a false sense of security with some bullshit story just so he could kill me later.

"I wish I could help you, Darian. I really do."

"Give me something," I said flatly. "Or I'm walking."

Camden's brow furrowed. "You're not a typical Shaede. The entire supernatural community knows that."

He had that right. Shaedes—though their own species on the supernatural family tree—could be created in rare circumstances. Azriel had been made a Shaede in the womb. Padma, his mother, had been made a Rakshasa-Shaede hybrid by Xander. And I, had been reborn a Shaede when Azriel's ethereal form had passed through mine. Since the time of that rebirth, however, I'd been changed. By Azriel in his attempt to sacrifice me in order to reawaken a race of Fae warriors who'd been transformed into stone gargoyles ages ago. I had become midnight and dawn, shadow and dusk. A creature who lived between the realms of human and supernatural. A guardian of the faerie realm. My fingers moved involuntarily to caress the emerald around my neck, the key to *O Anel*. Unfortunately, my status as "other" kept me from fitting in anywhere, with anyone.

"You frighten the Arx," Camden continued. "You're an anomaly and it's unknown to them exactly what your power might be. You're a threat, and threats to humanity are dealt with swiftly and effectively. Their leader, Mitchell Redmond, is a powerful man in his own right. His followers are like those of Mithras in their fanaticism. Once he sets his sights on something, he stops at nothing until he gets what he wants."

"And he wants me dead?" It seemed completely farfetched. The only creatures, human or otherwise, I was a threat to were those who'd done wrong and needed to pay. And as for my power . . . to be honest, I had skills but no actual power. Nothing extraordinary at any rate. "I'm sorry, Camden. But it just doesn't make any sense."

"Darian." Camden raked his fingers through his dark hair and his shoulders slumped with frustration.

I had a tendency to rub people, Fae, Shaedes, and now Werewolves, the wrong way. If he knew what was good for him, he'd save himself the aggravation and walk away now.

"I owe you a life debt. That's no small thing. You might not trust me, but I'll swear a blood oath to you, if that's what it takes to assure you that your safety is my number one priority. I'm not the only one looking out for you. You want answers and you'll get them. As soon as those answers don't further compromise your security. This is just the start of what I'm afraid is a long and bumpy road ahead. In the meantime, the building is yours." He extended his hand, a key grasped in his fingers. I looked down at the offering, unwilling to take it, but he cocked a challenging brow and refused to move until I plucked the key from his grasp. "A crew will be here in the morning to set up a security system and start on renovations to make the space more inhabitable. Be here by eight if you can." He reached into his pocket and produced a matte black business card. "And if you need anything in the meantime, call me."

I plucked the card from his outstretched hand. Despite my skepticism, I didn't sense an ounce of deception from him. In fact, some strange intuition tugged at the back of my mind and urged me to give him my trust. The pomposity of it all screamed Xander and as soon as Camden and I parted ways, I was going to do my best to get to the bottom of it.

"I'll play." I tucked the business card into my back pocket. "For now."

"Good." Camden headed for the door and chuckled. "Because honestly, I expected this to be a hell of a lot more difficult. I'll be in touch."

I watched as the haughty Werewolf sauntered out of the building that was now my new home base. Once I knew he was out of earshot, I pulled my phone out of my pocket, scrolled through the contacts, and hit send.

By the fifth ring I was ready to strangle someone. Before voicemail could pick up, a groggy voice answered on the other end of the line and I let out a sigh of relief.

"This better be good. I was in the middle of a killer dream."

Asher's snark just wasn't as good over the phone. I rubbed away the ache of loneliness that stabbed at my chest and drew in a deep breath. I was stuck in Seattle while Asher, Raif, and Xander were in Banff setting Xander's kingdom straight. I missed all of them and was more than ready for them to come home. But they were home, weren't they? Seattle wasn't where they belonged. And I was going to have to come to terms with that.

"Darian? Everything okay?"

I snapped out of my depressing thoughts. I could feel sorry for myself later. Right now, I needed to handle business. "Do you know anything about Xander contracting a Werewolf to look out for me?" It wouldn't be the first time the Shaede King had thrown his weight around and ordered someone to follow my every move. "Or anything about an old storefront in Capitol Hill down by Lake Union that he might be trying to sell?"

"Huh?" I had no idea what the time difference was between Seattle and the Canadian town but it was obvious Asher might've needed a couple of minutes to wake up enough so he could comprehend my questions. "I wouldn't know about any properties on the water, but I'm sure he didn't contract any Werewolf. Do you really think he'd hire out for something like that? Besides, Misha keeps enough of an eye on you for his peace of mind."

I'd always known Xander had introduced me to Misha to keep me in his periphery while he was away. Despite our rocky history, we still cared about each other, though Xander's definition of "care" was a little more obsessive than mine.

"Hmmm. All right." Well, that put me back at square one, damn it. I wasn't completely shot down, though.

"What about T—"

A sharp stab of pain shot through my head as Asher's words slurred and became incomprehensible white noise in the back of my mind. His voice muffled and I locked my jaw as I breathed through the pounding at the base of my skull.

"What was that?" I couldn't tell if my own words were slurred or not. All I could focus on was the headache that threatened to split my cranium in two. "I think your phone is cutting out." Or my brain was. Jesus.

"*Mfmf Tymf splin . . . .*"

Gibberish. I couldn't decipher a single word Ash said. My head continued its relentless pounding and I sucked in a sharp breath. I needed to get back to Misha's and lie down before I passed out on the damned concrete floor. I cradled the phone in my right hand and my head in the left as I doubled over. "Ash, I need to go. I'll call you back later. Sorry I woke you up."

I hit "end" and stuffed my cell into my back pocket as I dragged in ragged gulps of breath. By small degrees, the pain began to subside, and my heart no longer pounded against my ribcage as though trying to find a way out. Stars swam in my vision and I swayed on my feet. I'd be lucky to stand up straight let alone drag my ass back to Misha's. A wild rush of anxiety stole my ability to think as the worry churned like an angry sea in the pit of my stomach. Something was seriously wrong with me and getting worse by the day. And there was no one I could go to for help.

A chill breeze blew through the warehouse and the ring on my thumb sent out a flare of ice that traveled the length of my arm. Goose bumps rose on my flesh but somehow the chill managed to calm my nerves and dull the pain in my skull. The fine hairs at the base of my neck stood on end as I sensed a presence close. I pulled one of the daggers from its sheath and turned a slow circle as I scanned my surroundings. The chill air drained from the warehouse as though carried away on a breeze and the flare of cold from my ring retreated as well.

Damn it, there was something seriously wonky going on. It had been suggested to me more than once that the old worn silver ring on my thumb was enchanted. Though how, and by whom, I didn't know. And since the day I'd put it on—I'm sure it had been years ago—I hadn't been able to take it off. I couldn't help but suspect that was connected to my headaches. I needed to get to the bottom of it, though. Before I went out of my freaking mind.

I took one last tentative glance around before I locked the door and left. I was exhausted, on edge, and didn't have the patience to walk the several blocks back to Misha's place, and so I joined with the shadows and allowed the air currents to take me where I needed to go.

For months I'd been under the impression the strange state of my life couldn't get any stranger. The sinking feeling in the pit of my stomach told me I was about to prove myself wrong.

[5]

I had a lot on my plate, and I hadn't helped my situation by demanding that Misha give me another job right away. But my pride wouldn't allow me to go to him and admit I might have bitten off more than I could chew.

I stumbled out of the guest room and headed straight for the liquor cabinet. I snatched a port glass and the unlabeled bottle that contained the swirling gold faerie wine. I poured a generous shot into the glass and downed it in a single swallow. The thick, heady liquor glided down my throat, smooth as silk, and settled as a warm glow in my stomach. I poured a second glass and brought it to my lips. Misha cleared his throat from behind me and I rolled my eyes before I swallowed the contents of the delicate glass and poured a third.

"Another headache?"

My eyes drifted shut as the wine went bottoms up. I set the empty glass on the bar, corked the bottle and put it back on its shelf. Misha had warned me to use the wine sparingly, but for some damned reason, it was the only thing that calmed the throbbing ache in my brain. Last night's episode had been a doozie. Definitely warranted a third pour.

"Yeah, but whatever." It's not like I had any sort of explanation for it. "It is what it is. I'll be fine in a few hours."

"You're drinking too much." Misha's eyes narrowed with disdain as he retrieved the empty port glass from the counter and carried it into the kitchen. "It's not meant to be a cure-all, Darian."

I knew that, but god how I wished it was. "I just needed to take the edge off." I wasn't interested in a lecture. Misha could save his breath.

"What happened last night?"

Where to begin . . . . "Well, I got the building for a freaking steal."

Misha snorted. "As though there were any doubt. Good. I've missed having a little privacy around here."

He acted pleased to be rid of me, but I had a feeling he was going to secretly miss me. "That was the least interesting part of the night, though."

Misha's brow arched. "Really?" He let the word hang, not exactly a question. He shared my suspicious nature and considering the recent shit storm of assassins raining down on my head, he had to have known the hang up with the building had more to it than a simple real estate negotiation.

"What do you know about an Alpha Werewolf named Camden Walsh?" If anyone had a bead on Seattle's supernatural heavy hitters, it was Misha.

Misha's eyes narrowed. I had his full attention. "His business dealings are legitimate. He's well regarded and respected by the majority of the supernatural community. He's the highest ranking Alpha in the U.S. if not the world. He's a male with considerable power and sway."

Misha managed to reinforce the meager knowledge I had about the Werewolf. In fact, Camden was a bigger deal than I'd thought. "Is he honest? Trustworthy?" That was my biggest concern. Could I trust the things he'd told me last night?

"He's an honorable male." The Fae couldn't lie, but was this another bending of the truth? Honorable didn't always mean trustworthy.

I could work with honorable, though. I didn't completely trust anyone in this world except for Raif and Asher. Xander sometimes fell under the category of trustworthy. Aside from those three—

I sucked in a sharp breath as pain stabbed through my skull. I'd been on the verge of a thought, but before I could grasp it, the too familiar headache rushed in to steal it away. I was getting pretty damned sick of feeling so off kilter. There wasn't enough faerie wine in the world to fix me.

"Are you all right?" The genuine concern in Misha's tone was more disconcerting that the fucking headache.

"Fine." There was no point in discussing an issue that didn't have an explanation or a solution. "Camden claims to be representing a third party. Someone who apparently has my best interests at heart. Says he knows who put the bounty on my head."

"And . . .?"

Misha and I had been speculating on who would be the most likely suspect for months. I wondered if what I was about to tell him would confuse him as much as it had me. "Have you ever heard of a human organization known as the Arx?"

Misha's full lips pursed as he regarded me. "Please." He gave a dismissive wave of his hand. "Those fanatics? Don't tell me they're involved. What an absolute waste of time and energy."

It appeared as though Misha didn't share Camden's opinion of the group's stature. "What do you know about them?"

"What do lions know about ants?" Misha replied. "Other than they're a nuisance."

Misha's lack of concern threw me for a loop. Especially after Camden had made them seem so formidable. "The Werewolf seems to think they're a little more than a nuisance. He says they eradicate anything they perceive as a threat to humanity."

Misha snorted. "And they consider you a threat to humanity?"

Again, my feelings were a little bruised that he'd so easily disregard me. Not that I considered myself hot shit or anything. But he could have at least pretended to be a little impressed.

"Camden says their leader is a guy named Mitchell Redmond. And that his followers are zealots."

"Cult leaders are charismatic," Misha replied, again unconcerned. "And their cults are fleeting. They burn bright for a time and then implode. Creating a black hole in the wake of their destruction. The Arx is nothing."

"How long have they been around?"

Misha shrugged. "Five hundred years, give or take."

I supposed five hundred years could be considered fleeting to a long-lived creature like Misha. "Fleeting or not, it's the only lead I have right now."

Misha nodded but he averted his gaze. Damn, I wanted to know what swirled in that shrewd mind of his. "What now?" he asked. "Are you planning to storm the fortress and rid the world of the Arx before they rid the world of you?"

"I'm hardly prepared for anything like that." My gaze wandered to the ring at my thumb and its chill reached out over my skin. "And I'm not even sure if I can take the intel at face value. Especially since it's coming from a mystery 'benefactor' as Camden called him."

"I see," Misha replied. "And so, I surmise your next move will be to determine the identity of this mysterious third party?"

"Obviously." He knew me better than I thought.

"Unknown variables are unacceptable." I was glad Misha wasn't any more thrilled than I was with the introduction of this new, anonymous player. "And what exactly is Camden Walsh's role in all of this?"

"He owes me a life debt." The explanation seemed ridiculous. I'd helped him out, sure. But he didn't owe me anything. There were so many missing details from the events surrounding the night I'd saved Camden from whatever Mithras had planned for him, that I couldn't process any of it. I didn't know if it was something Lorik had done to me, or if I was just losing my damned mind. "Before Lorik kidnapped me and traded me to the Raksasha for the return of his soul, he'd been courting Mithras. Trying to become part of his syndicate. He had us jumping through all sorts of hoops. One of them was delivering a Werewolf to Mithras's compound. I helped to free Camden . . . ." I rubbed at my temples. ". . . somehow. And I guess he feels like he owes me a debt of gratitude or some shit."

Misha inclined his head. He didn't press for any further details and I was glad I didn't have to try to dig around my dysfunctional brain to find them. "At any rate, I have a feeling we'll be working together." But how, and to what end, I didn't know yet.

"I realize you have no other option at this point, but tread carefully, Darian." Misha's serious tone coaxed goosebumps to the surface of my skin. "You may be beyond your depth, despite having Camden in your corner."

Didn't I know it? Getting in over my head was sort of my thing, though. That and a self-destructive streak that reared its ugly head every time my life seemed to be gliding smoothly. "I really don't have a game plan at this point." Admitting it made me feel a little less stressed. "But I think it's a good idea to keep Camden close rather than tell him where to stick it."

"I agree." Misha leaned against the granite countertop of the wet bar and drummed his fingers on the surface. "I can do some digging as well, see what I can find out. The Arx believe themselves esoteric, but it's their human arrogance that lends them a false sense of security. I can confirm the validity of Camden's claims and perhaps from there you can form some plan of attack."

It was as good a strategy as any. Misha was connected. He'd at least know someone who knew someone who knew someone who knew something about the Arx and what they were up to. God, the more I thought about it, the more ridiculous it seemed. But at this point, I didn't have any other choice. It was either trust

Camden or wait for more eager assassins to try to put an end to my existence.

"Considering the circumstances, you don't have to follow through on the contract I offered you." I figured it would only be a matter of time before Misha got down to business. "You obviously have other problems that need your attention right now. All of these distractions will pull your focus."

"No way." I could've taken the easy out but thanks to my stubborn streak, that wasn't ever going to happen. "I'm not backing out."

Misha gave me one of his signature long suffering sighs. Who would he be exasperated with when I was gone?

"You're insufferably obstinate."

"Yup."

"There will be hell to pay if this job is botched."

"Oh, ye of little faith." Misha and I had only been working together for a little over a year. I didn't have enough of a track record to give him peace of mind quite yet. I leveled my best laser death stare on him. "I don't botch jobs. Ever."

Misha smirked. "Fine. I'm holding you to it, though. Don't let this business with the new building, or the Werewolf, distract you from what you're being paid to do."

I think he knew I needed him to take a hard line with me. If anything, to keep me focused so the anxiety of my current situation wouldn't eat me alive.

"No problem." I was a professional first and foremost. Considering I'd taken out the shifter the other night while dodging a barrage of bullets, you'd think Misha would recognize that by now. Oh well. Some people were tougher to impress than others. "But I would like a little more background on the mark."

Misha's lips thinned. He wasn't happy about my digging for more info and a shiver of trepidation danced down my spine. Secrets didn't make friends. "I have nothing further to offer you." His crisp formality threw up yet another red flag. "I've told you, killing him won't violate your precious code, Darian. That should be enough reassurance for you."

It should have been. But it wasn't.

"Whatever." I had a name and that was enough. If Misha didn't want to be more forthcoming, then I'd take care of business on my own. But it rankled that he didn't trust me enough to divulge more details while simultaneously expecting my blind trust in return. My mood had soured to the point of no return and I wasn't interested in moping around Misha's kitchen all night. "I'm going out." He didn't need an explanation, but for some reason it made me feel better to act like a spoiled kid rebelling against curfew. "See ya later."

I allowed the shadows to swallow my corporeal form as I left Misha's house with dramatic flair. I was pissed and I wanted him to know it. Whether or not he cared was another matter altogether.

For a while, I roamed the streets of Seattle as nothing more than feathery wisps of midnight. Shadows curled around me like lengths of dark ribbon, dancing against the backdrop of street-lights and headlights. Before long, I found myself standing in front of my blown-to-shreds building at the heart of Belltown. Regret stabbed at my chest as I took in the sight of my beloved studio. Almost one entire side of the top floor was missing, and the exposed brick was marred with black scars from the explosion. The building had been condemned and was scheduled to be torn down. I couldn't bear the thought of the place being razed to the ground. It had been my safe space for so long. My little haven in the heart of the bustling city.

Losing this place was like losing a limb or a vital organ. I wasn't sure how I'd coped without it so far.

I might have told myself that I was okay with camping out in Misha's guestroom and now, getting ready to settle into a new place. But the prospect of change scared the ever-loving shit out of me and sent my anxiety into a tailspin. My gut curled into a tight knot as I drifted on an air current to the second story of the building. Rubble littered the once pristine bamboo floors and deep grooves made from shrapnel ran like claw marks down the remaining three walls. Everything that could have been salvaged —which wasn't much—had already been tucked away in a storage unit. The space was bare aside from the wreckage that remained and the shadows that only added to the twisted ugliness of the destroyed space.

If the Arx, or more to the point, Mitchell Redmond, was in fact responsible for what had happened here—the total destruction of my haven, not to mention my peace of mind—the bastard was going to pay for it.

Rather than dwell on any immediate plans for retribution, I reclaimed my corporeal form and picked my way through the rubble to the space where my kitchen used to be. All that remained was the crushed remnants of the island and refrigerator and the sturdy brick wall. I crossed the space and laid my palm to the cool bricks before allowing my fingertips to trace the edges of the rectangles along the mortar lines. Maybe I could get the demolition crew to save the bricks so I could put them to good use at my new place. A little old familiarity to go with the new . . .
.

One of the bricks gave way beneath my fingertips, and then another. Funny, it almost seemed as if they were meant to be that way, not connected to anything but given the appearance of being secured in place. A deep throb of pain radiated through my skull and I gritted my teeth as I pulled two of the bricks loose. Three more . . . four . . . five . . . eight . . . until I stared, jaw slack, at the door of a small safe.

"What in the actual . . . ."

Another stab of pain shot through my skull and I doubled over as I cradled my head in my palms. The headaches—which were weird enough—seemed to come at the most inopportune moments. Like now, as I stared at a wall safe I couldn't remember having ever installed. It was mine, though. I knew it without a doubt. Tears streamed down my cheeks as I fought against the searing heat that continued to stab through my skull. My hand moved as though on its own to turn the dial to the right, left, and right again. I turned the handle, and the door gave way and swung open to reveal a pile of cash, IDs and passports, envelopes, and other miscellaneous items. The world seemed to tip on its axis as my vision blurred, blocking the contents of the safe from further scrutiny. A tremor shook my body as I sucked in a sharp breath and forced myself to fight through the pain to retrieve the contents. I'd be damned if I let a headache—no matter how painful—keep me from this piece of my life that I'd somehow managed to forget.

Another wave of pain stole over me and I swayed on my feet. I clutched the envelopes and other mysteries to my chest as I went down on one knee. I might just pass the fuck out, but at least I'd have these treasures in my arms.

A dark shadow near the ceiling lurched in the periphery of my vision. My head snapped up and whipped to the right. Before I could react, the smudge of cloudy darkness slammed into me, knocking me to the floor. The seemingly gossamer entity hit me again, as solid as a battering ram as it shoved me a good twenty feet across my destroyed studio, toward a gaping hole in the center of the floor. Whatever attacked me, it wasn't another Shaede. This was a creature I'd never encountered before. It seemed best to fight fire with fire as a means of defense, and I let the shadows swallow my corporeal form.

I'd like to see whatever the hell this was use its muscle against a gossamer thing.

My incorporeal state helped to dull the throb of pain that echoed through my skull and allowed me some small amount of clarity. I had to assume that whatever this creature was, it was another assassin with its sights set on the million-dollar bounty the Arx had placed on my head. It came at me again, and I caught an air current as I backed away. It shouldn't have been able to see me through the cover of shadow, but it had no problem picking me out. The dark mass moved with blinding speed as a roar erupted from somewhere within its center. I braced myself for impact despite knowing there was no way it could hurt me, as long as I was cloaked in shadows.

Wrong.

So, *so* wrong.

It hit me dead on. Shadows scattered from around me, forcing me back into my solid body. It shouldn't have been possible, but I was too shocked to contemplate the hows and whys. Adrenaline dumped into my bloodstream and my heart hammered against my ribcage with frantic beats. I slammed into the remains of my kitchen island and my spine cracked, momentarily immobilizing me until the vertebrae could fuse and heal themselves.

The black cloud of doom didn't have any qualms about kicking me while I was down. It moved with blinding speed, struck with unimaginable strength, and kept me on the defensive, locked in the confines of my skin. It tossed me around as though I was nothing more than a ragdoll. Blow after cruel blow, never giving my body a chance to completely heal before breaking me once again.

I didn't know how much more I could take. Whereas the black cloud had no problem lashing out despite its insubstantial appearance, I couldn't get a single shot in. A billowing, kinetic ball of darkness that was neither solid nor air. The fine hairs on my arms stood on end and my teeth chattered from the force of magical energy it exuded. Whatever the hell it was, it was powerful. And quite possibly the one thing that could manage to wipe me from the face of the earth.

The undulating black mass pulled back and let out another deafening roar before rushing at me once again. This would be the killing blow. I hoped whatever this thing was, it was able to spend the cool million it was about to receive . . . .

Silence descended on me, wrapping me in a cocoon of cool air. The pounding in my head increased to the point I thought my skull might split right open. The black cloud roiled in an angry swirl and dissipated into the air like bits of dust. I squinted through the pain to see someone walking toward me, his gait confident and predatory. I shielded my eyes against the dazzling brightness of his presence, though I couldn't be sure if the aura that surrounded him was real, or an illusion created by the intensity of my headache.

"You're okay, Darian." The words were spoken through the silence, not to my ears, but right in my head like a thought. "I've got you. Everything's going to be okay."

God, I hoped so. Because I was about to check the fuck out.

[6]

You're okay, Darian. I've got you.

A calm overwhelmed me and filled my chest so that my heart ached. My entire being awakened with the whirlwind of emotions those words evoked. Couldn't remember how or when I'd heard them before, but I knew without a doubt they'd been said to me more than once and by the same individual. A sense of peace and comfort overtook the fear and anxiety and by slow degrees, my body ceased its trembling and I was able to take a deep breath.

I was safe. Protected. Nothing and no one could hurt me. But how? Why? And who was it that provided me with this unshakable knowledge? This sense of calm?

"Hello?"

It seemed silly to call out to someone when I wasn't sure there was anyone around. Not even my supernatural eyesight could penetrate the inky darkness that surrounded me and if not for the strange peacefulness, I'd have been freaking out over the possibility that I'd gone suddenly blind. That was it, though. Somehow, I inherently knew I was being prevented from seeing and that it was for my own good. It stirred up a hell of a lot of whys that I knew I wouldn't get the answers to. At least, not right away.

"Is anyone here?"

Hell, I didn't even know where "here" was. I knew I wasn't at my studio, and I couldn't smell the water, so I wasn't at my new place either. Likewise, my senses didn't pick up on anything reminiscent of Misha, or of Xander or Raif. I wasn't anywhere familiar. With anyone familiar. The sensory deprivation should have sent my anxiety into a tailspin. Instead, I couldn't help but give myself over to the calm that insisted on holding me in its warm embrace. I didn't want to do anything but stay right where I was.

A strange energy signature brushed my senses. Familiar and yet . . . not. My pulse quickened with my breath, but it wasn't fear that stirred my blood. More like anticipation. Or yearning. As though I was about to wrap my fingers around something that had been just out of my reach for far too long.

"I know you're there. I can feel you."

So many questions needed answers and I was antsy as hell to get them. Patience wasn't exactly one of my strong suits, but I held it together and remained still, giving my mysterious company the time he, she, or they needed to shed a little light on my current situation. The seconds ticked by like hours as I sat there in the quiet dark. Waiting.

Cool skin met mine. Fingertips brushed along my cheekbone. A pleasant shudder rippled over my skin and my eyes drifted shut as I let out a slow breath. A single, innocent touch was a homecoming. As inexplicable as it was simple. I wasn't afraid. Not even close. Instead, I leaned toward the touch and let my head tilt into the contact as a large palm cupped my cheek. If I was under the influence of magic, it was heady stuff.

I might as well have been trapped in a dream. And if so, I never wanted to wake up.

A blast of cold flared from the ring that circled my thumb and snaked around my wrist, up my arm. It wasn't an uncomfortable sensation per se, but it sent a momentary rush of foreboding through my body. The sensation retreated as quickly as it appeared, leaving me once again in the state of near sensory deprivation.

"How are you feeling?"

The question came out of nowhere. A disembodied voice that was so generic it might as well have been computer generated. A little disconcerting considering my current situation. I wasn't afraid though. I wasn't prepared for a fight. I wasn't thinking of a way out. I was so goddamned calm you'd think someone had slipped me a few Xanax or something.

"Fine, aside from not being able to see anything." Or smell, hear right, etc. Somehow, I didn't think I needed to elaborate. My unknown host knew exactly what was up.

"It's necessary. I'm sorry, Darian. There's a way around it, and you'll get there, but for right now, this is for your own protection."

The familiarity with which he spoke to me combined with the enigmatic statement piqued my curiosity. I wasn't even sure how I knew the voice belonged to a "he" but somehow, I had no doubt. We'd met before. But he didn't want me to see his face or hear his voice. It only made me want to reclaim the use of my senses that much more.

"Not to burst your bubble or anything, bud, but that explanation isn't going to work for me."

He laughed as though totally expecting my snarky response. "I'm sure. But for the time being, you're just going to have to trust me."

I let out a derisive snort. I'd been through this song and dance already with Camden. If my strange rescuer had met me before, he had to have known that I didn't trust anyone who hadn't earned it.

"Ask me anything. If it's in my power, I'll give you an honest answer."

Cryptic. Fae, perhaps? A twinge of pain tugged at my skull

and I drew in a cleansing breath. "Within your power, huh? All right, I'll bite." It's not like I had anything better to do while I sat here in the dark. "What in the hell was that thing that attacked me in my apartment and what in the hell were you doing there?"

"That thing," he said, "was a Délash. And I was there to protect you from it."

The most basic answers possible, and yet, they didn't tell me anything I needed to know. I guessed we'd have to break this down into tiny pieces. "A what?" First things first, identify this new and very dangerous threat.

"Délash. It's hard to explain. It's not a living thing. Not really, anyway. More like sentient power."

So basically, the black cloud of doom that had tossed me around my building was raw power that possessed the ability to think and reason. Like that wasn't scary as fuck. "Gotcha. Okay then, who controls it?" Someone had to be pulling the strings. My money was on the Arx which honestly, was a little hypocritical considering their whole anti-supernatural, human preservation thing.

"I can't tell you that." Despite the monotone of his voice, I sensed the disappointment. Don't know why he was so bummed. I was the one with the target on my back.

"Why not?"

He let out a sigh that I couldn't help but think I'd heard a hundred times before. As though whoever this was had at one point been perpetually frustrated by my stubborn tenacity.

"It's for your own safety." God, I was tired of hearing that boilerplate response. "But I promise you, Darian, as soon as it's possible, you'll know everything."

Hmmm. A bunch of non-answers that got me nowhere. Whoever this guy was, he had a reason for protecting his identity. Maybe he was Camden's third-party player. Or maybe he worked for whoever sent the black cloud of doom after me and was trying to stay on the DL. But if that was the case, why help me at all when he could have just let it kill me.

"Whatever. Tell me, don't tell me. That's your prerogative. Why protect me from it? Just another supernatural Good Samaritan out on a stroll or what?" There was no way he'd simply stumbled across my building and noticed the tussle. He'd known where I'd be and had followed me to the building. Maybe he was less of a protector and more of a stalker.

"It's my job to protect you."

Yup. Definitely a stalker. What next? I already had mysterious secret societies paying for my death, clouds of power hunting me down, even more mysterious saviors keeping me in the dark—both literally and figuratively—while I tried to piece everything together. I seriously needed a drink.

"Did Xander hire you to follow me?" As good a guess as any that the arrogant Shaede King would be behind this.

A space of silence passed, and I swear the air cooled by several degrees. A chill danced along the surface of my skin and I shuddered.

"This has nothing to do with Alexander Peck."

Whoever this guy was, he wasn't a fan of Xander. Interesting. "All right. Then who hired you to watch me?"

"No one hired me. I'm your protector, Darian."

Seriously. What in the hell was this guy talking about? The sense of calm that had overtaken me was quickly replaced by gut churning frustration. Maybe I wasn't safe at all. Maybe I was being held by one of the Arx's assassins, simply playing with me before delivering the killing blow.

"Sorry, buddy. But you're going to have to find a new job. Because I didn't hire you and I sure as hell don't need a protector."

I was answered with a chuff of laughter. "Gods, I've missed you."

What. The. Actual. Fuck. "Funny. Can't say I feel the same way."

Another space of silence passed, and a strange melancholy settled over me, sucking all of the breathable air from around me. My chest tightened and I rubbed at my sternum to banish the sensation that refused to abate. I tried to draw a deep breath, but my lungs were reluctant to cooperate.

"You do miss me, Darian." The melancholy wasn't mine. "You just don't realize it."

I didn't know how much more of this I could take. A panic attack was creeping up on me, I was blind and at the mercy of god only knew who, and the dull ache at the base of my skull was beginning to throb in a way that seriously soured my already bad mood. I hated feeling helpless and right now I was completely at the mercy of someone—or something—that could just as easily be fucking with me than trying to keep me safe. I reached for the daggers that should have been sheathed at my hips only to find them gone. Well, shit. Looked like I was officially screwed.

"Calm down, Darian. I'd never hurt you. I'd never let anything or anyone hurt you. I'm leaving, but I'll be close. Watch out for the Délash. I'm going to fix everything. I promise you."

Watch out for the Délash? I waited for something. A small clue on how I could avoid it.

Another flash of bitter cold flared from the ring that circled my thumb. It swept me up in its icy chill, bringing goosebumps to the surface of my skin and causing my teeth to chatter. I wrapped my arms around my body as I guarded myself against what might as well be a blizzard. As quickly as it started, the storm passed, and in blinding brightness, my eyesight returned to reveal my surroundings.

Alone.

I stood in the center of the building I'd leased from my myste-rious benefactor only a couple of days ago. The fresh water scent of Lake Union rushed through my nostrils as did the musty, unlived-in smell of the building. All of my senses had been dulled to keep me from recognizing anything about where I was or who

I'd been with. But why? And how? I didn't know of any creatures capable of such a feat. Not even witches could conjure that type of magic.

No doubt about it, I was way out of my league. Problem was, I had no idea who I was out of my league with.

With slow steps, I wandered the warehouse space. More to center myself and calm my racing heart than anything else. I stopped at an old beat-up desk at the far corner to find my daggers and katana, along with the pile of stuff I'd grabbed from the safe at my building before the dark cloud of doom had shoved me across the floor. The same guy—Fae—creature—warlock—force of nature—whatever—that had brought me here had managed to salvage my treasures and left them for me. Maybe he wasn't all that bad after all. Either that, or he was trying to lull me into a false sense of security. If that was the case, dude didn't know me half as well as he seemed to think he did. I never felt secure. Rarely trusted. My inner circle was as tight as the ring that refused to leave my thumb. He might have wanted me to be patient and let the answers present themselves in due time, but what he didn't realize was that I was way too tenacious to just sit back and watch my life unfold before me.

Or maybe he did realize it . . . . Fuck. I had no idea what to think at this point.

Time had flown since the Délash's attack. The first rays of the morning's sunlight now filtered in through the foggy, unwashed windows of my new place. That damned cloud must have packed a serious punch to render me unconscious for several hours. My conversation with my unknown rescuer couldn't have taken more than twenty minutes which meant I was missing a serious chunk of time. Nothing about the previous night and current morning made an ounce of sense and I knew I wasn't going to get any real answers anytime soon.

Damn, I hated to be left in the dark.

I reached for the stack of manila envelopes, papers, and

whatnot scattered on the desk's surface when a loud knock at the front door nearly startled me out of my skin. I let out a shaky breath as several choice curse words sprang to the forefront of my mind. Was the entire freaking world trying to rattle me?

Another knock came on the heels of the first and I hustled to the front door. I wasn't a morning person by any stretch of the imagination and the fact that I hadn't even been to bed yet only added to the 'tude I was about to rock. I yanked open the door, prepared to tell whoever was on the other side exactly where they could shove it, but immediately swallowed the urge as I took stock of the man's jeans, work boots, and clip board.

"Darian Charles?"

Camden had mentioned a crew would be starting renovations on the place soon. I'd totally spaced it out with everything I had going on. "That's me."

"Ned Smith." He reached out and I looked at his outstretched hand before bringing my gaze back to his. I smiled, hoping my expression was an I've-been-expecting-you sort of vibe rather than the I-have-no-fucking-idea-what's-going-on aesthetic I was trying to hide. "I'm the general contractor for the remodel on the building. We'd like to get started today if that's all right."

Since I'd leased the building as opposed to buying it, the cost for the renovations would fall on my mysterious landlord. Which was fine by me. I wasn't about to throw down a ton of cash for anything I didn't have the pink slip for. "Today, as in, right now?" I was too damned tired and overwrought to process anything. What time was it anyway? Couldn't have been later than eight in the morning.

"Yeah, we'd like to get started now if that's not a problem for you. I've got framers and laborers lined up for the next few days to rough out some stuff before the finish carpenters get here next week."

Wow. Ned's timeline seemed a bit zippy. I leaned an arm on the doorjamb and studied him for a quiet moment. The guy was as human as they came. Completely mundane. "You're not from some extreme makeover show or anything, are you?"

Ned laughed again. Not because I was funny, but because my apparently lame ass questions were making him anxious. Or annoyed. Probably both. "Nah. Just efficient. Is it all right if we get to work?"

Ned obviously wasn't the sort of guy who bothered with small talk. I liked him already. "Go for it. I'll just grab my things and leave you guys to it." The sooner they finished their remodel, the better.

"Great."

With that settled, Ned ignored me completely as he turned his attention to his crew and got everyone lined out for the day. I took that as my cue to get out. Rather than gather my treasures to take with me, instinct urged me to leave them where they were. I sensed they'd be safer here than at Misha's though I wasn't sure why. A low throb lingered at the base of my skull, and I had a feeling the headache was going to get worse before it got better. Which was why I'd planned to take my ass back to Misha's so I could guzzle a gallon or so of his faerie wine before I started investigating the items that I was sure were somehow connected to my mind-snapping headaches.

It was time to get to the bottom of things. And I was more than ready to connect a few dots.

[7]

"I take it you've completed your task?"

My step faltered at the threshold of Misha's front door. I regained my composure and closed the door behind me. I wasn't the only impatient one around here. "Not yet." I was going for unconcerned, but my voice cracked like a teenager coming in after curfew.

"I thought you wanted a paycheck?" Damn it. My investigation into the contents of the wall safe was going to have to be put on hold if Misha's annoyed expression was any indication. "If you're not up to the task—"

"Don't." I wasn't about to let the haughty Fae insult me or my work ethic. "If you even think about finishing that sentence you and I are going to have serious problems."

Misha cocked a brow. I wanted to wipe the smirk from his face. He'd wanted to get a rise out of me and it worked. Can't say I was a fan of his motivation tactics. "So, I can expect the job to be done by the end of the week?"

If I hadn't known better, I would've thought he was trying to push me into action to keep me from researching my mark. Or maybe even distract me from something else. I didn't like to think that he was trying to maneuver me. But if that was the case, anything less than compliance would throw up a red flag and I needed him unguarded. "Piece of cake," I replied.

Truth be told, I didn't like the implication that I couldn't get the job done. My ego always got the better of me and I had a sinking feeling I'd regret agreeing to his timeline. I'd wanted to research the mark a little before I went off and killed the poor bastard. Misha was pushing me into action, and whereas I didn't understand his motives, I knew he didn't want me thinking about anything for too long.

"Good." With business apparently settled, Misha turned his attention to the liquor cabinet. He poured two glasses of the faerie wine and extended one of them to me. I took the glass from his hand and tried not to drink mine in a single swallow. My head still pounded, and I was desperate for a little relief.

"Rough night?"

I eyed Misha warily as he sipped from his own glass. Either I was getting more paranoid in my old age, or he was privy to a hell of a lot more than he let on. I'd always been a little paranoid, so my money was on option number two. It seemed that with every passing day I found myself asking more questions than I could find answers to. And I didn't like it one damn bit.

"Peachy keen," I said with as much enthusiasm as I could muster. "How was yours?"

Misha studied me for a quiet moment as he took another long, slow sip from the glass. "Uneventful," he said after a moment. "I spent most of my evening reading."

Liar. "Oh yeah?" Well, it wasn't the entire truth, at least. No freaking way did he spend his evening with a book. I hadn't seen him pick one up once in all the weeks that I'd stayed here. "What's it about?"

Misha gave a dismissive wave of his hand. "It's a thriller. Serial killer with a vendetta, investigator with a history, the usual tropes."

Of course. I was seriously surprised Misha's pants weren't on fire right now. Anything for the Fae to navigate around the truth. No doubt he'd spent most of his evening reading something, but it sure as hell wasn't a work of fiction.

"Well, good for you. You deserve a little downtime." I forgot about trying to be polite and downed the remainder of the lustrous gold wine in a single swallow. It warmed a path down my throat and settled in a pleasant glow deep in my stomach. I regretted drinking so much, so fast, and I swayed slightly with the giddy rush. I set the glass on the bar top and stretched my arms high above my head as I tried to banish the wine's effects. "Time for this nocturnal creature to drag her tired butt to bed." I was so far from tired it wasn't even funny, but Misha didn't need to know that. "Peace out, homie."

Misha replied with a derisive snort. He liked my slang about as much as I liked his stiff, formal speech. "Rest well, Darian."

It was my turn for a disbelieving snort. But instead, I swallowed it down. "Thanks." The last thing I planned to do was rest. My problems were beginning to pile up, and I was running out of time.

I headed to my room, relieved that Ned's crew was in the process of getting my new place inhabitable.

I closed the bedroom door behind me and shucked my duster, tossing it onto a wingchair beside the bed. I headed for the dresser and pulled open the top drawer to dig through a stack of my clothes for the folded slip of paper with nothing more than a name and address written on it. The address wasn't far from my old building deep in the heart of Belltown. And the name, while seemingly mundane, could have belonged to any number of supernatural creatures.

"Levi Curtis," I said aloud. "I wonder what in the hell you've done to deserve to die?"

Rather than hang out in my room and hide from Misha, I decided to do a little reconnaissance. I became one with the light and left my corporeal form as I drifted through the pane of glass in the second story window and glided like a feather to the ground. I'd be damned if I'd kill anyone who didn't deserve it. I had no idea who this Levi was, but I was bound and determined to uncover his sins before I laid a single finger on him.

The trip from Capitol Hill to Belltown only took a matter of minutes thanks to a brisk early morning wind. It didn't take me long to find the address Misha had scrawled on the paper and I looked up to read the sign above the door, its neon tubing milky white and lifeless in the sunlight.

The Pit, huh? Sounded like a charming place. In all the years I'd lived in this neighborhood, how had I never noticed this place before? And yet, a strange sense of déjà vu tugged at the back of my brain minutes before I was struck with a railroad spike of pain.

Tears blurred my vision as I released my incorporeal form and doubled over with a groan. I cradled my head in my hands and squeezed my eyes shut as I drew in shallow drafts of breath. I couldn't keep going like this. The constant pain was beginning to take its toll, physically, emotionally, mentally. I was losing it and didn't know how much longer I could stand it. I continued to breathe through the throbbing pain and said a prayer to any god that might listen that I be spared from the ongoing torture. Maybe I had one of those brain eating parasites and thanks to my super-natural healing, I gave the damn thing a never-ending buffet. Bile rose hot in my throat and I shuddered at the thought.

I couldn't stand here on the street doubled over and sucking in breaths like I'd just run a marathon. Reconnaissance was all about stealth and I was about as stealthy as a bull in a china shop right now.

Looked like Levi and learning more about him would have to wait. At least I knew where to find him. It was a start, and I had six more days before the job had to be completed. This place, for whatever reason, had triggered a headache of epic proportions. I might not have been able to scout it out personally, but I knew someone who could help.

I didn't want to go back to Misha's, and Ned and his crew were hard at work on my new place. That left me only one option and it was pretty much the last place on earth I wanted to be right now. But I needed to lie down, get an ice pack on my head, and level the hell out before I crumpled under the ongoing strain. So, against my better judgment, I headed for the only place left where I could find sanctuary.

———

I STOOD BEFORE THE WROUGHT IRON GATE AT THE EDGE OF Xander's property and stared up the driveway toward the looming mansion. It reminded me of a scene from a gothic horror movie. Foreboding music, dark shadows, and the heroine taking her first steps toward her doom. I know, melodramatic. But no horror movie monster could be half as scary as Anya. And she was the last creature I wanted to tangle with today.

The Shaede manning the guard station let me in without a word. Everyone on Xander's staff knew I had full run of the place, and no one dared questioned my presence or authority. Just one of the perks that came with being a member of the king's inner circle. Of course, there were still those who speculated that we were lovers. A rumor that had been spread extensively over the past few years. Xander himself had been responsible for a lot of the talk but I didn't begrudge him. There had been a short period of time when I'd entertained a relationship with him. I loved Xander. I really did. Just never in the way he wanted me to. And there were days that I truly wondered why my heart could never belong entirely to him.

The trek to the house felt like my death march. I had no idea if I'd see Anya or not, but it was safe to bet we'd run into each other at some point. I mean, Xander's house was big but it wasn't *that* big. I let myself in and stood in the foyer for a moment as I took in my surroundings. Over the years, this place had become as much a sanctuary for me as my own studio in Belltown. But it was lacking the presence of the individuals that made it feel like home. I hated to admit how much I missed Asher, Raif, and even Xander. But their absence had opened a hole in my heart, and I was desperate for them to come back and make me feel whole.

Surely that was the explanation for the strange emptiness I'd been feeling lately.

"I thought you were living at Misha's," a cool voice said from the top of the stairs. I tried not to roll my eyes, but they acted of their own volition. "Or did he get tired of you and kick you to the curb?"

"How's it hanging, Anya?" Might as well get the antagonistic greetings out of the way now. "I heard Baby Gap is thinking about coming out with a line of leather-wear for toddlers. It's never too early to get them into some nice, snug cowhide."

In her pre-motherhood days, Anya had had quite the leather fetish. Dungeon mistresses had nothing on her wardrobe and I'd always wondered how she'd managed to get around without squeaking and squawking everywhere she went. Since little Dimitri's birth however, she'd adopted a more toned-down look. Not quite soccer mom, but not quite BDSM. Who knew there was a happy middle?

She drummed her fingers on the banister and her violet eyes narrowed almost imperceptibly as she studied me. She and Xander had formed an even tighter bond after the death of Anya's husband, and the birth of her son. She was the king's most trusted advisor, and in his absence, ruled as though she were queen. Not gonna lie, power suited her.

"As charming as ever." Anya descended the stairs slowly, as though chatting with me was the last thing on the planet she wanted to do. "What can I help you with today?"

Translation: How can I get you out of here as quickly as possible?

I gave her what I hoped was a friendly smile, though I suspected it was something closer to a grimace. "Honestly? I just need a place to crash for a few hours."

Anya must have sensed my exhaustion because her expression softened. She let out a huff of breath that was closer to a sigh, as her posture relaxed. "Are you all right? Because you look like shit."

I let out a bark of laughter. Following up her concern with an insult was the cherry on top of a stellar past twenty-four hours. "Look, I just need a breather." If she wanted, we could fight all day tomorrow. "Can I take a timeout here or not?"

Anya's lips thinned but her gaze remained soft. Maybe motherhood had changed her after all. "You know where your room is," she replied. "Or did you want me to carry you to the suite?"

Okay, so motherhood hadn't changed her *that* much. I headed for the stairs without another word and brushed past her just as quietly. I didn't turn to see if she watched me. Really, I didn't care. I had too much on my mind to worry about her and our petty rivalry. Once I got this headache down to a dull roar, I planned to call Camden and get the ball rolling on a few things. My to do list was getting bigger by the day and if I didn't do something now, the things that needed my attention would quickly be out of my control.

I opened the door to the suite that might as well have been an apartment unto itself. I didn't bother to turn on the lights, I simply crossed to the king-size bed at the far end of the room and collapsed onto its surface. Ahhhhh. Memory foam. There was nothing like it in the entire world and I swear, the mattresses in Xander's house had come straight from heaven.

The heavy drapes made it nice and dark. I settled my head on one of the downy pillows and let out a slow sigh. The dull ache in my temples had yet to subside and all I wanted to do was check out for a while and lose a few hours to empty, black sleep. Hopefully I'd feel more like myself when I woke up, though to be honest, I was starting to wonder if I even knew what "myself" felt like anymore.

Seconds after my head hit the pillow, I drifted off.

"Has anyone ever told you you're incredibly stubborn?"

I let out a snort as I sipped from the lip of my glass. The guy sitting next to me at the bar spoke with familiarity, though I couldn't remember ever having met him. "You and everyone else I've ever met. So, are you going to tell me about the job or what?"

I knew I was dreaming, but I was too damned tired to try and wake myself up. I gave into the fantasy and glanced toward the source of the warm voice that somehow resonated with power, unable to make out the details of his face. My gaze narrowed as I let out a measured breath. A mantle of calm settled over me and every muscle in my body seemed to relax at once. My head didn't pound and the familiar anxiety I felt on an almost daily basis was blissfully absent. Whoever my dreamland drinking buddy was, his presence was a more than welcome calm that I found myself greedy for.

"This isn't about a job, Darian. This is about us."

"Us?" I turned away and focused on the high-ball glass cradled between my palms. "There is no us."

"Wrong." The confidence in his voice sent a pleasant shiver down my spine. "I'm bound to you. The only thing that can separate us is death."

Why did it feel like this was somehow more than a simple dream? I couldn't shake the feeling that I was no longer lying in my bed at Xander's and had been transported to another time and place. I brought the glass to my lips and sipped. The liquid had no taste, the only indicator that I was simply lost in deep REM sleep.

"Bound, huh?" I let out a snort. "So, does that make you my slave?"

"Not a slave. A protector. I'm yours, Darian."

Mine. I'd heard those words before. In a dream? No. Someone had spoken them to me in reality. More than once. My gaze narrowed as I tried to make out the details of the face in front of me. I felt more awake now than I had when I'd laid down.

"Is this real?" The words tumbled unbidden from my lips. "Or am I dreaming?"

"Both." I sensed the smile in his tone.

Cryptic. "I don't like games."

"I'm not playing."

I reached over and gave my arm a solid pinch. Didn't even feel a tickle. "I want to wake up." If my brain wasn't going to get any rest, there was no point in trying to sleep.

"Not yet. Stay with me for a while." A pregnant pause saturated the air between us. "I . . . . I miss you."

His words gutted me. His absence was the hole in my soul that I'd been trying to fill for over a year. He was the pain that never subsided in my chest. The mystery I'd been trying to solve for months. "I miss you, too. I think."

He laughed and the simple sound was enough to make my heart beat a little faster. "I need you to know that I'm sorry. For everything that's happened and everything that's going to happen."

Apologizing in advance? That couldn't be good. "What's going to happen?"

"Things are going to get a hell of a lot worse before they get better, Darian. I just need you to be strong, okay?"

Strong? Lately I'd felt as sturdy as spun sugar. It wouldn't take much to crack me. I wondered what was coming. Pain? Suffering? Emotional trauma? Would I be beaten? Maimed? Tortured? It seemed I was always being tested. Put through the wringer. How much more could I possibly be expected to endure?

"Maybe you could find someone else to be sorry to." I wasn't interested in experiencing any more hardships. "I gotta be honest, I could sort of use a break."

"I know." His tone bore so much sorrow and guilt it coaxed a lump to my throat. "And I promise I'll give you one. Soon. In the meantime, keep your eyes open and trust me."

Tough words to swallow from a nearly disembodied dream voice. "Trust you?" I let out a bark of laughter. "Why in the hell should I do that?"

"Because you love me."

Right. *"Love you?" This dream got weirder by the second. "I don't even know your name."*

"Yes, you do. Think, Darian. What's my name?"

Mysterious hazel eyes invaded my memory as I let out a gust of breath. God, it was right on the tip of my tongue.

"Time to wake up, love. Be careful out there."

I sat up in bed, heart pounding. His name left my lips as a whisper, though I still had no idea who he was.

"Tyler."

White hot pain seared through my skull and I gritted my teeth. Goddamn it, I wished someone—anyone—could tell me what in the hell was happening to me.

[8]

I collapsed back onto the mattress with my head cradled between my palms. Tears escaped from between my tightly shut lids as I let out a shuddering breath. The headaches had been a near constant for so many months I'd lost count, and the unrelenting pain wore on me. The details of my strange dream faded as I came fully awake, and the name I'd spoken just moments before vacated my memory as though blown away by a cleansing breeze. I pressed the heels of my palms against my eye sockets, as if that would somehow abate the throbbing pain. I needed to find someone who could help me. Give me some kind of relief, before I lost my mind completely.

I was holding on by the barest of threads.

A knock came at the door moments before Anya's voice spoke through the heavy oak. "Should I have a place set for you at dinner? Or will you grace the household with your absence tonight?"

Heartwarming.

I pushed up from the bed and took several unsteady steps before crossing the room to the door. There seemed to be no escape from the pain—I couldn't even find solace in sleep. My head hurt too damned bad to shout back and forth with Anya just so she wouldn't have to meet me face-to-face. Right now, I needed solitude like I needed air.

The door might as well have weighed a thousand pounds as I pulled it open. A swath of light cut through the darkness, and I brought up my left hand to shield my eyes from the offending brightness. "Not that I don't appreciate the dinner invitation, but I'm not hungry. I'll be out of your hair as soon as—"

"Gods, Darian." The shock in Anya's tone bothered me more than the interruption. "What's wrong with you? You look like you're knocking on death's door."

Thank god I could always count on Anya to soften the blow to save my fragile ego. I blew out a slow breath as I leaned against the door to steady myself. "Headaches." There was no point in being dishonest. "They've been getting worse. I thought I might sleep it off here for a while, but that plan didn't work out so well."

"Headaches?" Anya's brow furrowed as she looked me over as though I'd lost my mind. "How is that even possible? And it must be one hell of a supernatural headache, because you look like shit."

She really was the best.

"Okay, well, it's been great chatting." It hadn't been great chatting. "But you'd better get down to dinner before—"

"Does *Ty-fmdpyst* know about this?"

A stab of pain shot through my skull and I sucked in a sharp breath. Anya's words became garbled and her face blurred in and out of focus. The same thing had happened the other night while I'd been talking to Asher. "Whatever you just said," I sucked in another breath and blew it out. "Don't say it again."

I didn't think it was physically possible for Anya to show actual concern for me, but her expression became even more serious as she took a tentative step toward me. "Does this have something to do with your *J-uftniptu* . . .?"

"Stop!" If she said one more word my brain was going to boil and explode inside of my skull. I dropped to one knee as I dragged in ragged gulps of breath to help manage the pain that ripped through me.

Anya bent down and put a hand on my shoulder. Despite the pain, I couldn't help but note that I must be in some seriously rough shape for her to treat me with any measure of kindness.

"I'm calling Xander."

"No." My hand flew up as though it could somehow stop her train of thought. I didn't know why I didn't want Xander to know what was going on with me, but I wasn't ready to reveal anything to anyone. Besides, he had a kingdom to rule and after the unrest of Saben's attempted coup, the last thing Xander needed was to worry about me and my problems. "Here." I reached into my pocket and pulled out the simple black business card with Camden's information. "Call this number. Tell him to send someone to get me."

The alpha Werewolf seemed to be more in the know than anyone regarding my situation. If I was going to ask for help—and god how I hated to—he was the best person to go to.

Anya took the card from my hand and studied it for a moment. "Let me help you to the bed and I'll call him."

"I'm okay." I didn't think my ego could sustain the damage of being helped back to bed. "Seriously. Just call Camden for me." I wouldn't be able to see the numbers on the phone, let alone get my fingers to work so I could dial.

Thankfully, Anya didn't argue. She turned and left me kneeling on the floor without another word. I didn't have the energy to drag my ass back to the bed, so I let my legs fall out from under me and crumpled to a heap on the floor. The pain began to ebb by small degrees, allowing me the opportunity to mull over the events of the past several days. And the conclusion I came to was that I was more confused than ever.

"Darian?"

I must've been lying on the floor for a lot longer than I'd thought. I looked up to find Camden staring down at me.

Concern marred the Alpha Werewolf's brow which struck me as a little funny since he didn't even know me.

"That bad, huh?"

Camden pursed his lips. "Well, it sure as hell isn't good."

He reached out his hand and I wasn't too proud to take it. He hoisted me up and I let out a deep breath that did little to numb the pain that clung to me. "Be straight with me. How much do you know about what's happening to me?"

Camden made sure I was steady on my feet before letting go of my hand. His expression became contemplative, as though he carefully chose his words. "I know enough to realize the pain is excruciating and that you think you're losing your mind."

He wasn't wrong. "Seriously. If I don't catch a break soon, someone's going to have to lock me in a padded cell."

"I think everyone's hoping it won't come to that," Camden said with a nervous laugh.

My gaze narrowed on the Alpha Werewolf. "And who would *everyone* be?"

"I think in the interest of your continued mental health, it's best not to discuss that particular detail."

Something didn't smell right. With every passing second, I became more certain that magic was somehow in play. It made me antsy to get to the bottom of what was going on and finally, I thought I knew where to start. "This has to do with a person, right?" Specifically, whoever had saved me from the murderous black cloud of doom the previous night. "It's a he." I wasn't sure how I knew that, but I was confident. "He's causing the headaches, isn't he?"

"It's complicated." I fixed Camden with a steely glare. "I know that's not what you want to hear right now," he added. "But, I suppose in a very roundabout, inadvertent way, yes. He's the cause of the headaches."

"Well then, tell him to stay the hell away from me and everyone will be fine."

"I think you know it's not that simple, Darian."

Sure I did, but that didn't mean I wasn't going to shoot for the easiest solution first. From the corner of my eye, I noticed Anya watching our exchange from outside the door. It's not that I minded her eavesdropping . . . . Wait a minute, yeah, I did.

"If you breathe a single word of what you've heard to Xander, Raif, or anyone else we're going to have a problem."

I didn't have to make eye contact with Anya for her to know I was speaking to her. She took a step over the threshold and threw her shoulders back. "As though I would bother any of them with your petty, melodramatic issues."

Her soft tone belied the harshness of her words. Maybe Anya and I were about to turn over a new leaf. I mean, I doubted we would be baking cookies and drinking wine while discussing makeup and boys anytime soon, but I hoped it was a start to something a little less antagonistic.

"Thanks." Just because I believed she wouldn't talk didn't mean I wanted to continue to have this conversation with an audience. I finally felt sturdy enough for my feet to support my weight and the room no longer blurred out of focus. I turned to Camden and leveled my gaze. "Let's go and let Anya get back to her dinner."

Anya didn't say a word. She simply stepped to one side and allowed us to pass.

"I appreciate you letting me crash for a while," I said as I brushed by her. "I'll try to keep my presence here to a minimum."

"You're always welcome, Darian." I paused at the top of the steps but didn't look back. "You know that."

A lump formed in my throat. Either I was getting sentimental in my old age, or the headaches were making me more emotional than usual. Rather than respond, I gave a quick nod of my head before I walked down the stairs with the Alpha Werewolf by my side.

"Where to?" Camden got right down to business and I appreciated that.

"My new place," I replied. I didn't care what state of construction it was in. I needed a little peace and quiet and somewhere safe to get my head straight.

"Perfect." Camden held out his arm as we hit the bottom stair. "After you."

I WAS PLEASANTLY SURPRISED AT WHAT NED AND HIS CREW HAD managed to accomplish in a day. Whoever was paying them obviously had deep enough pockets to light a fire under their asses. I couldn't have been happier. If they kept up the pace, the building would be livable in a matter of weeks. The place already had a homey vibe. As though the construction crew had some sort of insight as to what I'd like and what would make me most comfortable.

Interesting.

Camden settled atop a rung of a stepladder, legs braced out in front of him, and his arms folded across his wide chest. His alpha status was apparent in his relaxed posture that indicated he was rarely threatened. Definitely the sort of guy you wanted on your side.

"All right. Talk." No more beating around the bush. No more cryptic bullshit. No more sidestepping. I understood there were parameters that had to be respected. And certain secrets that, for now, needed to be kept. But that didn't mean I didn't expect Camden to be forthcoming with anything and everything else.

He gave a quick bark of laughter and flashed a wicked smile. "Honestly, I'm not even sure where to begin. There's a lot of shit to cover. It could take us days."

Lucky for me, all I had right now was time. "Okay, let's start with the problem we can tackle. The Arx."

Camden's posture visibly relaxed. "I was hoping you'd say that. But Darian, this is by no means going to be the least of your problems. It's just one we can discuss without it adversely affecting you."

Okay, so that didn't exactly put me at ease. But difficult or not, this business with the Arx was something that I could have some measure of control over. If I put whoever was at the root of my mysterious headaches on the backburner, there was a slight chance I could get some relief. Then again . . . . In all the chaos of the past twenty-four hours, I'd forgotten about my little side project for Misha. Which—as far as I could tell from my visit to the Belltown bar—might be somehow connected. I let out a slow sigh. If there was one thing I'd learned over the past few years, it was that nothing was ever random and there was no such thing as coincidence. I'd promised Misha the job would be done by the end of the week. A little tough to accomplish when I couldn't get close to my mark without experiencing skull shattering pain. Which made me wonder: was my mark the same guy who was the apparent cause of my headaches? If so, killing someone who claimed to be protecting me might not be the best idea.

All I could do was tick each item off my to-do list one at a time and hope everything worked itself out in the end. Wishful thinking, I know. But at this point, it was all I had.

"The faster we deal with the Arx, the better." I had bigger fish to fry, apparently, and was tired of wasting my time. "So if you have any suggestions on how best to exterminate an entire esoteric organization and get this bounty off my head, now is the time to throw it out there."

Camden gave a sad shake of his head. "There's no exterminating the Arx, I'm afraid. But we can set our sights on Redmond and at least eliminate the direct threat."

I threw up my hands and shot him a stern look. "I need more information than what you're giving me, Camden. If the organization itself can't be eliminated, I might as well surrender now." If that was the case, the least I could do was find some down on their luck individual to get the job done and leave this world with a good deed to hopefully redeem my soiled soul. "And if Redmond specifically is the one who has me in his sights, I need to know why."

Frustration set me into motion. I paced the confines of the empty building and let the cadence of my boots hitting the concrete floor distract my racing thoughts. Camden pushed himself up from where he'd been leaning on the ladder. A deep groove cut into his brow above his nose and his eyes flashed feral gold, giving me a glimpse of the wolf that lived beneath his skin.

"Redmond is a despot," Camden explained. "The Arx unquestionably follows his agenda. It benefits not only you, but the supernatural community at large to depose him."

I froze mid step and turned to face him. Threads tied together and Camden's roll in all of this became clearer. "You're going to plant someone sympathetic to the supernatural community in the Arx leadership."

He replied with a silent nod.

Wily SOB.

I didn't give a shit who he planned to insert into that role or why. As long as it would save my bacon, I was on board.

"Redmond uses the Arx to further his own interests. He makes a fortune though the connections he's made from a place of power: radical militias, militant hate groups, drug dealers, and black-market peddlers." His expression darkened and a shiver raced over my skin from the power I felt from a simple glance as his eyes flashed gold once again. "You'd be surprised at the price Werewolf blood fetches."

Redmond was clearly a low-life piece of garbage. I wouldn't bat a lash at ridding the world of him. My issue with anonymity would be tricky, but I had another, potentially bigger, problem that Camden probably needed to know about before we moved forward. And boy, was it a doozy.

"I'm more than happy to help the both of us and take the son of bitch out. I have a slight issue, though." I took a breath. Would he even believe me? "There's a sentient cloud of magic following me around and it doesn't like me all that much."

Camden nodded. "The Délash. I know."

Wow. He really did keep himself informed. It was good for me, though. The less I had to explain, the better. And likewise, since my mysterious protector was nowhere to be found, the more blanks he could fill in, the less out of control I'd feel.

"Have any idea how to get rid of one of those?"

Camden's rueful laughter was the only explanation I needed. "You'd have a better chance of wiping out the entire Arx on your own than you would getting rid of the Délash."

Okay. So that sounded bleak as fuck. Pessimism wasn't going to win the day, however and so I decided that just because no one had ever apparently gotten rid of a Délash, didn't mean it couldn't be done. Where there's a will, there's a way. And stubborn willfulness had nothing on me.

Unfortunately, we hadn't made much ground. But on the plus side, the pounding in my head had finally relented so at least I could think clearly. I needed to be proactive. Idle time was the enemy of an anxious, overactive brain. "I can find a way to take care of Redmond. But until we find a solution for my Délash problem, I'm going to need someone around who has my back."

"I think you already know that someone has your back, Darian."

Yup. My mysterious, faceless, voiceless protector who couldn't even be troubled to give me a name or phone number to call if I got into a pinch. So far, I'd rate this creature's service a one out of ten. Would not recommend.

"Fair enough." At this point, there was nothing else to say. If Camden was confident in this unknown player's ability to protect me, I'd play along, for now. That left only one thing for me to worry about. "There's something else. Misha contracted a job for me. Very few details on my mark, and thanks to the brain busting headaches, I haven't been able to do any recon on him."

"I can help you with the recon," Camden replied. "You at least have a name?"

"Yeah. His name's Levi and he works at a bar in Belltown called, The Pit."

Camden's eyes went wide with shock and my anxiety crested with a rush of adrenaline through my bloodstream.

"Levi. You're sure?"

"Yeah. Why?"

"Fuck." The barked expletive caused my heart to stutter in my chest. "I swear to the gods the situation gets more tangled by the second."

Great. Apparently, things had just gone from bad to worse. My eyes went skyward. It would sure be nice if someone up there cut me a little slack. Oh hell, who was I kidding? I knew for a fact we weren't even close to the eye of the storm yet.

[9]

C amden blew out a frustrated breath as he paced. "Okay, so we know there's not much that can be done about your memory issues yet. But we need to do something about the headaches. ASAP."

I was literally ready to try *anything* to get rid of the skull-splitting pain that seemed to only get worse. So far, Misha had the only thing that gave me any kind of relief and I was starting to trust him less by the day. "Faerie wine numbs the pain, but it doesn't get rid of it permanently."

Camden let out a derisive snort. Guess he wasn't a fan of the shimmering gold drink. "You shouldn't consume anything offered to you by a Fae creature. They're not to be trusted."

His blatant disgust told me what I needed to know about the Werewolf's opinion of Misha's kind. Not that I necessarily disagreed with him. The Fae were tricky to be sure, and though I was suspicious of Misha's recent motives, I still liked him. "Really, I can cope with the memory gaps" —because honestly, up until now the minor missing details here and there hadn't seemed too troubling— "but I *really* wish my headaches would go away."

A flash of cold flared from the ring that circled my thumb and wound a path around my wrist and up my arm. I sucked in a sharp breath as a wave of energy stole over me in a swirling vortex that I was certain only I could feel. My legs turned to Jell-O beneath me, and my knees shook as though they were about to give out. Power flooded me. Coursed through my veins and infiltrated every cell that constructed me. My breath raced and my heart beat a mad rhythm in my chest. Camden took a tentative step toward me, his brow furrowed, and I threw up a staying hand. Goosebumps spread over my skin and my teeth chattered from the icy chill that soaked deep into my bones and settled at the base of my skull.

I wanted to be afraid of what was happening, but all I felt was energized.

"Darian? Are you all right?"

"Yeah." Not sure how I knew it, but I totally was. "I'm okay."

My simple reassurance seemed to be enough for Camden and he relaxed. As the cold began to ebb from my body, I let my own tension ebb as well. Something had changed and I had a feeling only I could sense it. Like a floodgate that had been opened to allow water to soothe the scorched earth, the power that flooded me now soothed me. I brought my left hand up and examined the worn silver ring that encircled my thumb. It was the source of the strange magic that twined around me like delicate lengths of ribbon. I still couldn't remember where I'd gotten it, but the dull ache that usually throbbed at the back of my skull remained absent as I contemplated the ring's origin.

Trippy.

It was like I'd said a magic word or some shit. It would've been nice to know exactly what that word had been . . . .

I wasn't going to assume that I'd been magically cured of the headaches simply because I could play with the ring on my thumb and not feel physical pain from the contact. Rather than jump in headfirst, I decided to test the waters a bit and walked to the table at the far end of the warehouse where my mysterious rescuer had left the cache of folders and envelopes I'd taken from my old place in Belltown. I reached out and laid my palm to the stack. Nothing. No pain! I had no idea what I'd done, but so far so good.

"Darian?"

"I don't want to get my hopes up or anything . . . ." I looked over my shoulder at Camden. "But I might have finally caught a break."

He took several steps toward me, his gait every bit that of a wary predator. "What do you mean?"

Hell if I knew, but I wasn't going to outright admit it. "It's my ring." No use trying to deceive a Werewolf. Besides, I wanted Camden to trust me. "I think." I held up my left hand and waved it in the air. "I'm not sure where it came from, but it's not just a random piece of jewelry."

Camden walked up to me and held out his hand as though to ask permission to examine the ring. I obliged and gave him my hand for inspection. His gaze narrowed and his nostrils flared as he inhaled a slow breath. "You're right. There's a tang of magic surrounding it."

Hell yeah I was right. "Any idea what kind of magic?" Werewolves had far keener senses than me.

"Yeah," Camden said, his tone as dark as his countenance.

My eyes went wide. "Care to elaborate?"

"Not particularly." A frown cut into my brow and he added, "It's not that I don't want to share that information with you, Darian. It's just that right now, I don't think we should press our luck."

"The magic in my ring, it's connected to all of this, isn't it?" I said with a flourish of my hand.

"Pretty much," Camden said on a sigh. "I know that's probably not what you wanted to hear."

On the contrary, it made a hell of a lot of sense and sort of put me at ease. "For now, I'm okay with it."

Camden's wolfish gaze narrowed as he studied me. "How do you know the headaches are gone?" He let out a chuff of laughter. "I mean, aside from the obvious."

It's not as though the pain had been constant, but I did miraculously feel a hell of a lot better. There was really only one way to find out and that was to dive headlong into something that had already caused me a migraine of epic proportions.

"I'm going to start right here," I remarked as I opened a thick manila folder. "I could barely hold this stuff yesterday without blinding pain." I tipped the envelope and its contents spilled into my hand. I looked up and met his eyes. "So far, so good."

Camden stayed rooted to his spot on the floor. Curiosity had to have eaten at him, but he showed me a great deal of respect by staying put and not inspecting the contents of the envelope. Most of it was immaterial as I tossed a couple of fake IDs, passports, and a few other forged documents onto the nearby table. Just a few necessities that might come in handy in the event I needed to bug-out in a hurry.

I continued to weed through the papers in the first envelope. Bank statements, info for a couple of offshore accounts, pictures that I recognized from previous jobs . . . . I paused at a white piece of lined notebook paper. Scrawled in black ink was an address that I remembered all too well. It was the location of the townhouse where I'd first met the great Alexander Peck. The handwritten note sparked something deep in my chest, a ghost of emotion that connected me to . . . someone. But not Xander.

I stared at the handwritten note and what I assumed was a name scrawled at the bottom of the paper. The ink blurred and I squinted as though it would somehow bring the letters into focus. I held the note out to Camden and he walked toward me. "Is there a name written at the bottom of this page?"

"Yes," Camden said slowly. His lips gathered into a contemplative pucker as though he wondered whether he should say it aloud. "Tfymgbv."

"Stop." I knew he'd spoken the name clearly, but it sounded like gibberish to my ears. Whoever had written that note had been effectively erased from my memory but for what reason, and by who, I had no idea. Anya had spoken that name to me as well. The name of my mysterious protector? Someone everyone apparently knew, but I wasn't allowed to remember. Who in the hell had made that decision? And how had they wiped this person from my mind?

The Werewolf's brow furrowed. "Are you okay?"

I gave a quick nod of my head. I wanted to smile despite my frustration. "It just sounds like garbled nonsense when you say the name. But on the plus side, no headache."

A corner of Camden's mouth quirked upward, and I sensed it was the most optimism I was going to see from him, at least for a while. I wanted to jump up and down and shout my elation. *No headache! Booyah!* I didn't know how the magic in my ring had gotten it done, but I was suddenly incredibly grateful I hadn't been able to take the damn thing off.

On the not-so-plus-side, it didn't look like I'd glean much from the stack of stuff I'd salvaged from my apartment. At least, as it pertained to my mysterious rescuer and the holes in my memory. Whatever—or whoever—wanted me to forget, had done a damned good job of making sure those empty spaces stayed nice and blank. Damn it. I was hoping to make some serious headway, but right now, I'd settle for even a small victory.

"What now?"

I set the remaining papers back on the table and turned to face Camden. "Good question." I was willing to take baby steps despite my impatience. Anything was better than remaining sedentary.

"Let's tackle the Levi issue first. It seems the most manageable."

I quirked a brow. "If you say so." I was skeptical, but I needed a dose of hope that I hoped Camden could supply.

"For some reason, someone wants Levi dead. Fast. And from the way you make it sound, your handler is equally anxious for you to get the job done."

I hated to voice my suspicions of Misha, but he was definitely acting weird. "Yup. And he's never given me a job with so little info on the mark before."

"So, someone either paid a good chunk of change for Misha to look the other way, or he's complicit in whatever is going on."

I was hoping for option number one. I could handle him being bribed to push me into a job that might be morally questionable. If he was in on it . . . that was another story. "And not being able to do any intel on Levi makes it tough for me to determine which it is."

"I think that's the point. Someone—and we don't know who that is yet—is trying to back you into a corner."

"Or draw me out into the open," I suggested.

Either was a possibility. With as much stress as I was under lately, I would have likely gone through with the job whether I had all the details or not. Probably. Maybe. Hell, at this point, I didn't know how I'd react. "I'm feeling the pressure for sure."

"What if we could buy you a little time and save an innocent life in the process?"

I quirked a skeptical brow. "Innocent?"

"Believe me, Darian. Levi hasn't done anything to deserve to die."

My pulse skittered in my veins with the rush of anxious energy. I should have trusted my gut to begin with. Nothing about this job seemed legit. I studied Camden for a quiet moment. "You want to hide him, don't you?"

Camden offered up a wolfish grin. "Yes. Well, maybe. I need to make a couple of calls, but it might be our only option. And we'll have to convince Misha, and whoever wants the job done, that he's dead."

It was a great idea. Something I never would have thought of in my current state of mind. It was nice to have someone around to bounce ideas off of. "If it comes to that, we'll have to make it *very* convincing." Supernatural creatures weren't easily deceived. "So what exactly is this Levi?" He had to be fairly important, or incredibly powerful to be on someone's hitlist. "Fae . . . .? Shifter . . . .?"

"Human," Camden replied.

"Human?"

Camden chuckled. "He's a very well-connected human."

That made sense. When humans got tangled up in the affairs of the supernatural it was never good.

"Since his connection to your . . . problems make it difficult for you to have contact with him, I'll take care of the details. I won't bring you in until I need you."

I wasn't used to giving up control. It made me twitchy. But I didn't really have a choice other than to allow Camden to take the lead on this one. "Fair enough, but I need something to do or I'll go insane. What about Redmond?" There had to be something I could do to be proactive instead of just waiting around for some greedy assassin to kill me for him.

"The Arx wants you dead." Camden went back to his perch on the stepladder and folded his arms across his wide chest. "I don't think being an annoyance to the guy paying to get the job done is going to help your case at all."

Being an annoyance was what I did best. A smile spread across my lips and for the first time in a long time I felt a spark of happiness. I'd be like a mosquito. Buzzing the head of that bastard nonstop. He thought he could just put a price on my head and that would be the end of it? I laughed. Not by a long shot.

"Darian." Camden's warning tone only fueled my fire. "Whatever you're thinking, reconsider."

Too late. The gears were already turning. It felt good to reclaim a little of the fire I'd lost over the past year. If I had Redmond and his Human Purification Society to thank for it, then so be it. "Not sure if anyone told you or not, but I'm not very good at behaving."

"I've been well informed." Camden's reply was saltine dry. I loved when my reputation preceded me. "I can't keep an eye on you *and* manage this issue with Levi. Your . . . benefactor won't be happy if anything happens to you."

Benefactor. Protector. Whoever this person pulling the strings was, they could give Xander a lesson or two on high-handedness. "I can look after myself." I'd been doing it for a long damned time and no one had managed to kill me yet.

"We're supposed to be tackling the issue with Redmond together."

I quirked a brow. "Together?" I'd never been much of a team player, but I could understand Camden wanting to present a united front. Our interests were separate but similar. And we weren't exactly dealing with someone who was powerless.

Camden leveled his gaze. One-hundred percent alpha and used to being obeyed. I could rock the alpha vibe as well. If anything, my attitude might encourage him to put on the gas regarding the Arx's morally bankrupt leader to be rid of me faster.

He didn't respond to my questioning our "team" status and I didn't expect him to. His intense golden gaze told me everything I needed to know. "Fine." I let out an exasperated sigh. "I can be careful." I'd spent my entire existence living just under the radar. I knew how to be low-key. Sort-of. "Does that help?"

He eyed me with a fair amount of suspicion. I liked Camden. He didn't trust easily, and it was obvious he didn't take any shit. "No."

"I'm not sitting around doing nothing." I'd go out of my freaking mind and wind up getting myself into worse trouble than if I went off alone in search of Redmond. "So you'd better come up with a comprise."

Camden chuckled. "A compromise, huh? All right. I'll deal with Levi, and you can do a little reconnaissance on Redmond. On the condition that you allow someone from my pack to accompany you."

I opened my mouth to protest. Camden held up a staying hand and the air crackled with power. No one argued with an alpha, apparently.

"If I don't get a choice, how is this a compromise?"

His smile widened. Good natured and at the same time, dangerous. "It isn't. But I figured calling it that would make you feel as though you had some measure of control over the situation."

Har. Har. Wasn't he clever? I swallowed down the indignant retort that sat on the tip of my tongue, knowing damn good and well it wouldn't do me a bit of good to argue. "It's better than nothing." The concession was tough for me to make. "But I want it to be clear that whoever you decide to send along *isn't* a babysitter." I could take care of myself, for shit's sake. "All right?"

Camden responded with a curt nod. "Backup. Not a babysitter."

Backup I could handle. Though, I suspected it was just more wordsmithing on Camden's part to keep me from pitching a fit. "Tomorrow night?"

Camden's arms dropped to his sides, a gesture I assumed signaled he was ready to call it a day. "I'm surprised you're waiting that long." He headed for the door and said over his shoulder, "I'll send someone over at nightfall. But Darian . . ." He turned to face me. "I'm putting my neck on the chopping block by allowing this. Do me the courtesy of exercising some degree of caution."

He'd obviously been given the skinny on my reckless nature. "I can do that." I wasn't interested in getting killed and I knew how to be safe when I needed to be. "No worries."

Camden let out a chuff of breath. "Sure." He pulled open the door and let himself out.

Looked like I had a pet project to keep myself busy for a while. A smile spread across my lips. For the first time in a long time, I felt almost . . . normal.

[10]

"I've been told that you operate under a strict code of conduct. Is that correct?"

I looked around the posh office space. It had to have cost a fortune to decorate it. But if the client could afford the price tag for a space practically wallpapered with original Monets, Manets, and van Goghs, then surely she could afford to pay my asking price.

If I decided to take this job, it would be an epic payday.

"That's right." I'd opted to come unarmed. The client was human and not a threat. I had the night's shadows to protect me if I needed it and I wanted to portray an image of professionalism. Though, my black jeans, boots, and long-sleeved shirt, coupled with my long, black duster wasn't exactly business casual. "If you're looking to take out a work rival or the woman who slept with your husband, or the neighbor who cuts you off in traffic every morning, I suggest you find another professional. I'm not interested in avenging those sorts of wrongs. I only mete punishment on those who truly deserve it."

The client—an old-money heiress, according to my research—nodded and gave me a sly smile as she looked me over. "Good. Because I'm not interested in hiring you to do anything petty. I'm hiring you because someone does, in fact, deserve to be punished. And if I could do the deed myself, I would."

Sure. No one shelled out thousands of dollars for what I did because it didn't work into their schedules. Somehow, those who paid my salaries thought passing money my way would keep the blood off of their hands. That's not how it worked. But it wasn't my job to school the woman sitting in front of me as to her part in all of this. She'd have to live with her decision here today, just like I'd have to live with my decision to carry out the deed for her. We all accepted our parts of the guilt whether we wanted to or not. She'd find that out soon enough.

We'd agreed on no names prior to our meeting. Not that we didn't already know everything about each other. It simply made her more comfortable to pretend that we had anonymity between us. I could give her that if it helped to make her feel more comfortable, ridiculous as it was.

"There isn't much time. I've got ears everywhere and I've found out he's scheduled a flight to Brazil. Leaving at the end of the week. If he's allowed to leave the country, he'll disappear and won't ever be held accountable for his crimes."

The end of the week was two days from now. It didn't give me much time to vet the mark on my own. "I don't usually work with such a tight timeline," I replied. "I can follow him for the next couple of days to be sure—"

She produced a stack of glossy photos from her desk and tossed them across the surface toward me. They fanned out and I glanced at the bloody, grisly images before meeting her eyes.

"All his victims," she said.

"Looks like serial-killer territory." Seemed a little over the top. "Police involvement?"

She nodded. "I have people on the inside," she replied. "All of the murders were determined to be unconnected, and he had a credible alibi so the police eliminated him as a suspect."

"Seems like your evidence isn't convincing, then."

Her eyes narrowed. "You and I both know that alibis can be fabricated and police can be bought."

Anything could be fabricated with enough motivation and the money to get it done. Including crime scene photos. And cops weren't immune to bribes when they were big enough. I leaned back in my chair and slung an arm over the rest as I crossed my legs. My client shifted in her seat and tapped a manicured nail on her desktop. I sat in silent regard long enough to make her squirm.

"Please," she said at last. A sob seemed to lodge in her throat. "If you don't do this, he'll get away. He'll kill again. Who knows how many. He has to be punished for what he's done."

"It'll be a quick death." Torture wasn't my thing. "Hardly punishment."

"It'll be punishment enough." She dabbed at her eyes with a tissue. "But more importantly, he won't be around to hurt anyone else, ever again."

I stayed silent. Studied her. Waited for some sort of tell that would let me know if she was playing games with me.

"I'll double your fee," she said.

The job already offered a larger than normal payday. Double would set me up comfortably for the next year. Plus, I had my eye on a building in Belltown with a loft that would make a great place to live. I'd been wanting to move out of my current apartment, because neighbors, and get a place that offered me the privacy I desperately needed. I wanted that building and real estate in Seattle didn't stay on the market for long.

"Triple." If I was going to do this, without the vetting I wanted, I was going to make it worth my while.

She pursed her lips and let out a huff of breath. "Fine. Triple your fee."

"Half upfront," I replied.

She pushed away from her desk without hesitation and crossed the office to a large safe against the far wall. A few quick turns of the dial had the heavy door swinging open. She pulled two fat manilla envelopes from the safe and came back to her desk.

"Seventy-five thousand," she said as she tossed the envelopes in front of me. "You'll get the rest after he's dead."

Intuition tugged at my center, but I ignored it. Seventy-five would be more than enough earnest money to secure the building. I scooped up the envelopes and tucked the bulky mass into my duster.

"I'll be back in two days." Her brow furrowed. "It's not too late to back out if you're having second thoughts." I wasn't sure if that last bit was for her or me.

"No second thoughts," she assured me. Her voice had turned to steel. "Get it done."

"He's as good as dead."

I answered with a nod and left. I just hoped we were both prepared to face the consequences of our actions.

———

I'D NEVER KILLED ANYONE IN THE SUBURBS BEFORE. STEALTH WAS impossible in a place where people knew their neighbors and were suspicious of anything out of the norm. I let the shadows cloak me as I stalked my prey, which really, felt so much more sinister considering the wholesome backdrop of the cul de sac. A tremor vibrated down my spine, but I shook off the worrisome discomfort. I had my goal in sight—the building in Belltown. My earnest money had secured it for a week and there was already another buyer hungry to get their hands on it.

I couldn't shake the feeling that something wasn't right. I watched my mark through his living room window, his behavior pretty damn casual for someone who'd supposedly murdered a handful of people and was preparing to leave the country to avoid a possible arrest. And really, why would he flee if he'd had an ironclad alibi as the client had suggested. That damn twitch of doubt itched at the back of my mind once again and a stone settled in the pit of my stomach.

Shake it off, Darian. Focus. After tonight, your life is going to be exponentially better.

Just because the guy lived in the suburbs didn't mean he wasn't a dangerous predator. Gacy, Bundy, and others like them, had all been unassuming and seemingly harmless. I had to quit trying to talk myself out of this job. I was being paid to mete out justice.

I just prayed that the poor bastard deserved it.

I entered the house as a shadow.

My spine was about as stiff as a cooked noodle and I gave myself a mental gut check. Now wasn't the time to go soft. I needed to keep my eye on the prize.

That building in Belltown was as good as mine.

I drew a short, sharp blade from a sheath at my back. Quarters were too close for my saber and besides, the situation didn't call for it. This would be quick and efficient.

Why was I hesitating?

I stretched my neck from side to side, still engulfed in the warmth of shadows. My mark emerged from the kitchen, glass of wine in one hand, a book in the other, as he settled down in a wingchair at the far end of the living room. He seemed too at ease for someone who'd recently been interrogated by police for killing multiple people—including the client's own sister. I still didn't know his alleged motives for the killings, but did it really matter why? I was being paid to rid the world of this trash, and that's what I was going to do.

I waited for him to sit and open his book. I guess there was sort of a poetic justice to killing him while he was settled and relaxed. I kept to the edge of the room where the light didn't quite reach and he paused for a moment, his brow furrowed, before settling down into the comfortable chair. He set the glass on the coaster resting on the end table and opened the book. He crossed a leg over his knee and focused his attention on the pages in front of him.

I slid through the dark until I was poised behind him. What I was about to do would be a mercy in comparison to the butcher job I'd seen in the crime scene photos. I let those grisly images guide my hand as the blade sank into the gentle flesh of his throat. He started, and let out a surprised gurgle as he grasped at the wound, his eyes wide and disbelieving as he slumped in the pristine white chair and bled to death.

My stomach soured at the coppery tang of blood. Headlights shone into the window as a car pulled into the driveway and I retreated to the front door, sliding as nothing more than feathers of darkness through the wooden planks. A garage door opened, and closed, but rather than retreat, I waited, watched through the bay windows as a woman entered from the garage and made her way through the house calling, "Mark? Honey, where are you?" as she made her way to the living room.

A scream of pure terror and anguish rent the silence. I remained frozen in place, my own heart thumping wildly in my chest as she screamed and cried and ran for the kitchen, coming back seconds later with a cordless phone. She was nearly incomprehensible as she tried to speak to the 911 operator, and still, I couldn't bring myself to leave. I waited, watched as she threw the phone down and dragged the body to the floor where she laid herself over his chest and sobbed.

Sirens preceded blue and red flashing lights, and I kept to the shadows as I watched police converge on the scene. Neighbors peeked out from their windows, and others more emboldened, stepped out into their driveways to watch the spectacle. The sobbing woman was escorted from the house as police tried to calm her long enough to question her.

"H-h-he," she drew in a ragged breath. "He was a good man," she said. "I can't think of anyone who would want him dead." She began to cry again. "No," she said to the detective, "I don't think there's anything missing. "He was sitting in his chair. His book was on the floor beside him. I just—I just don't know how . . . who . . . . Oh, god. Mark."

She broke down into sobs once again.

My stomach boiled with anxious energy and my pulse thrummed in my ears. Something wasn't right. I'd sensed it from the second I'd taken the contract. Sure, Mark could have lived a double life. He could have killed those people. He could have done a lot of underhanded things. But my gut told me, I'd been duped. The police didn't seem to know anything about Mark Harris. From the bits of conversation I picked up as I flitted between the officers combing the scene, he had a spotless record. He'd never even gotten a speeding ticket. He hadn't been questioned in connection with the murders the client claimed he'd committed. She'd lied to me. And I was going to find out why.

————

I FOUND THE CLIENT ASLEEP IN HER BED.

Without an ounce of caution, I ripped the covers from her and jerked her upright, unconcerned with who might be within earshot. She had the money to pay for security, but it seemed tonight, she wasn't worried about her own safety or protection. Too bad for her. She'd crossed the wrong person and I wasn't about to show mercy.

"Who was he, and why did you want him dead?" I snarled close to her ear as I shook her awake.

"I—I told you," she spluttered as the sleepiness vanished from her eyes, replaced rapidly with fear. "He was a murderer. He killed my sister."

"Bullshit." I didn't tolerate liars. "Tell me right this fucking minute or I swear to god, the next breath you draw is going to be your last."

"He's dead?" She asked on a breath.

I didn't answer. I was too goddamned sick to my stomach to acknowledge it.

"What does it matter?" Tears glistened in her eyes but didn't spill over the lids. "I paid you to do it. The rest of your money is in a safe in my study. You can have it all right now. I'll get it for you. You did your job, and now you can walk away."

"What did he do?" I asked again, low. "Tell me right fucking now."

Her lips formed a hard line as she locked her jaw down tight.

Apparently, she needed a little coaxing. I brought the blade, still dark with Mark Harris's blood, to her throat. "You'll go out the same way he did. Only, I won't make it quick."

"I'm glad he's dead," she seethed through gritted teeth. "No one tells me no."

That's it? He'd turned her down? All of that effort, the photos, the story about her sister, the urgency that he was about to flee the country.

97

The entire production to spur me into action and all of it because he'd said "no."

I didn't even need to know what he'd turned down. I didn't care if it was an affair, a business venture, or an invite to a party. I'd killed an innocent man tonight. His blood was on my hands. All because I'd been too damned greedy and impatient to do my due diligence.

I took the blade and stabbed once, between her ribs and into her lung. I dropped her to the floor and grabbed the phone on the bedside table, jerking the cord from the wall. She floundered on the carpet, the air gurgling in her chest as she pressed a hand to the wound and fought for breath. She tried to stand and stumbled. Blood poured from the wound and the rattle in her chest grew louder as she suffocated. Her eyes widened with the realization that her life was about to end, and I turned my back on her and wandered through the house in search of the study.

My shadowed hand penetrated the steel. Anything I touched turned to shadow, and I dragged out multiple items of no consequence until I found was I was looking for. I tucked the envelope, seventy-five thousand dollars, and the price of my conscience into the folds of my duster.

Never again would an innocent die at my hand. And anyone who tried to manipulate me would pay the price.

I joined with the night as I left her downtown penthouse, and never in my life had I felt so deserving of the darkness that swallowed me.

[11]

I didn't go back to Misha's. Instead, I camped out at my soon-to-be new place, surrounded by the unfamiliar, yet comforting sounds of the waterfront. Memories plagued me, but they were a reminder of what was at risk if I'd blindly followed the Fae's directive to kill Levi without asking any questions or doing my research beforehand. Camden's offer to help had taken some of the burden from my shoulders, but not enough to give me peace of mind. I was too charged to sleep and so I paced every square inch of the place until the sun rose, acquainting myself with the shadowed corners and learning every creak and groan of the building's bones. I'd need a sleeping bag and maybe an air mattress if I was going to stay here during the construction, but I was more than ready to have my own place again along with some much-needed privacy.

Ned and his crew showed up with the sunrise. I left them to it and decided to set up camp at a nearby coffee shop to do a little work on my own. I trusted that Camden had the Levi situation under control, and though I'd (sort of) promised him I'd exercise caution regarding Redmond and wait for backup, I decided doing a little research of my own in the meantime wouldn't hurt.

A simple Google search pulled up enough information on Mitchell Redmond to keep me busy for most of the morning. I found it curious that such an arcane organization as the Arx would choose a leader with such a high profile. He wasn't tough to track down. Then again, leaders like Redmond craved power and notoriety as well as the money and clout that came along with it. Reminded me a lot of Mithras. Most supernatural creatures weren't short on ego, but gods had ego to spare. Redmond could've given the war god a run for his money. From what I'd managed to learn, he wanted any potential opponent to know he wasn't afraid.

The more I thought about it, the more I knew that's how I'd play it if I were in his shoes.

Mitchell Redmond was the perfect figurehead for a militant hate group.

Wealthy. Respected. High-profile. A shrewd businessman with a reputation for going for the jugular. Not afraid of the camera. Influential friends. He'd attended swanky parties and red-carpet events all along the west coast. Dated a couple of actresses, models, and one Olympic athlete. Looked like Redmond was a fan of slalom. I continued to scroll through the many pictures and articles, learning a little more about the man but nothing particularly helpful. Redmond's high-profile lifestyle proved he wasn't afraid. Of anyone or anything. And why should he be? He had a virtual army at his back. And it also made sense that Camden's plan was to depose him and put a supernatural usurper in his place. The only way to destroy an organization like the Arx was to attack it from within and wait for it to implode.

I still didn't understand the logistics of how the wily wolf planned to get that done. Camden was the most powerful alpha in the northwest—and according to Misha, perhaps the world. It wasn't too farfetched to assume that he'd had spies inside of the Arx for a while. I still didn't know how my mysterious benefactor tied into all of this, or why the Arx considered me a big enough threat to humanity to put a million-dollar bounty on my head, but I had to hope I'd get some answers soon.

I might have been losing my mind, but I wasn't an idiot. I could put two-and-two together, memory issues or not. There was always a bigger fish. And Camden kept company with someone far bigger than him. My mysterious benefactor/protector/whatever was a next-level supernatural creature. Whoever this individual was, Camden was obviously getting help from him as well.

If Camden was so confident the Arx could be brought down, I had to assume my self-appointed protector was on Mithras's level power-wise.

Perhaps some sort of god?

The air left my chest in a whoosh of air. What in the hell had I gotten myself into?

I tended to keep to myself. My inner circle was tight: Xander, Raif, Asher, and I supposed I could count Misha as well. Though his recent behavior had me rethinking his inner circle status. Aside from Mithras, I couldn't remember having ever encountered another supernatural creature that I might consider god-like. Then again, how would I even know? If Mithras had been walking around Seattle, odds were good he wasn't the only god kickin' back with the human and supernatural populations.

I swear, I learned something that changed my perception of the world every day.

A dark shadow caused the daylight outside the coffee shop window to dull, and a rush of adrenaline dumped into my system. My stomach curled into a tight knot as beads of sweat pricked at my skin. Anxiety really was a bitch. I was afraid of something I couldn't identify. On edge because of a threat I couldn't defend myself against. I didn't handle helplessness well, which was why I'd decided to move on Redmond—I needed a situation I could control rather than spending my time looking over my shoulder, waiting for an assassin's blade or a sentient cloud of raw power to take me out.

"How are you doing over here?"

I looked up from my phone screen at the waitress who'd been buzzing around the café, wiping down tables. The place was mostly self-serve which I liked. She must have been bored—or an overachiever—thanks to the lull in customers.

"I'm good." I looked down at my almost empty mug. One of the best things about Seattle: there was no shortage of great coffee. Caffeine was supposed to be good for headaches, or so I'd heard. I'd take whatever help I could get to make sure the pain in my head stayed gone. "Thanks."

The bell above the door gave a cheery jingle and she departed with a quick nod and a smile as she headed to her place at the counter.

"You might want a refill. I have a feeling it's going to be a long night."

I'd been so preoccupied with the bustling waitress I'd totally missed the woman who'd walked up on me. Jeez, I was totally losing my edge. I stretched my head from side to side before turning my attention to the feminine voice and realized in an instant that she wasn't a woman. Well, not exactly.

Werewolf. Her energy signature was almost identical to Camden's. She must have been a member of his pack and most likely my backup-slash-babysitter.

"You're early." Camden had said he'd send someone at nightfall and it was barely noon. "And how in the hell did you know where to find me?" If I'd been followed without knowing it, I wasn't simply losing my edge, it was gone entirely.

She gave an unconcerned shrug as she settled into the chair opposite me. "I'm not overly patient. And I'm a tracker." She tapped the upturned tip of her nose. "Locating people is sort of my specialty."

Interesting. I tried not to let the blow to my ego show as I looked her over. Tall, solidly built, with a blonde pixie cut and brilliant blue eyes. She had that same feral gleam in her gaze that Camden possessed. A glimpse of the animal that lay beneath the surface of her skin. I had no doubt she was formidable. Camden wouldn't have chosen her to accompany me otherwise.

"I'm Kira, by the way." She brought a paper coffee cup to her lips and sipped from the opening in the plastic top.

"Darian. Nice to meet you." It seemed silly to introduce myself since I was certain Kira had been well-briefed, but no one could accuse me of being less than cordial. I'd come a long way since my stoic, anti-social days.

I waited patiently for Kira to do her own assessment of me. A quiet moment passed, and her serious expression gave way to a shrewd half-grin. "Are you ready to stir up a little trouble, Darian?"

My kind of girl.

"Absolutely." I was tired of having a target on my back and wanted Redmond and the Arx out of the picture A-S-A-fucking-P. "Do you have a game plan?"

Kira's mouth screwed up into a pucker. "Camden only wants us doing reconnaissance for the time being. Personally, I think it's a waste of time."

A girl after my own heart. But knowing what I now did about the Arx's cocky leader, Camden was right to want to exercise a little caution.

"It won't be tough to find Redmond." Hell, a simple Google search had told me everything I needed to know. "He's not afraid of living his life in the spotlight."

"Maniacal cult leaders," Kira said with a derisive snort. "So much ego."

I wondered how many cult leaders she'd met to make that assertion. "He doesn't have any reason to exercise caution. He takes a security team everywhere he goes and he has the power of a global secret society behind him. I'm sure he thinks I'm more worried about saving my own skin than coming after him."

"Like I said" —Kira took another sip from her cup— "so much ego."

I gazed into my nearly empty mug as though I could find the answers to all my problems in the lukewarm coffee left in the bottom.

"Humans have no business meddling in the affairs of the supernatural or any other creatures for that matter." She leveled her gaze and her lips formed a hard line. "I don't trust any of them."

Her pointed look made me think she was trying to get a point across. I just wished I knew what it was.

"Can I ask you something?" It had been eating at me for almost a year. Kira answered with a tentative nod. I could ask. Didn't necessarily mean I'd get an answer though. "What did Mithras want with Camden when he had him kidnapped?"

Kira blew out a breath. "Mithras is a war god. He gathers strength from combat. If he'd managed to kill Camden in battle, he would have absorbed his opponent's strength and abilities."

No wonder Mithras had wanted him so badly. "From what I've been told, Camden is the most powerful Werewolf in the U.S. Maybe even the world. I'm not even half as strong and I'd managed to kill the body he'd inhabited. Camden would have likely gotten the job done."

Kira looked at me as though I'd just sprouted a second head. "We have rules. One of those being that an alpha only engages in ritualistic combat when a formal challenge has been issued. Mithras didn't follow the rules. He took Camden with no intention of it being a fair fight. He wanted him weakened and easy to put down. His only interest was in acquiring power."

The night Lorik and I had been instructed to deliver the wolf to Mithras, he'd been shackled by a silver collar around his neck. The details of that night were hazy in my memory and it rankled that I couldn't recall it with more clarity. But it didn't take a genius to know the silver would have weakened Camden and tipped the odds in the favor of the war god. Omnipotent, he wasn't, which was probably why he'd wanted the Alpha Werewolf's power. Even gods had a pecking order, it seemed.

Kira cocked a brow as she studied me. "You make it sound as though killing Mithras had been an easy task."

Hadn't it been? I tried to recreate that night in my mind but all I could conjure were flashes of memory shrouded by fog. I knew it had been a hard-won fight. I knew I'd almost kissed my ass goodbye at least once. I knew he'd taken on the form of a minotaur. I remembered being alone—or had I been? Damn it. Had something or someone come to my aid? Lorik? I swallowed a snort. He might have kept me safe, but only because he'd needed me good and alive when he'd handed me over to Padma. He hadn't helped me.

Who, or what could kill a god?

Another god. That's who.

"Darian?"

I broke from my reverie to find Kira watching me. Wary.

"Not easy." The gaps in my memory were seriously pissing me off. "Not even close."

Kira relaxed back in her seat as though my answer had somehow proven something to her. Maybe she was trying to gauge my ego which used to be a little on the overblown side. Over the past few years, however, I'd been knocked down a peg or two. I knew exactly what sorts of things lurked in the shadows and beyond. I wasn't even close to as tough as I used to think I was.

"I gave my word to Camden that we'd only do a little field work," Kira said. "But the extent of our visibility while we do it, is up to you. The city is crawling with assassins waiting for an opportunity to kill you. I'd understand if you wanted to keep a low profile tonight."

She had a point. It seemed like I couldn't go anywhere without someone trying to kill me. And of course, there was the matter of the Délash to consider. I sensed the evil cloud of power and destruction would have no problem taking out the competition to get its—whatever—on me. The damn thing didn't have hands, claws, feet, or anything else. But it sure as hell could pack a punch. And it wanted a piece of me.

Despite all of that, I refused to cower and hide.

"Laying low has never really been my thing. I want to get my eyes on Redmond." If anything to get a read on him. There was only so much I could glean from an internet search. "He should be easy to find. He's not exactly hiding out or anything."

Kira nodded. "True. Finding him is one thing, though. Guaranteed his security detail makes the secret service look lax in comparison. So tonight will definitely be a-look-but-don't-touch situation."

Men like Redmond stayed in power because they weren't stupid enough to put themselves in harm's way. They kept their pawns close and played them well. The Arx supplied Redmond with a nearly inexhaustible supply of foolish followers willing to lay down their lives to protect him in the name of their cause. Another cloud passed over the sun, casting a dark shadow outside, and I bristled. My gaze wandered to the open windows and I craned my neck toward the waning light.

"I'd never heard of a Délash until Camden told me about it," Kira remarked as though learning of the existence of a sentient cloud of doom was no big thing. My ears perked at the mention and I forced my lip to keep from curling into a sneer. Kira knew what had me on edge and I didn't like it.

"Yeah?" It sort of pissed me off that yet another person knew more about my situation than I did. "What all did Camden tell you?"

"Not much," she said with a shrug. "Enough for me to know I

never want to tangle with one. I gotta say, I'm impressed. You seem to amass some seriously powerful enemies."

Not sure if that was the kind of feather I wanted in my cap, but whatever. I shivered as I forced my gaze from the window. "Can't guarantee you won't tangle with one if you hang out with me." The new threat to my life could've been hanging out in one of the side alleys for all I knew. Just waiting for me to leave the coffee shop.

"I won't have anything to worry about." Kira's expression almost hinted at a smile. "It's not after me."

I pursed my lips. Dry humor or not, she had a point. From what I'd gathered, the Délash was a creature with a one-track mind. It wouldn't be a threat to anyone other than its target—and whatever came between it and its target. Something told me Kira wouldn't throw herself in its path given the opportunity.

Again, whatever. I wasn't her problem and the Délash sure as hell wasn't her problem. But Redmond was, and that was the only thing we currently had in common.

"So where do you want to start?" I didn't want to talk about the Délash anymore. I didn't need the added stress. Redmond and the Arx were my current priority. I'd deal with one threat to my life at a time. I already had a pretty good idea of where to find Redmond, but this wasn't exactly my show.

"There's a gala tonight at the Chihuly Garden. He'll be there."

I swallowed a snort. The wily Werewolf had played me. She wasn't my wingman. I was hers.

"Hope you have a nice dress." She pushed out her chair and took the paper cup with her. "I'll meet you at your place at eight."

I cocked a brow. "My place?"

Kira answered with a chuff of laughter. "You're not as low-key as you think. See you in a few hours."

I wondered if her words were meant to stir unease or serve as a warning.

Neither was good.

[12]

The Chihuly Garden at the Seattle Center was by far one of the city's brightest gems. Room upon room of blown glass sculptures created dreamlike landscapes, each one more impressive and surreal than the last. I expected to see the Cheshire Cat perched atop one of the towering glass structures, ready to lead—or mislead—Alice on her way home. I would have thought we'd left the city behind for a magical realm if not for the people mulling around, champagne glasses in hand, and voices low so as not to drown out the sound of the string quartet playing nearby.

To say I felt ridiculously out of place was an understatement.

"You clean up pretty good."

Kira stepped up beside me looking as relaxed as I felt awkward. She rocked a blush pink evening gown that complemented her fair complexion and blonde hair. I'd opted for a black —of course—cocktail dress that more than likely made me appear pale and sulky. Then again, I pretty much always looked pale and sulky, so I could hardly blame the dress.

"Back at ya." Kira was truly stunning. Beautiful with that natural deadly edge all supernatural creatures possessed. Eyes from all over the room were drawn to her and though she acted as though she didn't notice, I knew she was aware of every tiny detail around her. Werewolf senses were keen as fuck.

"So . . . ." I snagged a couple of champagne flutes from a passing server and handed one to Kira. "I was thinking. What if we run into Redmond and he recognizes me?"

A feral light sparked behind Kira's eyes and she gave me a wolfish grin. "That's the plan."

I pursed my lips. "I'm bait?"

"Sorta. I mean, of course he knows who you are. But he probably thinks he still has a certain level of anonymity. How should you know who he is? Maybe seeing you here will plant a seed of doubt in his brain and make him feel a little more exposed. If he worries you know who he is and what he's up to, it'll put him on edge. Camden wants him rattled."

Reconnaissance my ass.

This wasn't a stealth mission at all. Tonight's appearance was an outright act of aggression. We were throwing down the gauntlet and daring Redmond and the Arx to pick it up. I wondered if my mysterious benefactor knew what Camden was up to. Not that it would matter one way or the other.

"Why do it in a public place, then?" Redmond was a pretty public figure. It's not like it would've been tough to seek him out on his home turf.

"Because we don't want a fight," Kira said. "You have to think like a strategist, Darian."

I was definitely a stab first and ask questions later sort of assassin. The subtleties of warfare didn't concern me. I did my necessary research, and if my mark was properly vetted as scum of the earth, I delivered the killing blow. Assassins didn't typically take the time to introduce themselves to their targets prior to killing them.

I tilted my head, as much of a concession to my own ignorance as Kira was going to get. Tonight was an, "Oh, hey!" wave to Redmond. *I see you, I know what you're up to, and you're fucked.*

Whether or not he'd find the little introduction threatening or not was yet to be seen.

As was Redmond who, so far, was MIA.

Kira and I mulled around the exhibit, travelling from room to room, as we snacked on the fancy hors d'oeuvres and drank champagne. Not a bad way to spend a Friday night. I was still blessedly headache free and felt more like my old self than I had in a long damn time.

There was no sign of Redmond. As much as I wanted to put this business with the price on my head to rest, I didn't know if I was on my game enough to confront the man who'd taken out the contract face to face. Kira seemed like she could hold her own, and though I didn't know the Werewolf well, I trusted that she acted in my best interest. I'd saved her Alpha from the machinations of a wily god. I supposed that meant the pack owed me a debt.

Kira fell back several paces as I wandered into the next salon. A tall form caught my eye, the broad shoulders and honey wheat hair unmistakable. I knew that form. Knew the silky strands of that hair. Knew the dark velvet sound of his voice, without even having to hear it. My stomach did a twisting backflip as my heart fluttered madly in my chest. What was he doing here? When did they get back? And why in the hell hadn't anyone told me?

As though he sensed my presence, Alexander Peck, King of the Shaedes, turned to face me. A broad, cocky smile curved his full lips and his bright eyes lit with a joyous and at the same time, mischievous light.

"I think I quite like catching you off guard, Darian."

Frozen in place, I couldn't get myself to move. I didn't know if I wanted to hug him, hit him, or both. The past year had been so gods-damned lonely. There was a point in time when all I'd wanted was to be rid of him. But right now, I couldn't imagine my life without him.

"I guess you've taken care of your usurper." As though there

110

was any doubt. Xander would never allow anyone to snatch his throne out from under him. "Who did it?" I couldn't help but rib him a little. "Asher? Or Raif?"

Xander's grin grew into wide, arrogant smile. "Come now, Darian. You should know me better than that."

I couldn't help but smile myself. "I do know you better than that. I just wanted to see your reaction."

Several feet separated us, and I still couldn't bring myself to close the space. I didn't know what I was afraid of. This was Xander. We had a history, sure. But we'd made our peace with each other and he was one of very few people I knew I could always count on.

I rocked forward on my feet. Shifted my weight to my toes. As my balance tipped, I forced my right foot forward. Xander moved in sync and we fell into a comforting embrace that instantly warmed me from the inside out.

"Gods, I've missed you," he murmured into my hair. "Life simply isn't exciting enough without you in it."

"Ditto." A lump grew in my throat and I found it difficult to speak past the thickness. "Misha isn't half as antagonizing as you are."

Xander chuckled and the warm tenor of it vibrated through me. "So tell me, little assassin, what are you hunting tonight?"

The Shaede King was nothing if not well informed. I had no doubt he already knew what I was doing here. He just wanted to hear me say it.

"You know. Same shit, different day. If you must know, I'm hunting a megalomaniac cult leader hell bent on protecting humanity from the supernatural. Oh, and he's also put a million dollar price on my head."

Xander's bright blue eyes hardened for the barest moment. Always trying to protect me. But he should have known better than that by now.

"Misha is supposed to be keeping you out of trouble," he said almost conversationally. I didn't miss the bitter undertone, though. And I also knew Misha would get a stern talking to later. Not that it would do much good.

"Since when has anyone ever been able to manage me, *Your Highness?*" I made sure to let him hear the disdain in my tone. "I can take care of myself."

"That seems to be a constant theme with you, Darian." Likewise, he made sure to let me hear the overbearing concern in his tone. "And yet, I find myself ever looking after you."

I could have taken the remark as an insult, but Xander and I had always had an adversarial relationship. He cared for me. Wanted me to be safe. And he was high-handed enough to think that he could manage me.

Which was why he wound up constantly disappointed.

"Funny, I don't recall ever asking you to."

His eyes narrowed as his expression tightened. "I am the king." His go-to explanation for imposing his will on me. I knew in the finality of his tone that it was the last he would speak on the subject.

Like it or not, Xander would always have his nose in my business. And as annoying as that could be, I'd learned over the years how to work around it. My annoyance couldn't squash my excitement at having him home, though. And even more than that, I couldn't wait to see Raif and Asher again.

"That's right," I agreed with a bright smile. "You are the king. And you've been away from Seattle for a long time, so don't let me keep you from having a good time tonight."

"Are you kidding?" His bright eyes sparkled with amusement. "It's only been a few minutes, and already I'm having more fun than I've had in almost a year."

As much as I loved pushing Xander's buttons, I was here for a reason. I cast a quick glance over my left shoulder to see Kira studying me from across the room. There wasn't a supernatural creature in the city who didn't know Alexander Peck, Shaede

High King. But the gossip mill would certainly be churning once word of his return spread.

"I'd love to stand around and chew the fat with you all night, but I'm actually sorta busy." Truth was, I wanted to ditch this place and head straight to Xander's house to seek out Raif. It would have to wait, though. I needed to get my head in the game and focus. Though the last thing I wanted was to tear myself from Xander's side. "Have a wonderful rest of your night, your highness," I said with a slight nod. "I'll catch ya later."

It took every ounce of willpower I had to turn and walk away. Xander had made a grand re-entrance into my life, no doubt exactly how he'd planned it. Relief flooded my limbs and settled my churning stomach. I wouldn't have to face the impending threat to my existence alone. The comfort that came from knowing someone had my back—someone tangible and not a mysterious, faceless figure—gave me strength to put one foot in front of the other as I walked toward Kira.

"Is it a powerful feeling?" A smug half-smile curved Kira's lips. "To know you can easily bring a king to his knees?"

I rolled my eyes. My tumultuous relationship with Xander had been gossip fodder for the supernatural community for years. It no longer fazed me.

"Alexander Peck kneels for no one." And gods, wasn't that the truth. "Especially me."

"Uh-huh." Kira let out a chuff of laughter as she led the way out of the salon and on to the next exhibit.

The slightest tremor raced over my skin, the sensation of Xander's eyes on me as I walked away. Had we met in another place—another time—I had no doubt that we'd be together. More than once over the past year I'd asked myself why it hadn't worked out between us. And though I couldn't latch on to a definitive answer, I knew that "why" was what caused the inexplicable, empty ache in my chest.

Focus, Darian. I couldn't afford distractions. Of any kind.

Kira remained silent as we continued to stroll through the exhibits, her attention seemingly focused on the blown glass art. Her predatory energy signature brushed against my skin in a ripple that coaxed goosebumps to my flesh. I was glad she was on my side.

Kira beside me, Xander behind me, and the prospect of seeing Raif again before me, sent me into sensory and emotional overload. My stomach roiled with nervous anticipation, my mind raced with innumerable thoughts, and my limbs twitched with the urge to turn and leave this place and head straight for Capitol Hill where I knew my best friend would be.

My gaze wandered from a bright, twisting sculpture and landed on a man who stood at the opposite end of the exhibit. His shrewd gray-blue eyes swept over me quickly, and just as abruptly, shifted toward the group of people that surrounded him. Kira's hand reached out to nudge me as though she'd accidentally bumped me. I didn't need a signal from the Werewolf, however, to tell me I'd laid eyes on Mitchell Redmond.

He looked more or less as he had in the pictures of him I'd found online. Though perhaps a little more underwhelming. For someone with as much power as he supposedly possessed, he presented himself as a rather forgettable creature. And maybe that's the look he was going for. Sort of business professional-meets-televangelist.

Part of me wanted to march straight up to him and drive the pointy end of my dagger right between his ribs. The other, more defiant side of me, locked eyes with him again and graced him with a wide, inviting smile.

Come and get me, motherfucker.

Redmond's eyes narrowed almost imperceptibly but he returned the gesture with slightly less charm behind the straight, white teeth of his smile.

Kira turned her back to Redmond and his cohorts and tilted

her head as she studied a large grouping of blown glass globes. "He's nervous," she said. "I can smell it from here."

"Good." I wanted him nervous. I wanted him to know that I wasn't afraid of him or anyone he sent after me.

"We've done what we came here to do," Kira replied. She caught a passing server and exchanged her empty champagne glass for a full one. "But I want him to leave first."

A good old-fashioned stand-off. On any other day, I would have enjoyed sticking around to make Redmond sweat, but since seeing Xander, all I wanted was to get the hell out of here. That wasn't an option, though, and so I decided to use the opportunity to my advantage and educate myself on this new threat to my life.

"Who's in the entourage?" I asked as we waited for his group to move on to the next exhibit. "Anyone I should be made aware of?"

"I know a couple of faces," Kira replied. "Other members of the Arx. No one particularly important. Lackeys. Private security. "The guy on his left, though, is his second in command. Lance Landry. I'm assuming the others are business associates or hangers on. Redmond loves attention."

All power mongers did. I gave Lance a once-over. Definitely ex-military. Likely special forces. His body language and expression told everyone he was spoiling for a fight and it didn't matter much who brought it to him. Guys like that were unpredictable and dangerous. He looked my way and flashed a wide, cocky grin. Oh yeah, he was going to be trouble.

"What's Redmond's specific beef with Camden?" I was sure the Alpha Werewolf's motives for deposing Redmond weren't entirely altruistic. "It's only fair that you give me some information."

"Power," Kira said with a shrug. "That's what the Arx fears the most—aside from their own, of course. Camden has power and he's 'other.' That makes him, and likewise, our entire pack, and the supernatural community as a whole a threat to those who seek to destroy, rather than understand that which is different from themselves."

Fear could be a hell of a destructive force. Especially when it was coupled with hate. The Arx feared what they didn't understand, and it helped to fuel their hatred of all supernatural creatures.

"Are they truly that dangerous?" The threat to my existence aside, I couldn't understand how supernatural beings could feel threatened by a group of humans who lacked our advantages, no matter the size of their organization.

Kira bristled as she gave Redmond a sidelong glance from across the room. "Don't let your arrogance get the better of you, Darian. The Arx has nearly unlimited resources at their disposal." She turned to face me, her expression grave. "And none of us is infallible."

Point taken. "So we stay the course." It seemed the best way to assure my own safety was to ally myself with Camden and his pack and work to eliminate Redmond. "And bring them down from the inside."

"That's the plan," Kira replied.

She turned her back fully to Redmond. He and his cronies took it as a cue to wander from the exhibit room and we waited a beat before I followed beside Kira as we made our way from the exhibit toward the exit. She remained silent, though I knew her keen senses were on high alert. Tiny pinpricks grabbed at my skin and my stomach swirled with nervous energy. The urge to look over my shoulder was almost too strong to resist but I forced myself to appear calm and relaxed.

Redmond and his organization were dangerous. But something scratched at the back of my brain. The knowledge that somehow, the Arx were the least of my worries.

Something bigger—and badder—waited for the opportunity to take my life.

[13]

Kira left me outside the Seattle center with a promise that she'd be in touch soon. I put my worries on the backburner as I shed my corporeal form and headed straight for Xander's. Elation inflated my chest as I hurried toward Capitol Hill. Tendrils of my ethereal self passed through the bars of the gate, too anxious to see Raif to worry about the guards stationed there or what they might say.

It took every ounce of willpower I had to recognize decorum and regain my physical form to ring the doorbell rather than barge right through to the foyer.

Heavy footfalls made their way to my ears before the ornately carved door swung wide. Tears spilled from my eyes and a wide smile curved my lips as I flung myself into Raif's arms.

The air left his breath in woof of air, followed by the deep rumble of laughter. "I missed you, too, Darian," my best friend said as he held me tight.

"Damn it, Raif . . . ." I couldn't finish my sentence. Not only because of the sudden thickness in my throat, but because of all the many sentiments that fought for supremacy in my mind.

. . . I've needed you.

. . . I've missed you.

. . . Don't leave again.

. . . I'm so alone and lost.

. . . Something is seriously wrong with me.

. . . I don't know what to do.

"I know," he replied in his clipped warrior's tone. "We need to talk."

Turned out, I didn't need to say anything to him. He knew me better than anyone. Well, almost anyone. And I'm not sure why it struck me that there was certainly someone who knew my mind and heart better than Raif. But he was here now, unlike whoever it was that my mind had wandered to.

Straight to business. God how I loved him.

He led the way downstairs to the formal conference area that I'd come to think of as Xander's war room. I hadn't been in this part of the house for the better part of a year. The glossy mahogany table brightened with the reflection of the overhead lights. Raif took a seat at the head of the table where the king usually sat and motioned for me to sit beside him.

"How'd it go?" I wasn't ready to dive into the shitshow that was my current state of affairs. And besides, I was dying for the gossip on Saben and his miserable attempt to toss Xander from his throne. "Did you and Ash kick his ass into next year?"

Raif chuckled. I'd forgotten how menacing his sapphire stare could be and I almost felt sorry for anyone foolish enough to take up arms against him.

"Of course." I wouldn't expect anything but a straight answer from my friend. "But that's the short version. I'm afraid it would take all of tonight and most of tomorrow to tell you the full story."

My curiosity burned, and not for the first time I wished I'd been with him for this adventure. My heart dropped as I locked eyes with Raif. "I take it you're here to tie up a few loose ends before you pull up your stakes and head back to Banff."

"Darian," Raif replied in a scolding tone. "Always the pessimist. We have so much to discuss."

Boy, did we.

"Well, let's get to it then," I said with a grin. "Start at the second you guys got home and don't stop until the part where Saben is dead."

"And always the deflector," he remarked before fixing me with a stern expression. "We'll talk about that in good time. We need to talk about *you*."

"Yeah," I said, defeated. "I know." I took a deep breath. Averted my gaze. "What have you heard?" That I'm a dead woman walking? That I've lost my mind? That I've managed to get myself into yet another scrape I probably won't be able to get myself out of? I could speculate all day.

"Where should I start?" Raif teased. "In all of my years, I've never met anyone so incapable of staying out of harm's way."

"What can I say?" I tried to keep my tone light. "Go big or go home."

"Indeed."

Raif studied me for a quiet moment as though trying to delve into my thoughts. Or dissect them. He observed me as he would a stranger he was trying to get a bead on and that tore at my heart.

"You think I'm different?"

"Not different." He paused as though wanting to choose his next words carefully. A deadly gleam lit his eyes and hardened his proud features. "But someone has altered you and it angers me more than you possibly imagine."

Altered. The word sent a skitter of nervous energy down my spine. A flare of cold stretched out from my thumb, causing my hand and fingers to tingle. "What do you know?"

"Enough."

I let out a derisive snort. "Care to fill me in?"

"Let's start with what we have the best odds at controlling." Raif, always so pragmatic. "The leader of the Arx has offered an impressive bounty for you. It would be an easy feat to eliminate him, but it's not so simple, is it?"

"If only." I propped my elbows on the shiny tabletop and pressed my palms together as though in prayer. "And seriously, how is it that everyone seems to know about this secret society, but me? Am I *always* out of the loop?"

Raif hiked an unconcerned shoulder. "The Arx has been in existence for a very long time. And never anything more than a mild annoyance. Humans are fragile, and their lives, short. The leadership is always changing. They've become bolder in recent years, and more dedicated to their suspicions and hate. But this too will be fleeting. It's the immediate threat to your life that concerns me. And it's all that should concern you."

Okay, maybe he had a point. But Camden didn't seem to think their threat was fleeting.

"The werewolves appear to have an agenda in regard to the Arx," he said, rather than asked.

Raif always had the inside track. Why did I even need to get him up to speed.

"They do," I confirmed. "They want to take Mitchell Redmond out while inserting someone to take his place. Someone who will destroy the organization from the inside out."

"A supernatural in charge of the Human Purification Society," Raif said with a snort. "It's a brilliant plan, if not a little risky."

"I agree, but it's not my call to make. Essentially, by helping them, I'll be helping myself. I don't see a better way to save myself at this point."

"I agree," Raif replied. "Besides, the Arx is a thorn in the supernatural world's side. I doubt they offer much value to those of their own kind either. The world is better off without such organized hatred. It might feel like the long way around, but I believe it will be the quickest and most efficient solution to your problem. I've reached out to the Alpha. They have our allegiance and aid."

I smiled. "Thanks." Knowing Raif had my back meant more than anything to me.

"One obstacle addressed," he said. "On to the Délash."

My eyes widened though I tried to hide my surprise. "You know about the dark cloud of doom?"

Raif pursed his lips. "A very cavalier nickname for a creature that could end you in a blink of an eye."

Yikes. I knew from experience that the sentient mass of dark energy was dangerous, but hearing Raif confirm it really hit the point home.

"What do you know about it?"

"Not enough." He let out a measured breath that was more disconcerting than an outright sigh. "It's as unpredictable as those who wield its power."

The Délash was certainly a very menacing weapon, which made its wielders even more frightening. "Who controls it?"

Raif's expression turned grave. "I don't know how to tell you without causing you excruciating pain."

Of course. Everything swung around to my mysterious headaches and whatever caused them. "How did you find out about my headaches?"

Raif tilted his head in an expression that said, *Please. I know everything.*

I wasn't satisfied with an expression as answer, however. "Tell me."

"Anya," Raif said.

Of course. Tattletale.

"But I found out what I needed to know by going straight to the source."

"The source of my headaches?" How could Raif have possibly known who, or what, that was? "How?"

His eyes met mine and he gave a sad shake of his head. "Poor Darian." The genuine pity in his voice tore through me. "Always at the mercy of those too foolish to understand their own selfishness. I pray the gods will give you better."

Jesus. From the way he spoke, you'd think I had some terminal illness that was about to take me out for good. A wave of fresh anxiety crested in my chest, and I took a deep breath to still the tremor that threatened to roll through my fingers.

"Tell me what the hell is going on." I couldn't take being in the dark for another second. "I don't care what kind of pain it causes me."

Raif let out a frustrated breath. "I'll do my best to choose my words carefully. First, what do you remember of the past several years?"

Boy, that was a loaded question. "Everything, I guess. But at the same time, it feels fake. I mean, I know that my memories are real, but there are holes. Bits and pieces of whole memories that I can't recall. It's like I can't see what's supposed be there."

"It's because the individual who fills those spaces has been erased from your mind."

His explanation didn't surprise me a bit. I more or less knew that my memory loss had something to do with the mysterious stranger that had saved me from the Délash, as well as the group of ambitious gangbangers who'd tried to get their hands on the Arx's million-dollar pay day a while back. What I hadn't realized was that my supposed savior had played a bigger part in my life than I'd realized.

"Erased?" It seemed crazy. "How? Why?" Anger and confusion rushed in to chase away my fear and anxiety. "And who in the hell would do something like that?"

"Darian." Raif gave a sad shake of his head. "You've frightened the wrong creatures."

Why in the hell did everyone find me so goddamned threatening all of a sudden? You'd think I was the Dark fucking Phoenix or something. "I haven't done anything." I hated feeling like I was making a plea for my innocence. Especially to Raif. I held my hands up in supplication. "I'm not dangerous." Raif gave me a pointed look and I amended to, "Well, only to anyone who deserves it."

Raif combed his fingers through his short, tawny hair. "This is more complicated than I thought it would be."

He was visibly frustrated and I knew exactly how he felt. If I didn't get some solid answers soon, I'd crawl right out of my damned skin.

"You've been keeping company with a very powerful supernatural creature for the past several years. One who has"—Raif paused as though unsure how to say the next few words—"bound himself to you."

He studied me for a brief moment, and I realized he was waiting to see if his words caused me any pain. There was definitely a shitload of shock, but so far, my head felt fine. "I'm okay," I replied. "Keep going."

"Because of something he's given you," Raif explained, "his power is, in theory, limitless."

Okaaay. "What do you mean, 'in theory?'"

"Because I'm not sure I believe that any creature in this world can be truly omnipotent," Raif explained. "But . . . ." He sighed. "I suppose anything is possible."

"Would this be the sort of power that could freeze bullets in midair and scare off dark clouds of sentient doom?"

Raif gave a silent nod.

"Wait. Because of something he's given me?"

I reached down to trace the ring that circled my thumb as a derisive snort came from the doorway. We turned in unison to see Xander leaning against the jamb, still dressed in his black tie attire.

"He's an arrogant, thoughtless, careless, maniac. And as far as I've seen, he doesn't care at all that he's put your life in danger."

Did everyone but me know who this guy was? I was damned sick of being the last to know what was going on in my own life.

"Tell me how you really feel, your highness."

"You know exactly how I feel." I didn't miss the double meaning in Xander's words. "But those meddling fools with their overinflated egos made sure you wouldn't remember."

Fools? As in plural. The knot in my stomach tightened. What I wouldn't give to have those missing memories back, because whatever had happened, it must have been bad for someone—or some group—to have wiped it from my mind.

"Who are they?" If I could identify the threat first, I could determine what to do next. "And what exactly do I have that's got them so pissed off?" I caressed the cool silver. "I mean, I can just give it back if that's the issue."

Xander pushed himself away from the doorway with an angry huff of air. He folded his arms across his strong chest as he regarded me for a quiet moment. "I should have left him in that PNT cell to rot."

A spark of familiarity ignited in my mind. As though I'd heard those words from Xander before, or something like it. My brow furrowed as I dug deep into my memories, desperate to latch onto anything that might help me remember.

My lack of control over the situation caused a fresh wave of panic to wash over me. "Someone tell me what the hell is going on before I freak the fuck out."

"Ty—"

Before Xander could get the word out of his mouth, pain scalded a path through my skull and down my spine. The sensation of being cooked alive in my own skin was a fresh new torture and I shoved the chair out from under me as I shot upright, my arms braced on the table as I tried to breathe through the pain. My knees wobbled, and finally buckled. I went down hard, my chin striking sharply against the tabletop as I crumpled to a heap on the floor.

So much for being headache free.

Xander responded with a string of angry, unintelligible

words. The sound of Raif's chair scraping against the floor followed and seconds later, two pairs of strong arms hoisted me up to stand.

"I'll kill him," Xander said from between clenched teeth. "If it's the last thing I do."

"Xander," Raif warned. "Enough."

I held up a hand, both to let Raif and Xander know I was okay and to stop whatever argument might be about to start. Not gonna lie, it bothered me that my friends had the missing pieces of my memory but couldn't provide them.

"Darian—"

"I'm fine, Raif." I cut him off before he could voice any words of concern. A chill crept over my left hand, snaking out from the mysterious ring around my thumb and I shivered. Just the other day, I'd made the blinding pain disappear. All it had taken was two simple words. "I wish the pain would stop."

The cold intensified until my teeth chattered. Both Raif and Xander took tentative steps away from me which frightened me even more than the inexplicable cold that enveloped me. But the pain stopped almost instantly. I straightened, my eyes closed as I released a breath of relief.

"How did you know to do that?" Raif asked.

"No." Xander's scowl darkened as he exchanged a worried look with Raif that did nothing for my already edgy anxiety. "How did she do it without *him*?"

Raif's brow furrowed, likely echoing my own perplexed expression. "Perhaps he doesn't have to be physically present . . . ."

"I have no idea what you're talking about," I said. "But keep going."

If they talked around whatever it was that caused my iron spike headaches, maybe I'd reclaim some part of my lost memories.

Raif seemed to consider his next words carefully. "I don't recall him ever having to be close to her to protect her. As far as I know, their bond makes it possible for her to call upon his power when she needs it."

Wow. This was so not the way I envisioned a Raif/Xander homecoming. Maybe a call first with a heads up, dinner, Raif and Asher telling me the story of how they won Xander's kingdom back . . . . Instead, we'd all been thrown into action without any downtime. And once again, it was all my fault.

"I don't know what I'm doing," I began. I looked down at my thumb before bringing my hand up. "But I think I know how I'm doing it."

Xander's expression was far too knowing for my peace of mind.

"They'll kill her," he said more to Raif than to me. "And we're powerless to do anything about it."

"We might be," Raif agreed. "But she's not."

"*She* is sitting right here." I wasn't going to put up with them talking about me like I wasn't even there. "And if this"—I pointed to the ring—"thing is giving me any sort of strange power, I have no idea how to control it."

"Yes, you do," Raif said. "Think carefully Darian about your words."

I knew what I'd said, but it seemed so absurd. I'd only been half serious when I'd said the words. "I wish?"

Raif answered with a nod.

"What in the hell is this thing?"

"It's your doom," Xander said darkly. "And I promise you, I'll do everything in my power to rid you of it."

Xander knew more about the mysterious ring, and what it was doing to me than I was comfortable with and it bothered the hell out of me. The Shaede King had a tendency to manipulate situations to his benefit. But at this point, I had no choice but to trust him.

It was either that, or let whoever had it out for me, kill me.

Damn it, I wasn't ready to die.

[14]

My cell vibrated, interrupting my train of thought. I pulled it from my pocket and checked the caller ID, Misha.

"Shit." I held up a hand to silence the conversation as I swiped my finger across the screen and put the phone to my ear. "Hey, Misha. What's up?"

"Where are you?" His voice bore the tone of someone who wasn't interested in small talk.

"Xander's." There was no point in lying to him. Lies never attracted anything but trouble. But that didn't mean I had to tell him the whole truth, either.

"Have you forgotten something?"

He wasn't interested in where I was. He was pissed off that I hadn't gotten a job done. Understandable, I suppose, though I still didn't know what about this Levi guy had Misha's panties in a bunch.

"Not at all." I made my voice equally cold, unwilling to let the Fae intimidate me. "I told you I'd have it done by the end of the week. Is it the end of the week yet?"

"No," Misha replied stiffly. "But I also recall telling you that the client would appreciate the timeline being moved up."

He'd hinted more than told, but I didn't give a shit either way. "Tonight was no good." Misha didn't need to know why. A good assassin bided their time and struck at the perfect moment. "I haven't let you down yet, so why worry?"

"I'm not worried." He almost sounded offended that I would suggest such a thing. "I want it done."

"*You* want it done . . .?" I let the question hang for a moment. "Or the client does?"

"The client," Misha replied. "Will you be coming by later?" He forced his tone to a more conversational level.

He'd never asked me anything like that before and I didn't ignore the red flag. Something was up with Misha, and goddamn it, I didn't have room for anything else on my already full plate. "Not tonight." I needed to talk to Raif about Misha. Maybe he or Asher could do some digging for me. "But I'll be by tomorrow."

"Very well, Darian. Goodnight."

"Later."

I ended the call and I stretched out my arms. Tension pulled my shoulders close to my ears and I forced myself to relax as I set my phone on the glossy tabletop. Thanks to supernatural hearing, I didn't have to repeat my conversation to Raif and Xander. The three of us sat for a quiet moment. We'd had a lot to process in the past few hours and the night wasn't over yet.

Xander's intense gaze met mine. "Misha has been good to you while we've been gone?"

He never missed a single detail and had picked up on my nerves. "Sure." I didn't know how close Misha and Xander were. And I was still suspicious that Misha had been a spy for the Shaede King, keeping me under his wing and reporting straight to Xander. "He's a pain in the ass." I met Xander look for look. "Sort of like you, but we get along okay."

Xander wasn't exactly buying it, but my response seemed enough to placate him for now.

"I've got a job to do for him, but as you saw tonight, I've been a little preoccupied."

"Tell me about the werewolves." Raif seemed disinterested with Misha and was ready to get back to business. "Xander says you've allied yourself with them?"

Raif, always thinking like a warrior.

"Something like that."

"Camden Walsh is a very powerful male," Raif replied. "A king in his own right. Obviously, you realize that his interest in you isn't solely because of the bounty on your head."

I paused as I took in Raif's somber expression. I looked at Xander, similarly serious, and drew in a deep breath. "Sorry," I said on an exhale. "But this is seriously crazy. You've been gone for a year, and here we are, sitting in the war room, hashing over details without missing a beat as though no one ever left. It's *seriously* trippy."

I hadn't allowed myself to feel overwhelmed, but it was starting to catch up with me. Why did I have to exist in a state of constant chaos? I wanted someone to blame for it, but the truth was, I had a way of finding trouble, even when I wasn't exactly looking for it.

"I understand how you feel, Darian." Raif's tone was gentle, though no less stern. "Unfortunately, we don't have time for pleasantries. We have a lot of catching up to do and not a lot of time to do it."

"I know." I let my head fall back onto my shoulders before stretching it from side to side. "I just need a break."

Xander snorted. "That's easy. Simply change the company you keep."

I looked at him. "*You're* the company I keep."

His full lips pursed, and he looked away. Seriously, what was wrong with him? I mean, Xander was always a pain in the ass, but he seemed particularly peeved right now. Could it be my mysterious benefactor that had his designer undies in a bunch?

"Back to Walsh," Raif said. I could always count on him to keep me on task. "Have you sensed any duplicity from him?"

"Not at all." And that was the truth. "He's been upfront—well, as upfront as he can be—since day one."

"What did he tell you exactly?"

"That he represented a 'benefactor' who wanted to help me out with the property I wanted to buy—"

"What property?" Xander interjected.

I rolled my eyes. Lord, but he was high-handed. "None of your damn business, that's what property." I turned my attention back to Raif. "Anyway, he said he represented some mystery person that he couldn't speak to me about for obvious reasons." I tapped my temple with a forefinger. "He also said that he owed me a life debt for helping him escape Mithras and that he knew who had put the price on my head. He more or less said it would be advantageous for us both to take Mitchell Redmond out and that we should work together." I took another deep breath. "But after meeting with a member from his pack, I get a sense that I'm less of a partner and more someone he's been asked to keep watch over." And I didn't like that one bit.

"I see." Raif's expression remained passive as he processed everything I'd said. He never gave anything away, just one of the things I loved about him. "And that's why you were at the event at the Chihuly Garden tonight?"

"I thought I was there to do a little recon. But I think Camden wanted to dangle me in front of Redmond to shake him up."

Xander's hand slapped down on the tabletop with enough force to make the wood creak. Angry fire lit his gaze, but he could save his indignation.

"Please." I rolled my eyes at his dramatic display. "I would have done the same thing if I'd been in his position. Besides, I wanted to get my eyes on the bastard."

Raif hiked a shoulder as he looked over at his brother. "She's right. It was a good idea."

Xander seemed equally disgusted with the both of us, but we didn't give him the satisfaction of a reaction. In fact, I was about to ask if maybe he wanted to go check on Anya and the baby. He was sort of a third wheel at this point.

"And what is your opinion of Redmond?"

I shrugged. "Without having talked to him . . . I think he's arrogant and drunk on his own power. He doesn't go anywhere without bodyguards though he looks like he can hold his own in a fight. But," I paused as I leaned in toward Raif. "He's human. How hard can it be to take him out?"

"The Arx has power, Darian," Raif said. "Don't underestimate any of them."

"How is it that I've never heard about these guys before?" It never failed to amaze me, how little I knew about the arcane workings of the world. Just when I thought I'd heard or seen it all, something new crawled out of the wood word to prove me wrong. "And how is it that you know about them?"

"Do you know there is a President of the United States and a governing body?"

"Yeah . . . ."

"Does their existence cross your mind every day?"

Raif certainly had a way of getting his points across. "Nope."

"For the most part, the Arx doesn't affect us," Raif explained. "Had they displayed hostility to us or ours, then we would pay them more heed."

"Exactly," Xander agreed. "And now, they'll regret the day they set their sights on you."

It warmed my chilly heart to know that Raif and Xander considered me as "ours." It felt good to have my support system back and it boosted my confidence.

"Camden didn't want to tell me exactly why the Arx considered me dangerous enough to kill. And since I know you know way more than you're letting on, I think it's time you told me why."

The haughty brothers exchanged a silent glance that offered little in the way of reassurance.

"Seriously, spill it."

"I'm not sure how much you can be made privy to without it causing you pain." Raif's brow furrowed. "I'm not willing to take the chance that something worse than a headache might await you if we decide to be completely candid."

What could be worse than the skull-splitting headaches? Oh yeah, the fire in my blood a few minutes ago. Until now, the headaches had been the only adverse reaction from trying to remember anything. I knew better than anyone that things could always get worse.

"At this point, I'm willing to risk it. Whatever it is." I'd wished the pain away twice now. There didn't seem to be any reason why I couldn't do it again. I was tired of being left in the dark and I didn't want to be a helpless participant in my own destiny any longer. I needed to know as much as I could, as soon as I could, so I could form some sort of plan.

"If I had it my way, I would have told you months ago," Xander said, his voice thick with disdain. "It's unfortunate that I have to tell you now, when the truth could hurt you."

Xander had been withholding information from me? Big freaking surprise.

"Be careful," Raif warned. "Tell her enough, but don't do anything that might alert the Synod."

"Synod." Somehow, the word rang with familiarity. "More dangerous than the Arx."

"Infinitely." Raif replied.

Well, that didn't sound good.

"Okay, now that we have that cheery baseline established, who are they and what do they have to do with the latest clusterfuck in my life."

"The Synod is the ruling body of a supernatural race of . . . ."

Xander paused, as though searching for the right word. I felt like we were on one of those gameshows where one person had to help another person guess a word without saying the forbidden clues. "Gods, I don't even know how to describe them. They're higher beings. The highest on the supernatural ladder. They are self-proclaimed protectors. And fancy themselves wish granters," he said at last.

"Wish granters?" That would explain why wishing my headache away had worked. "Like a ge—"

"Don't." Xander interrupted. "For once, Darian, just listen."

I huffed out a breath. Nothing got under my skin like being put in my place by Xander. I folded my arms across my chest and leaned back in my chair as I gave him and Raif my full attention.

"They . . . form an attachment to those they wish to protect. And that connection can only be severed by death—or if the individual no longer needs protection."

"Okay." A mild throbbing pulsed at the back of my head, but I kept the discomfort under wraps. "What does that have to do with me?"

"One of them formed an attachment to you."

Raif let out an amused snort. "I suppose that's one way to put it."

Silence settled over us as I digested what Xander had just told me. It didn't take much to connect the dots. Obviously, my mysterious benefactor—the same individual that had saved me twice from ambitious assassins over the past year—was the mystical being in question.

"Why?" I knew the who—sort of—but why would any creature on god's green earth want to do something as drastic as attach themselves to me? Not that I even understood what that attachment entailed. But seriously. I wasn't the type of person anyone wanted to keep company with for any length of time, let alone till death.

Xander's expression grew pensive, his gaze penetrating. I hoped he kept his mouth shut and didn't try to unearth feelings I'd thought we'd put behind us. I had enough to deal with right now. I didn't need any more unnecessary drama.

"Even you have to admit, Darian, you have a tendency to find yourself in trouble," Raif said with affection. "How could a creature with a strong protective instinct resist watching over you?"

Xander scowled at his brother and sank lower into his chair. His Royal Poutiness had better snap out of his mood. We still had a lot of ground to cover, and I wasn't about to deal with his attitude.

"Okay, fine. Whatever." I brushed my hand through the air, unwilling to discuss my bad luck and its relationship to my occasional lapses in judgement. "But why can't I remember it? And why does that make me dangerous enough to justify killing me?"

"Because your so-called protector gave you something that makes you dangerous."

I brought my left hand up and showed my thumb to Xander and Raif. "Is this it?"

Their silence was all the affirmation I needed. "For what it's worth, I have no idea how it works." Aside from nearly freezing me to death, and maybe helping with my most recent headaches, I couldn't think of anything else the ring had done power-wise."

"*He* knows how it works," Xander replied bitterly. "That's all that matters."

I eyed the Shaede King warily. "You know *him*. Don't you?"

"I do," Xander replied without guile. "And I wish to the gods I didn't."

Obviously there was a little bad blood between my supposed protector and Xander. "What did he do to you?" Whatever it was, it wouldn't have surprised me if Xander deserved it.

Xander's gaze hardened. "He put you in this position," he said after a moment. "That's enough."

It might have been enough, but that wasn't all. I'd get the rest of the story, eventually. But for now, I was content to let it slide. "Fair point. That doesn't explain why I can't remember any of this or why I'm being subjected to excruciating pain to keep me from trying to remember."

"The Synod is attempting to keep you apart," Raif said.

"And you know this how?"

"He told us."

My gaze narrowed. "When?"

"Three days ago," Raif said. "Your phone call to Asher threw up a red flag. We talked to Anya as well, and he contacted me not long after that."

My curiosity was quickly turning to anger. Always in the dark. And always at the mercy of high-handed know-it-alls who thought they could decide what was best for me.

"What else do you know?" My voice lost its fire as a weariness stole over me. I was so tired of all of this I was ready to turn my back on Seattle and never return. I could back out of the lease on the waterfront building. I had a nice nest egg set aside. What was stopping me from taking off for good?

The truth, for starters. Not to mention my pride and my own burning need to recover the memories that I'd lost.

"Only that your situation will continue to become more dangerous by the day as long as he continues his quest to destroy the Synod."

"They're afraid . . . . And what they're so worked up over isn't our relationship but the fact that I found a way to shake loose from the leash they had on me."

The words resounded in the back of my mind, dreamlike, but I knew with certainty that they'd been spoken to me at some point. A sense of trepidation followed on the heels of the words. A worry that sent a wave of anxious energy through my bloodstream.

"Darian?" Raif's brow furrowed. "What is it?"

"Nothing." I gave a quick shake of my head. "Just tired."

Raif's expression of concern remained, though he didn't push me on the matter.

"So we talk him out of this plan, whatever it is," I said. "Danger averted."

"It's not that easy," Raif said. "Imagine someone twice as stubborn as Xander."

Xander shot a dirty look at his brother and I stifled a laugh. I honestly couldn't imagine any living soul who could be twice as stubborn as the king. Whoever this guy was, he had to be a piece of work.

"Then we take him out." Saying the words sent a stab of pain through my chest. Why would it pain me to kill someone I couldn't even remember?

"We can't do that either, Darian." Raif sounded as tired as I was. "Your life forces are bound."

Meaning, if he died, I died. Lovely. When I finally got face-to-face with this guy, I was I going to show him with my fist how much I appreciated him putting me in this position.

"I'm tired and it's late." As happy as I was about Xander and Raif being back in Seattle, I couldn't keep having the same cyclical conversation. "I'm going to hit the hay. I'll see you in the morning."

Despair welled in my chest and choked me with its bleakness. It seemed impossible to escape my situation and I needed some peace and quiet to work things out in my head. I slid my chair from the table and pushed myself to stand. My eyes met Xander's and held them for a moment before I turned and left his war room. I hurried up the stairs and reached for the door when Raif spoke out to stay my hand.

"Darian, a word."

I allowed myself a sigh as I turned to face him.

"I really have missed you." I said it as more of an apology for my abrupt exit. "I wish I'd known you were coming home. Xander sort of caught me off guard tonight and the timing was . . . ."

"Unfortunate." Raif finished for me.

"Yeah." I rolled my head from shoulder to shoulder and tugged at the décolletage of my dress. God, I wanted to get back to my place and get out of this uncomfortable thing. "I'm just struggling to wrap my head around all of this."

"I think we all are." Raif offered a sympathetic half-smile. "It's hard to understand how we can have a whole picture of your life while you are only allowed glimpses. And I don't want to pile on more than you can handle, but you need to know . . ." he paused as though unsure if he should say more or not.

"Spit it out," I replied. "At this point, nothing more can surprise me."

"Your relationship with this, protector, who's been wiped from your memory, it's more than you think."

Great. I had a way of rubbing everyone the wrong way, maybe we had an antagonistic relationship as well.

"How so?"

Raif sighed. His gaze darted toward the staircase, letting me know there'd be repercussions from Xander for what he was about to tell me. "You are in love with him, and likewise, he is in love with you."

Well. Knock me over with a feather. Suddenly Xander's morose attitude made so much more sense.

"I take it this isn't a casual dating sort of thing."

"Your souls are bound," Raif remarked solemnly. "This goes far beyond anything casual."

The weight of his words settled atop my shoulders as a dull ache began to throb in my head. We were getting dangerously close to too much information and I was too damned tired to press my luck any further. This new and unexpected revelation did nothing to assuage my fears. In fact, all it did was ramp them up a few hundred percent.

"Thanks for the info, Raif." I was on overload and couldn't muster up anything more articulate. "I'll see you tomorrow."

I turned and let myself out.

Definitely not how I wanted to celebrate my friends' return to the city.

And certainly not how I wanted to learn about the apparent love of my life.

[15]

I walked through Capitol Hill, wishing like hell I'd changed out of my evening gown and heels before heading over to Xander's. I could have traveled as shadow, but I needed the night air to clear my head and the click of my heels on the sidewalk offered my brain the distraction it needed to keep from over-thinking everything I'd heard tonight.

It was a lot to fucking process.

Seattle never slept, but it was late enough that the streets were relatively empty. Music played from the open door of a pub and I glanced inside at the people bellied up to the bar before contin-uing toward the waterfront.

Click, clack, click. Click, clack, click.

One, two, three. One, two, three. I counted in time to each footfall, forcing myself to acknowledge only the cadence of my steps.

The air left my chest as a force crashed into me from behind, knocking me into a solid wall of muscle. My arms were seized behind my back in an iron grip, and I kicked off my heels, using the body in front of me as a catapult. I dug my feet in to his chest and propelled myself upward as I used the leverage to climb assailant number two's body and flip myself over assailant number one, to land without a sound on the pavement behind them. I remained in my corporeal form, rather than allow the shadows to protect me. No way would I let them think they'd scared me.

But damn it I hated it when anyone got the jump on me. Especially when I wasn't dressed—or armed—for a fight. A dress with pockets was a godsend, but they didn't have room for my magic daggers or my sword. I'd tucked a shorter, less impressive dagger into a sheath beneath my dress, though. I might have been disadvantaged, but I sure as hell wasn't helpless.

My attackers had managed to shuffle me into a side alley before I freed myself. I was more comfortable taking the fight from the street. No need to involve any Good Samaritan who might happen to come along and want to help.

My would-be assassins were going old school tonight. No firepower. One pulled a long, thick bladed knife from a sheath at his thigh, while the other held two, shorter daggers in each hand. Their energy signatures brushed my senses. One Shifter . . . and one Fae. Fuck. The Shifter I could handle. The Fae would be tougher.

I set my sights on the weaker opponent first. I'd need all of my focus to beat the Fae and as soon as the Shifter was out of the picture, the better. I wasn't thrilled about my attention being divided, but those were the breaks. The Fae hung back and let his partner take the lead. Smart. He could let the Shifter kill me and then kill his partner and get the money without sustaining so much as a scratch in the fight. I took a step back, deeper into the alley and reached behind my back to where I'd secured the dagger in a sheath sewn into the fabric between my shoulder blades.

It wasn't much, but it was enough. I held the dagger in my right hand, absolutely disgusted as my bare feet scraped against the cold, littered pavement. Thank the gods I couldn't get tetanus —or worse—because I was pretty damn sure I'd already cut myself on a piece on broken glass. I put my pain and any distractions on the backburner and focused on the Shifter who slowly closed the distance between us. His eyes were yellow-gold and a wicked scar marred his left cheek. Probably scored with a silver blade. He bared his teeth and a low growl rumbled in his chest. The Fae stayed back toward the street as though blocking my escape route and watched with an almost disinterested expression. I'd make sure to change his demeanor soon enough.

"Get on with it." I was tired of waiting for the Shifter to make his move. "Seriously. It's two against one. What are you waiting for?"

A sneer curled his lip as he lunged for me. Pushing buttons really was my thing. I took a defensive stance, knowing the short dagger wouldn't make it past the larger knife and his longer wingspan. But where he was bulky and slow, I had speed and agility. I let him think I'd hesitated and he used the opportunity to slash at my throat.

I joined with the shadow, swirling past him as a ribbon of darkness. I became my solid self with a downward sweep of my arm and cut with my short knife through his jacket and into flesh. He let out a snarl and whipped around to face me, no longer cocky and relaxed. A glint of fear reflected in his eyes and his gaze darted to the Fae who watched from the edge of the alley, completely unconcerned.

The Shifter might've thought they were working together, but he was sadly mistaken. No doubt the Fae hoped his partner would tire me out and die in the process, thereby leaving him an easy kill and a fat payday.

"Your friend's not much help," I remarked with a jut of my chin. "I wouldn't share the bounty if I were you."

The Fae smirked. Yeah, he'd definitely be tougher to kill. The Shifter came after me again, the glint of his blades flashing with the wild swings of his arms. I knew the Fae wouldn't join the fray until his partner was dead or on the run. So I turned my attention solely on the Shifter, determined that he'd pay for making me fight in a damned cocktail dress.

I mean, seriously.

I entered the battle-dance with deadly intent. If Redmond wanted me dead, I needed him to know that he'd better send an army to get it done. One small dirk against the larger Bowie knife put me at a disadvantage, but I made up for it with speed, and my ability to meld with the shadows. The sound of metal on metal echoed off the brick walls that enclosed us as I passed from shadow to my solid self. My breath sucked in on a hiss as the Shifter got in a lucky shot, the knife sinking into the exposed skin of my forearm. He leaned in hard, to try and push the blade into my ribs but I became shadow, giving him nothing but the pavement to cushion his fall. The Fae chuckled, and I pushed him from my mind, refusing to let him get into my head and distract me.

I'd deal with him soon enough.

My current opponent was stronger, agile, and damn good with the knife. If I'd come armed for a fight, this would be over already, but since I had only the dirk to protect me, I was working for the advantage. Sure, I could melt into shadow and simply escape, but running wouldn't do me any good. If I didn't send a clear message to those who meant to do me harm, I'd be running for the rest of my life.

Damn it, I was tired of this shit. The Shifter rushed me again, and rather than dodge his attack, I met him with a forceful kick to the gut that caught him off guard and sent him sprawling into the opposite wall. Without a second to spare, I flipped the knife in my grip, brought it up to aim, and let it fly. The blade buried itself to the hilt in the Shifter's forehead and his eyes went wide as he slumped to the ground.

The Fae pushed himself from the wall, the same self-assured smirk still curving his lips. He put the twin daggers away and instead, drew a long saber from a sheath at his back and twirled it in a dazzling display before leveling the blade at me. Well, shit.

This wasn't going to be an easy win. I began to think that retreat —so I could live to fight another day—might be the best option.

The sword dropped to the ground with a ring of metal and the Fae grasped at his throat as a low gurgling sound echoed in his chest. Crimson flashed from the gaping wound as blood poured from his jugular and pooled on the dark pavement. He dropped to his knees and I sucked in a sharp breath as Asher's face came into focus. He kneeled to wipe the blood from his own blade on the Fae's shirt as he jerked his chin toward the street.

"Let's get out of here."

I nodded. Too stunned—and grateful—to speak. There wasn't a better wingman on the planet.

I'd been too shaken up to grab my shoes, so I walked barefoot beside Asher as we made our way to the waterfront. A shuddering breath escaped my chest and I hated that I felt so vulnerable.

"Thank you." Shame at my own weakness heated my cheeks and I kept my gaze straight ahead. "I'm not sure I would have made it out of that alley alive if you hadn't shown up."

I knew Asher's presence was no accident. With Xander back in the city, he'd be my shadow from now on. And damn, was I grateful for it.

"Please," Ash scoffed. "You would have walked out of there just fine without me. It just would've taken you a little longer."

He knocked his shoulder against mine. Traitorous tears stung at my eyes and I swallowed past the thickness in my throat. God I'd missed the little shit.

"We make a good team."

"Hell yeah we do."

A couple of quiet seconds passed while I composed myself and put my soft emotions in the little mental box where they belonged. Survival meant compartmentalizing and I was good at it.

"So, are you glad to be back in Seattle?"

"Of course," Ash said with his typical youthful enthusiasm.

"Seattle is much more exciting. Probably because you're here," he added with another shoulder knock. "I gotta say, I've never known anyone who gathers adversaries like you do."

Adversaries. It was my turn to scoff. I supposed that was one way to put it. "You know me, always stirring up trouble."

Asher laughed.

"Is that why you're back?"

He didn't answer me right away which didn't fill me with any warm, fuzzy feelings. I hated that those closest to me felt like I needed looking after. I'd been independent for so long and my pride took a hit every time one of my friends had to get me out of a scrape. Which seemed to happen a hell of a lot lately. Ash's brow furrowed as he tucked his hands into his pockets.

"You're not okay," he said, low. "And when you're not okay, he's not okay."

He being Xander.

"You shouldn't have told him."

Asher shrugged. "Even if I hadn't, Anya would have."

Anya. The little rat.

"Snitches get stitches, you know."

Asher laughed. "She cares about you too. She just shows it differently than the rest of us."

"I guess." I didn't have the energy to truly be upset with her. If I'd been in her position, I would have done the same. "I hate to admit it, but this shit is wearing me out. I've got way too many fires to extinguish."

Asher nodded. He didn't say anything else about my current predicament and I was grateful for it. I was tired of having to talk around something that may or may not cause me skull shattering pain. My building came into view and a sense of calm washed over me. Already this place was beginning to feel like my home base. A new sanctuary. I pointed and took a right toward the front entrance and Ash followed.

"I like it," he remarked. "Reminds me of your old place a little."

"Me too." It definitely fit my vibe.

"Doesn't hurt that it's close to the house."

Xander's place could hardly be considered a "house." It was more of a royal compound.

"A year or so ago, I would have argued that it's way too close." I unlocked the front door and Asher followed me inside. "Now, though, I'm pretty thankful for the proximity."

Asher took a look around the unfinished space. Though Ned and his crew were practically miracle workers, there was still a lot that needed to be done. He straddled a folding chair presumably left by one of the construction workers and folded his arms across the back.

"Alexander won't like you living in an unfinished place."

Of course he wouldn't. But since when had what "Alexander" liked or didn't like matter to me?

I hiked a shoulder. "I've got a cot and a sleeping bag. I don't need anything else."

Asher snorted. "Don't worry, I'm not going to be the one to tell him."

I rolled my eyes. So high-handed.

I'd been living under Misha's watchful eye for almost a year. The last thing I wanted was to move right in under Xander's almost obsessive protection. I needed some room to breathe. A quiet space to clear my head. I didn't care that it wasn't finished or furnished. It had four walls and a roof and that's all I needed.

"Raif will want to install a security system," Asher remarked.

He'd outfitted my previous place with a state-of-the-art system. "Probably." That didn't bother me. A little added security couldn't hurt. "And I'll let him."

Ash's brow furrowed. "You're worried?"

I supposed that I usually put up such a good front of bravado that it seemed unlikely anything would worry me. I couldn't hide it this time, though. Shit was coming at me from all directions, and I just didn't have the fortitude to keep it all at bay.

"Yeah." I blew out a breath. The concrete floor chilled my bare feet and I wiggled my toes to help the blood circulate. "I need to get my memories back and figure out what the hell I did to deserve having them wiped in the first place. And I've got the Arx and this bounty on my head to deal with after that."

Asher didn't seem surprised to hear about the Arx which just confirmed that Xander made sure everyone in his inner circle was as well informed as he was.

"We'll tackle it as a team," he assured me. "I've got your back, Darian."

He did. "And I've got yours."

His answering grin was one hundred percent mischievous charm. "I can't wait to get into some shit with you."

So cavalier. I supposed it came with the territory when you walked around with a nickname like Lyhtan Slayer.

"Don't get too excited," I chided him. "You might get more than you bargained for."

"Gods, I hope so!" He rocked back in his seat before pushing himself to stand. "It's been a minute since I was in a good fight."

I cocked a brow. "You mean tonight doesn't count?"

He grinned and the expression was nothing if not wicked.

"What happened in Banff?" I was tired of talking about my problems and wanted to focus on something else. "A year is a long time to be gone."

His expression didn't dull. The memory of whatever had gone down there still glinted with excitement in his bright eyes.

"We sent Saben to the shadows for eternity," he said. "We made an example of him so that any other ambitious usurpers would know what they were up against."

The workings of Xander's kingdom were pretty much lost on me. I hoped that someday, I'd be able to see it for myself. "Why come back, though? There's nothing for him here. He could have called Anya home and stayed put."

Ash leveled his gaze. "Do you really believe he would have stayed there while you're here?"

I looked away. Xander's feelings for me were no secret. But I didn't want to be the reason he left his home—and his people—behind.

"It could happen again," I reasoned, though for Ash's sake, or mine, I didn't know.

"Maybe." His tone showed little concern. "And if it does, we'll deal with it. But really, it just makes sense for him to be here. Think about it. Seattle is a major hub for supernatural diplomats. There are kings, and alphas, and head honchos from every faction of our world here."

I'd never really considered it, but Seattle did have an unusually large concentration of supernatural creatures in residence. It was the home base for the PNT—the ruling supernatural body of the Pacific Northwest. If anything political was brewing, Seattle was likely where it would go down. And international borders didn't mean anything in the supernatural world. We might have lived on the same planet as humans, but we existed apart from them.

"Fair enough." It actually made me feel a hell of lot better to know that business had brought Raif, Xander, and Asher back and not simply my own recent shit-show of events. "So I guess it's business as usual from here on out?"

"Yep." Asher yawned and stretched his arms high above his head. "Getting into trouble with you is just a bonus." He headed for the door and paused with his hand on the knob. "Oh, and don't be surprised if you see the occasional security detail doing a sweep of the area. Just don't want you accidentally stabbing someone who doesn't deserve it."

I rolled my eyes as though the notion was ridiculous, but honestly, it was probably a good idea for Asher to give me a heads up. "Thanks. And tell your high and mighty king that I appreciate his concern for my welfare." Xander would get a kick out of that one.

"He'll never believe you said that," Asher replied with a wide grin.

"Exactly. Why else would I have you deliver the message?"

"Damn, it's good to be home." Asher pulled open the door and stepped outside. "See you soon, Darian."

"Goodnight. And thanks again for your help."

His smile remained, but a shadow of worry hid behind his eyes. "Any time."

My friends and closest allies were home, and for the first time in a year, I felt like the odds might be tipping in my favor.

[16]

I woke the next morning just as exhausted as I'd been when I hit the sack. I'd slept for shit, my brain too full for me to settle down enough to find any kind of real rest. Yet another close scrape with ambitious assassins had nearly done me in. In fact, if it hadn't been for Asher, my ass likely would've been toast. It was embarrassing how much backup I'd been requiring lately. So much for being an independent, deadly assassin.

Aside from my bruised ego, and even sorer pride, I still couldn't wrap my mind around what Raif had told me last night. How was it possible to simply forget someone that I'd been in love with? And what did it mean that our souls were bound? How? When? Why? I had so many questions that needed answers and I had no idea who would give them to me.

Certainly not Xander. He'd been as closed lipped as possible.

I stood at Misha's door, unenthusiastic about seeing the salty Fae. He'd been all over my case lately and I had no idea why this job was so damned important for him to have his nose so far up my ass.

Was he simply anxious for the pay-day? Or did he know that

Levi didn't deserve to die and didn't want me to find out. Either way, none of it sat well with me.

Misha opened the door before I could ring the bell. He graced me with a wan smile, that for him, was downright cordial. "Darian."

"Morning, Mish." I wanted to rattle his chain a bit. If anything, to distract me from my dumpster fire of a life. "What's for breakfast?"

"The same thing that I serve every morning."

He held the door wide and I stepped inside.

"Ah. Nothing, then."

"I was under the impression this wouldn't be a social visit," he remarked as he led the way toward the kitchen. "But lucky for you, I have a pot of coffee on."

Not gonna lie, I needed the caffeine boost. "Awesome. Got any of that fancy creamer?"

He leveled his gaze. "Of course I do."

"Perfect. Sounds like we're in business."

I took a seat at the bar and waited for Misha to pour us each a cup. He placed the fancy china between us, along with some sparkling raw sugar and containers of cream and the flavored creamer he favored. I dumped a splash of creamer into my cup and gave it a stir before discarding my spoon on a saucer.

"So." I took a sip from the lip of my cup. "What's up? Don't try any of your fancy Fae tricks on me either. Be straight with me. Who is this Levi and why is this job so damn urgent?"

Misha's eyes narrowed as he studied me. "Why do you care?"

It was my turn to cut him a look. "You know why." He was well aware of my moral code and my policy for taking on jobs. And now that I suspected this Levi was marked for death for all the wrong reasons, I couldn't let it go.

"Fae tricks?" Misha feigned understated outrage well. "I am above *trickery*, and I am nothing if not upfront with you."

I cocked my head and fixed him with a stare.

"As up front as I am able to be," he amended.

"I'm not letting this go."

I'd decided last night that with all of the things in my life that were out of control, I needed to focus on something that was. Levi was that thing.

"I don't suppose you are," Misha mused. He paid close attention to his coffee for a moment, taking a few thoughtful sips before looking up at me. "Levi is a human who is very well connected to the supernatural world. In fact, he might be the most connected human on the planet. His associates are very powerful and very influential. And through no fault of his own, he has found himself in the midst of a brewing supernatural war.

"What did he do?" I was more interested in his perceived offense than his actual affiliation to any specific faction.

"He took the wrong side," Misha said simply.

"That's it?" My ire rose with his guileless explanation. "We don't kill people—humans, or anyone else—because they took the wrong side."

One of Misha's eyebrows rose haughtily over one eye. "Really, Darian? Speak for yourself. And may I remind you that taking the wrong side isn't exactly a sinless act."

I let out a snort. "How so?"

"How can I put this in terms that you'll understand? For instance, what about Nazi sympathizers?"

Well, the son of a bitch had a point. I couldn't argue with that logic. Sometimes the wrong side wasn't simply a matter of opinion or perception. "Exactly whose side did he take?"

"He chose friendship over family," Misha explained.

Unless his friends killed puppies and sold children on the black market, it still wasn't a murderable offense. A gray area. Sort of my comfort zone and neutral ground, in my opinion. I cherished my friendships more than any family I ever had. My friends were my chosen family.

The "wrong" side was still a matter of opinion in this case. Maybe this guy's family was a bunch of sadistic assholes.

"Why did he turn against his family?"

"I don't know." Misha's voice was free of deception. "All I know is that his family is more powerful than you could possibly comprehend, and it would behoove us both not to cross them."

In other words, get the job done and don't ask any more questions.

I'd faced some pretty nasty supernatural heavy hitters in the past several years. Misha didn't know me very well if he thought I scared easily.

"Got it." It wouldn't do any good to argue the point further. Misha wanted the job done and that's all there was to it. I turned to leave, through with his bullshit for the day. "I'll check in with you in a couple of days." So maybe Misha wasn't in on the plot to kill an innocent man, but he'd shown me that he was at the very least, unscrupulous about it.

"Darian."

The worry in his tone gave me pause. I affixed an expression of guileless curiosity to my face and turned to face him. "Yeah?"

"Please, don't do anything foolish."

Misha was genuinely afraid.

I studied him for a quiet moment. "Foolish for whom?" I asked him. "You, or me?"

"Either of us," he replied gravely. "Don't forget, your actions don't simply affect you, but anyone associated with you."

I inclined my head in acknowledgement before heading out the door.

———

MISHA'S WARNING ONLY SOLIDIFIED MY COMMITMENT TO CAMDEN'S plan. I trusted the Werewolf, and if he said Levi was an innocent man, I believed him. Misha was spooked. And it served to reason that whoever had come to him with the contract had scared him into ensuring the job would go off without a hitch. Fae creatures didn't scare easily. Whoever wanted Levi dead was a big-bad on the supernatural food chain for sure.

The last time I'd been to The Pit, the splitting pain in my skull had deterred me from going inside. Today, I was determined to walk through the door even if my head exploded by doing so.

Though I could have traveled as my ethereal self, I walked with the rest of the pedestrians, happy for the company of humans oblivious to the goings on of the supernatural world. Surely the black cloud of doom would keep its distance and not jump me in the middle of the day on a crowded city street. And if not . . . well, today might be the day I kiss my ass goodbye. Block by block, I let the cadence of my boots on the sidewalk drown out the thoughts of my overactive brain until a single crosswalk separated me from the old brick building, lifeless in the absence of its neon lights and nightlife crowd.

"I wonder, Darian, have you always been so stubborn, or is it a trait you grew into over decades?"

Though the light had changed, I didn't step into the crosswalk. The smooth voice that spoke from right behind me had me cemented to my spot on the sidewalk. Familiarity slithered over my senses and the energy signature from the creature looming over my left shoulder nearly sent me to my knees with its power. Whatever this individual was, he was dangerous.

I turned slowly to face him. He looked to be in his late forties, only the wisdom in his grayish eyes betrayed his true age. A shiver raced down my spine as alarm bells triggered my fight or flight instinct. I forced my shoulders back and willed myself to stay put and meet his unwavering gaze. Bravado was one of my better assets in a confrontation.

"Oh, I'm stubborn and then some," I remarked as I tried to recall where I might have encountered him before. "You obviously know me, but I'm sorry, your name's slipped my mind."

He smiled. It was genuine and softened his handsome chiseled features. "Merrick," he said. "And don't feel bad about forgetting. A great many things have slipped your mind."

The hairs on the back of my neck stood on end. A memory of him and I sitting together in the back seat of one of Xander's town cars came to me as clearly as though it had happened yesterday.

"Who are you?" Nothing about that memory made me think he was a friend. I rested my right hand on the pommel of my dagger, ready to draw if need be.

Storm clouds gathered in his eyes and the handsome smile faded from his face. "Wouldn't you rather know *what* I am?"

My gripped tightened on the dagger as my heart fluttered in my chest. If it came to a fight, something told me I'd lose this one. "All right," I said slowly. "What are you?"

"I am Jinn," he replied simply. "And you, Shaede, Assassin, and Guardian, have turned the Synod's world upside down."

I took a tentative step back, prepared to join with the sunlight and beat a hasty retreat. As though he knew my next move, Merrick held up a staying hand. "A truce." His tone was even and his voice no more than a murmur. "For a moment, at least."

"A moment?" I scoffed. Long enough for me to let my guard down and give him an opportunity to kill me.

"Be at ease," Merrick said. "As it relates to eternity, a moment can last a lifetime."

My grip on the dagger relaxed, though only a little. He might not have wanted to kill me right this second, but that didn't mean I was out of the woods. Though I didn't know if he was my enemy, I was certain that this Merrick wasn't an ally.

"What do you want?"

Merrick leveled his gaze and the force of it pinned me in place. "To strike a bargain with you."

I wasn't exactly sure what sort of creature a Jinn was, but I had a feeling a bargain struck with a Fae would be less risky.

"You don't say." I kept my voice as deadpan as possible. "What sort of bargain?"

"I can't give you everything without drawing unwanted attention to myself," Merrick said slowly. "But I can give you back a portion of what I took from you," he said. "And even that might result in my demise."

I let out a snort. He was playing games and I didn't like it. I couldn't think of a single thing that had been stolen from me. "Exactly what is that you think you took from me?"

"Your memories," he said simply.

My hands fell to my sides and my entire body numbed. I stared, unbelieving, as confusion, anger, and resentment swelled within me. For over a year I'd been battling debilitating headaches, dealing with the gaps in my memory, and trying to piece together the mystery of what had happened to me with only parts of the puzzle to guide me. And this man—no, this *Jinn*—standing in front of me was offering up the answers to all my questions, while admitting to causing the months of pain and distress that had tortured me.

Caution held my tongue. He could've been lying. I decided to keep him on the line for a bit, see if I could rattle him or get him to slip up and show his hand. Because if he'd actually been the one responsible for taking my memories, he wouldn't simply return them for no reason.

"I have no idea what you're talking about." The light changed again and another group of pedestrians side-stepped us to cross the intersection. "My memories are just fine."

"You're a surprisingly good bluffer," Merick replied. "I suppose in your line of work, duplicity is something of a necessity."

So far, the only feathers being ruffled were mine. I stood even straighter and stared him down. "I'm anything but duplicitous." I hoped he sensed the venom in my tone. "And if you don't watch your mouth, you're going to learn more about my 'line of work' than you'll care to."

Merrick chuckled and had the nerve to sound genuinely amused. My eyes narrowed. I thought about stabbing him with one of sentient daggers whether he could restore my lost memories or not.

"We are fools to think that we can control either of you," he mused. "But that mistake is a result of our own arrogance and will ultimately result in disaster. On the other hand, it is a credit to your character that you win the undying loyalty of those around you. And it is also what has put me in the position I'm in now."

The stop lights completed another cycle and once again, we were jostled by people maneuvering around us to cross the street. Merrick let out an annoyed sigh and snapped his fingers. The air thickened with powerful magic as everyone around us froze dead in their tracks. Cars stopped in the intersection as the world came to a complete halt. And all from nothing more than Merrick's fingers and his will to make it so. Though I didn't know much about the Jinn, aside from what I'd just been made privy to, I had witnessed enough to know that they weren't the sort of creatures to trifle with.

"That's a cool trick." One I'd seen before. I tried to remain calm despite my anxious nerves. "What else have you got up your sleeve?"

"That was nothing." Merrick gave a dismissive wave of his hand. "I'm simply tired of the distraction."

"Are you going to kill me?" A lick of fear slid down my spine. "There might be things that I don't know, and that I can't remember, but I have a feeling if you wanted me dead there wouldn't be much I could do about it."

"Contrary to what you might think, Darian, I'm not here to kill you, nor do I want you dead. Likewise, my opinion hasn't changed regarding your bond with Tyler. But circumstances have . . . affected my ability to remain impartial, and I find myself in need of your help."

Tyler. The name sparked something deep inside my chest. And like an ember brought too close to kindling, the spark grew into a fire that burned hot and bright in my soul.

"What could you possibly need my help for?" I affixed a mask of passivity to my face so Merrick wouldn't know how the name he spoke affected me. "Seems to me that a guy like you possesses the resources necessary to tackle any problem that comes his way."

"It would seem so, wouldn't it?" Merrick remarked. "But in this case, I am powerless."

Sure. I didn't believe that for a second. Without any effort, Merrick had managed to stop time itself. And while I tended to be a little too full of myself, I knew this man's—Jinn's—power and ability outweighed mine a million-fold.

"The suspense is killing me." I'd ooze with sarcasm until my dying breath. "What is it that you need me for?"

Merrick's expression grew serious as another wave of power washed over me.

"I need you to protect my son."

"Oh yeah?" Bullshit. No one packing this much supernatural mojo would need someone like me to protect his kid. "What's the little guy's name?"

A glaze of opalescent color washed briefly over Merrick's eyes. "His name is Levi."

Well, shit.

I let out a slow sigh.

"I'm listening."

[17]

Once again, fate's many threads wove together in an elaborate tapestry. Merrick was the needle, gathering the strands of my life into a complete picture. He claimed to have the answers to all of my questions. There was no way I could walk away from that. This contract had never sat well with me, and I was beginning to understand why.

Everything was connected.

"So this was a set up?" My knowledge of the Jinn was nonexistent, but I knew from the power that emanated from Merrick, that they were apex predators on the supernatural food chain. I wouldn't be able to kill one if I tried.

"On the contrary," Merrick began. "Levi, while powerful in his knowledge, is as mortal as the humans that surround us right now."

Interesting. Levi might not have been Merrick's biological son, but I could tell from the concern in his eyes that Merrick cared deeply about Levi. I took a quick look around at the hapless humans still frozen in time and space, none the wiser to the workings of the dangerous supernatural creatures that lived among them. Ignorance was certainly bliss, and I envied them theirs.

"About these humans," I said. "Don't you think we should do them a favor and let them get on with their day?"

"Of course," Merrick said as though just realizing that might be a good idea. "Shall we cross the street first?"

I shrugged. "Might as well."

We crossed the intersection in silence. Merrick walked with a slow, purposeful gait, his arms folded formally behind his back. The moment our feet hit the sidewalk on the other side, the world sprang back into action without missing a beat.

"You must be a blast at parties," I quipped.

A corner of Merrick's lips quirked with mild amusement.

We walked side by side for a few quiet moments. So many questions sprang to my mind, And next to me was someone with all the answers. The prospect of regaining even a fraction of those lost memories filled me with equal parts excitement and dread. There was no way all of the memories returned to me would be pleasant ones. I didn't know if I had it in me to relive any trauma or pain.

"Is it going to hurt?"

Merrick turned his head slightly and studied me from the corner of his eye. "Not physically."

Not the answer I'd hoped for. "I think I'd rather it hurt physically."

"Wouldn't we all," Merrick remarked.

His stoic demeanor made me wonder if the Jinn felt emotions. I suppose he had to have some capacity to feel if he was willing to make a deal with me in order to protect his son. Maybe Jinn were sort of like Vulcans. All logical and stiff level-headedness.

Before I could torture myself with any more doubts or worries, I found myself standing outside of the same dive bar I'd come to a couple of days ago. "He doesn't roam far, does he?"

Merrick gave me a wan smiled and I figured it was the closest thing to laughter I'd get from him. He reached for the door and pulled it open. "After you."

I gave him a sidelong glance before taking a deep breath and holding it in my lungs. My mind was clear, and my head free of pain. I had no reason whatsoever to believe—or trust—Merrick, but I was desperate for answers and he seemed willing to give me a few. Then again, this could've all been a trap, and once I walked through the door—BAM! Merrick collects a million-dollar bounty, and it's lights out for me.

Honestly, I wasn't sure I cared much anymore if someone managed to get the job done or not. I was so tired of having to worry about it.

"Sure," I scoffed as one foot crossed over the threshold. "Why not?"

The door closed behind me and the stale, musty air of The Pit flooded my nostrils. Good lord that was a welcome smell. A moment of disorientation caused me to sway on my feet. I took a stumbling step forward and caught the edge of one of the high tables to steady myself. Whoa.

Distorted images invaded my memory. It was like flipping through a book and only catching random pages without knowing the entire story. I'd stood at this table months ago, and I'd watched Merrick walk through the door and head for the bar.

The bar that Levi stood behind now.

Metal scraped against hard leather as I drew my daggers from their sheaths and whipped around. Merrick, that sly son-of-a-bitch, had poofed out of sight the second I'd walked through the door.

I kept the daggers at the ready as I pivoted once again toward Levi. The dark, windowless interior of the building was barely illuminated by the dim lighting, but I could still see the detail of the half-moon hollows of Levi's blue eyes and his once perfectly coiffed, sun-kissed curls, were longer now and unkempt. The bright smile that used to greet me every night, was replaced with an almost grimace. As though the act of turning his lips upward was too great a feat to accomplish. A slight buck of his chin acknowledged me as he reached for a glass, filled it with ice, and poured a couple fingers of liquor. He splashed something else into the glass and topped it with a maraschino cherry.

"Whiskey sour." He gave a sheepish hike of one shoulder. "Nothing flashy, but it's on the house."

"Thanks." I approached the bar, just as I had hundreds of times over the past several years, and Levi slid the glass toward me in our usual routine. The daggers hummed in my palms, unwilling to be discarded on the glossy wooden surface as I traded them for the glass. I propped myself up onto a stool and took a sip of the sweet-tarte cocktail and then raised my glass in a traditional toast.

God, this was weird.

"So . . . . It's been a helluva year, huh?" I did my best to maintain my composure, but my mind was spinning. Merrick had restored a portion of my memories, those pertaining to Levi specifically. I could understand why he'd been wiped from my mind. He connected me to . . . Tyler. And goddamn, I wished I could connect a face with that name.

"That's an understatement," he said with a snort. Up close, Levi looked even more haggard than I'd thought. Like he'd been put through the wringer. And boy, could I relate. "How are you holding up?"

I hiked a shoulder as I took another sip from the highball glass. "Splitting headaches, memory loss, feeling like I'm going crazy. Oh, and dodging assassins while trying to thwart the power-hungry leader of an extremist human secret society. Same old, same old. How about you?"

"Well, I've been shut up in this bar for three months, and I can't leave. Also dodging an assassin or two. One of which happens to be my friend and the best in the business. Oh, and I had a cold last week."

I smiled. That Levi could still bring a little levity to the situation eased the tension that pulled my muscles taut. At least I'd had some freedom. Despite the threat on my life, I'd come and gone as I pleased from Misha's and Xander's houses. I hadn't changed much about my daily routines because I'd refused to and because I had the supernatural advantage of rapid healing if injured. No one had forced me to stay inside and hide.

"House arrest?" I could picture someone as powerful as Merrick forbidding Levi from leaving. If only to keep him out of trouble. Maybe someday, Levi would tell me what it was like to be a human raised by supernaturals. I bet it was a trip.

"You could say that." He let out a slow sigh as he poured himself a drink. "The building is protected by Merrick's magic. It's the only place it can't get me."

"It?" That didn't sound good.

"The Délash."

Well, fuck. This was going to be a hell of a lot more complicated than I thought. "Wow. Looks like we have something in common. You must have pissed off the wrong people, too."

"Guess so." He let out a chuff of laughter. "I love Merrick. He's my father. But Tyler is like a brother to me. He's saved my ass more than a couple of times and there was no way I could sit back and let them do what they wanted to do with him."

Tyler's name was the one that had been shrouded from my memory with nearly unbearable pain. But since Merrick had spoken it, it no longer affected me to hear it. Had his utterance somehow hit a release valve?

Asshole.

"They?" A haze still shrouded my memory and I had trouble separating the gauzy strands of what was real and what wasn't.

"The Synod."

"Right."

Merrick had been true to his word, gifting me with at least

some of the memories I'd lost. I knew what the Synod was, the ruling body that presided over all Jinn. I also knew all too well what the Délash was and what it was capable of. That's as far as my knowledge went, however. I still couldn't discern much more about these mythological wish granters humans referred to as genies. God, what I wouldn't give for just a little more knowledge.

"Isn't Merrick a part of the Synod?" Some distant notion floating in the deepest recesses of my mind suggested as much, but I couldn't be sure.

Levi gave a sad shake of his head. "Not anymore. And even if he was, it wouldn't help me now."

I knew Levi had taken sides in a disagreement between the Synod and someone else. And now, with a portion of my memories restored, I had no problem connecting the dots.

"This is because of me, isn't it?"

"This is about what I think is fair and right," Levi replied. His lips quirked in a half smile, barely accentuating the deep dimples in his cheeks. "I consider us friends." Levi's smile grew, though only a fraction. "And even though this definitely includes you, what the Synod is terrified of, is Tyler."

There was still a black hole in my mind and heart where I knew he should've been. A void of emotion—unsettling indifference—confused me even further. What in the hell had we done to piss off these omnipotent beings so much that would make them feel they had no other option but to erase him from my life and kill Levi for? And besides that, what in the hell gave them the right to? Levi knew. But he wouldn't—or couldn't—tell me.

"So . . . ." I took another sip from my glass. The liquor warmed a path down my throat and into my belly. "What do we do now?"

The charming smile faded from Levi's supermodel-gorgeous face and his bright eyes dimmed with despair. "I don't know."

I stared at my glass, swirled its contents as though the answer to my question would appear from nowhere like some sort of alcoholic Magic Eight Ball. But the answers sure as hell weren't in that glass, and nothing was going to happen until I got off my ass and made it happen myself.

"How do you kill a Délash?"

I brought my eyes up slowly to meet Levi's. His brow furrowed and his lips puckered. "You don't. A Délash is sentient magic. Controlled by the Synod. It only goes away once it's performed the task set out for it.

I didn't buy it. Enough of my memory had been restored to corroborate what little Xander and Raif had told me. The Jinn were considered omnipotent beings. And call them gods, or whatever the hell you wanted, it didn't make them infallible. A Délash was nothing more than an extension of their magic. Get rid of the magic wielder, and you get rid of the magic. I'd killed a god once. I was pretty sure I could do it again.

"Every creature has a weakness," I said. "We just need to find it."

"Good luck with that," Levi said. "I wouldn't count on Merrick, or the Synod for that matter, to offer you up any help in that department."

Levi drew in a slow breath as he poured himself another drink. He wasn't the same person I'd known a year ago. The Synod and their stupid arrogance had dimmed his flame. The skin beneath his eyes had hollowed and darkened from lack of sleep, and he moved slower, almost lazy, as though he forced his fingers to obey even the simplest command. I could only imagine what it must've been like for him: a human thrust without consent into a violent, uncaring supernatural world. He didn't deserve any of this. It was at least partly my fault he was in this situation now. And I'd be damned if I didn't get him out of it.

"The Jinn don't know everything." They might've thought they were untouchable, but I was going to prove them wrong. I was going to kill their little pet. "There are missing parts." I'd sort of veered off my current train of thought, but my brain was buzzing, and I was having a hard time staying on track. "Like, I know you, I know our history, but there are just . . . blank spaces everywhere. If that makes sense."

"Yes and no." Levi kept his attention focused on his glass. "They don't want you to remember."

"Why?" I mean, seriously. What sort of threat could I possibly be to supposed omnipotent beings with egos big enough to think they were indestructible?

"Because." Levi leveled his gaze. "Together, you and Tyler are much too powerful. A force not even they can stop."

Huh. Not gonna lie, that did sound ominous as fuck. I've got skills, and a few magical tricks up my sleeve, but there are far more dangerous creatures than me out there. Which led me to believe that Tyler was packing a wallop in the power department.

My curiosity burned.

"So . . . let's just say for the sake of argument that their fears are well-founded." Ha! Not even I believed it. "If Tyler and I can get together, the two of us should have no problem taking down the Délash."

Levi cut me a worried look that sent a ripple of anxiety through me. "In theory. But to be honest, only Ty could answer that."

Ty. The nickname sounded comfortable. Like something I'd heard and spoken thousands of times.

"You're protected here, right?"

Levi nodded and took another healthy sip from his glass.

"So that must mean that you're not only protected from the Délash, but the Synod as well?"

Levi's eyes narrowed, but he nodded again, slowly.

"So . . . ." I waved my hand as though to speed up his brain to catch up with mine. "Let's bring Tyler here and see what happens."

Levi gave an adamant shake of his head. "No. The magic protecting me keeps him out too. Besides, if we even tried to see if we could get Tyler through the door Merrick would flip."

I shrugged. "What he doesn't know, won't hurt him, right?"

Levi kept his gaze locked on me, wary. If I hadn't known better, I would have sworn he was afraid. But of Merrick, Tyler, the Synod, or me, I had no idea.

"You have to trust me." Though at this point, I barely trusted myself. There was still too much missing from my memory for my peace of mind. And my motives in wanting Tyler here weren't purely selfless. I wanted my memories back. All of them. And if that meant using a loophole to go around Merrick—and the Synod—then so be it. "I wouldn't do anything to put you in danger." Levi was my friend. I'd never do anything to hurt him. "But don't you agree that we'll have a better chance of getting rid of the Délash if we have every advantage?"

Levi's chin dipped. As much of a concession as I was going to get.

"And don't you think that Merrick considered this very thing?" It was a stretch, but I was going for it. "Maybe he's giving us just enough rope to hang ourselves with."

Levi's lips pursed. "Not funny, Darian."

It was funny. Assassins need a little gallows humor now and then.

"Come on." I had to convince Levi this was a good idea. "Why else would Merrick not only intercept me, but give me enough of my memories back to know that killing you is something I *don't* want to do. Which, by the way, I hadn't planned on doing anyway. The Synod had to have found out that he'd protected the building to keep you safe from the Délash. And maybe, the Synod— Merrick included—knew that I couldn't come close to you as well, because getting near anything associated with Tyler caused me head-splitting pain."

"Where are you going with this?" Levi asked, his brow furrowed.

It made my head spin, too. "Okay, so let's say for the sake of argument that the Synod had the foresight to know that Merrick would ask me to protect you and that he'd make it possible for me to get close to you. What better way to kill two birds with one stone than to hire me to kill you? Thanks to Merrick's interference, I can enter the building, no problem. Maybe it disrupted the magic that's protecting you, too. I come here to protect you, because no way in hell am I going to let anything happen to you, and the dark cloud of doom conveniently waits outside for the magic barrier to be broken and, BAM!" I swiped my hands together. "Problems solved."

Levi's eyes narrowed as he contemplated my words. "It makes sense. And if that's the case, neither one of us is safe here."

"Of course it makes sense!" I was so close to getting the past year of my life back. Every inch of me vibrated with anticipation. "So if Merrick made it possible for me to get through the door, maybe Tyler can too by default. We won't know if we don't try."

"But what if that's exactly what they want? Maybe this is more about getting you in a position where the Délash can use me as a distraction to weaken you."

"What do you mean?"

"Maybe they figure you'll be easier to kill if you're too busy trying to keep me safe to worry about protecting yourself."

Damn, I'd never thought about that.

"Bringing Tyler here would also weaken you, because of the magic they're using to keep you apart. Between his presence, a Délash attack, and my being a distraction, you'd be easy to kill and their problems would be mostly solved."

"What about you?"

Levi shrugged. "If you're dead, Tyler dies. I'm no longer in their purview."

Fuck. He was right.

"This isn't about you at all." Anger boiled in my stomach and filled my body with indignant heat. "They're just tired of not being able to take us down and so they're using you as a pawn."

A corner of Levi's mouth hitched. "Seems like it, huh?"

So my memory loss and headaches were the Synod's way of

keeping Tyler and I apart. That much I knew. But it wasn't a flaw-less plan. Tyler had managed to be in my presence a couple of times. He'd used sensory deprivation as a way to keep the unbear-able pain at bay.

"If you're protected from the Synod and the Délash here, I still can't help but wonder if Tyler and I can be in the building together without any negative repercussions?" It might've been my only way to get my eyes on him and get some answers.

"Jinn magic shouldn't work here," Levi confirmed. "Though the wards Merrick put in place to make that possible are tempo-rary at best. The wards protect the building from him as well, so you can't wish him here."

"I can do that?" I swear my jaw dropped. "Like, just say that I want him somewhere and he just appears?"

Levi smiled and it was the first genuinely "Levi" expression I'd seen from him since I walked through the door. "That's barely scratching the surface of what you can do."

A shock of cold raced from the ring on my thumb, encircling my hand with an icy chill that chased a path up my arm. I wasn't the only one excited about the possibility of getting to see the guy all the fear and fuss was about. I wondered if I should let Raif or Xander know what I was up to. You know, just in case something went south. But ultimately, I wasn't willing to drag them into anything unless it was absolutely necessary. And since the Synod was the last group of supernaturals anyone wanted to tangle with, I decided it was best to keep them out of the loop.

For now.

I was more convinced than ever that if I wanted my life back, I needed to see Tyler. I needed to talk to him.

"I'm not going to let you be a pawn in their game anymore." I leveled my gaze on Levi. "How do we find Tyler?"

[18]

"He's around. Somewhere."

I cut Levi a look. "That's helpful."

He shrugged. "It is what it is. Since he became enemy number one of the Synod, he's sort of gone off-grid."

"Okay, so since he's off grid, we can't just call him up or shoot him a text. And apparently I can simply wish for him and he'll poof to wherever I am." That part of my memory was still a cloudy haze. Sort of shot down my mental image of rubbing a lamp to coax the genie from his home. Maybe Tyler had one to hang out in on a shelf somewhere. The ultimate tiny house.

"Only the charge can summon a Jinn," Levi agreed.

Charge, huh. Not sure I liked the sound of that. "But I can't do it from inside the building?"

"Right," Levi said. "It won't work in here because the building is protected from Jinn magic. You'd have to be outside for it to work. And I'm not sure what will happen if you try it, since the Synod has more or less blocked your bond. It might not work at all, and it might actually be a beacon for the Délash to find you."

Our bond wasn't entirely blocked. I'd made a wish or two over the past few weeks that had come true. Though Raif and Xander had been fairly shocked I'd been able to do it without Tyler right next to me. It didn't sit well with me, being able to order someone around with a set of words that they had to obey. More than ever, the absence of my memories infuriated me and I wanted them back like I needed air to breathe. Who did the Synod think they were to simply decide what was good for me? By taking away my knowledge of Tyler and whatever it was between us, they'd snatched my free will out from under me. I wasn't going to stand for it anymore.

"There's only one way to find out."

I set my drink on the bar and turned for the exit.

"Your wish might call the Délash," Levi said again. "It senses the use of Jinn magic."

Interesting. But I was banking on "might."

"I've wished." Wishes were such intangible things. It seemed impossible to be talking about the reality of having a wish granted. Jinn had to be packing a punch in the power department. "So far it hasn't triggered a murderous cloud of doom sighting."

Levi's brow furrowed. "That you know of. Do you want to take that chance again?"

Good point. I had enough to deal with. I didn't need the Délash showing up until I knew how to kill it first. We'd be falling right into the Synod's trap. Wishing might have been an easy fix, but I had other resources at my disposal.

"Camden Walsh."

Levi discarded his drink and braced his arms on the bar. "The Alpha Werewolf?"

"Yup." I couldn't believe I hadn't thought of him sooner. "He's working with Tyler. Sort of. He definitely knows how to get a hold of him."

Levi's eyes brightened and the knot of anxious tension in my chest loosened by a small degree. I didn't like seeing him beleaguered. Levi was pure sunshine and I wanted him to always be that way. "We just have to find a way to meet up without anyone knowing."

"Are you sure he can't come here?" The Pit was magically protected from the Synod thanks to Merrick. This was the absolute best place for us to meet.

"Merrick always covers his bases." Levi shrugged. "Whether he let you in or not, this place is protected from Tyler. He'll bend the rules but only so much. He won't risk falling out of favor with the Synod."

The more I learned about the Synod, the more I disliked their authoritarian ways.

I pulled my phone out of my pocket and selected Camden's name from my contact list. I fired off a text letting him know that our plans regarding Levi had changed and that I needed him to get ahold of Tyler ASAP and tell him I wanted a face-to-face. I traded my phone for the drink sitting on the bar. His response came back within seconds and my heart leaped into my throat as I picked up the phone to read the message.

Levi looked as anxious as I felt. "What did he say?"

I rolled my eyes. I swore I always overlooked the simplest solution. "He says they'll meet us at my building tonight at ten."

"I thought your building was a pile of bricks," Levi said.

My old place was, and I was still pissed off about it. "My new place," I said. "The one Tyler owns." Perfectly orchestrated. No doubt Tyler had planned on this all along. And if that was the case, why make me take the roundabout way to get to this point? My cheeks heated with annoyance and a fair amount of anger. The supernatural world played by its own cryptic rules and I never had been comfortable with it. "Camden set me up in a new place down by Lake Union. I hadn't known at the time that Tyler owned the building."

Levi laughed. "Sounds like something Ty would do."

Great. Like having one highhanded pain in the ass—Xander— in my life wasn't bad enough. Now, apparently, I had two. I texted

Camden to let him know we'd be there. "Well, looks like we're on. Ready to take on a Délash?"

"No," Levi replied. "But I guess I don't really have a choice."

The Délash I could handle. Meeting Tyler—the reason for the sucking wound in my soul—was something I couldn't even begin to get a grip on.

———

THE NEXT SEVERAL HOURS SEEMED TO LAST DAYS. MY ANXIETY ratcheted up with every minute closer to ten o'clock and I swore my heart raced at a hard spirt. I'd been waiting for answers for over a year and still, I didn't know if I was ready for it. Levi and I had decided against letting Merrick know what we were up to, though I couldn't help but wonder if anything got by him considering the near omnipotence of the Jinn. Levi argued that omnipotent didn't equal omniscient, but I wasn't so sure.

It was a gamble to take Levi from The Pit. Délash were nothing if not single-minded and they didn't stop until they reached their objective. Unfortunately, Levi and I both had targets on our backs. I was more concerned about the dark cloud of doom than I was Mitchell Redmond and his murderous machinations. And though he was the least of my concerns right now, he was on my to-do list and something that I'd have to deal with very soon.

I'd solve one problem at a time. And tonight was solely dedicated to Levi and my lost memories.

The construction crew had made considerable progress on my new digs. I hated to admit it, but it was giving my old loft a run for its money. Walls had been knocked out to leave the place wide open, with the bathroom as the only enclosed space. It's hard to get the jump on someone if there's nowhere to hide. The building was smaller than my warehouse space in Belltown, but the builders had done a good job of utilizing the high ceilings and had constructed a metal staircase against the western wall that led to an open bedroom loft that overlooked the kitchen and living room. They'd kept with the industrial feel, leaving the exposed duct work and the steel skeleton of the building visible.

I wished I wasn't too preoccupied to truly appreciate it.

Out of precaution, Levi and I had agreed that he shouldn't leave The Pit until as close to ten as possible. Camden had offered to escort Levi across town, reasoning that if he and I were separated, so would the Délash's attention be, and I felt as though I was becoming indebted to the alpha wolf, not the other way around. I was on goddamned pins and needles, waiting for them to show up. Levi was delicately human. If the Délash got a hold of him, he'd be dead in the blink of an eye.

By 10:01, I was pacing the confines of my new home like a wild animal caught in a cage. By 10:05, I was ready to go out looking for Levi and Camden. And by 10:10, my katana was strapped to my back and my daggers hummed at my hips. I threw open the door and nearly barreled into Levi and Camden who stood on the other side of the threshold.

"Are we interrupting something?" Camden joked and he lowered his poised fist to his side.

I let out an exasperated gust of breath. "Where in the hell have you been?"

The humor in Camden's eyes nearly sent me over the edge. How could they be so damn cavalier, considering what we were up against?

"I should have called." I didn't buy his apologetic tone for a second. "There were a couple of snags, but they're handled."

Camden might have been considered the strongest Alpha in the Pacific Northwest, and possibly even the world, but that didn't mean he was infallible. Levi was delicate cargo. We couldn't afford a single snag, not to mention "a couple" of them. I huffed out another breath as I stood to the side to let them in.

"What sort of snags?"

"Nothing on our end," Levi replied as they walked inside.

"On whose end, then?"

"Mine."

I'd waited so long for this moment. Despite our few blind encounters, it was as though I was about to meet him for the first time. He'd kept his memories of me. Of us. And I'd been left with nothing but a gaping black hole, and the headaches to warn me not to search the endless depths of the void for what I'd lost.

I was afraid of everything I didn't know and couldn't remember. And yet, I'd come too far to turn back now.

All eyes turned to the open doorway. Tyler stepped out of the night, a smile on his face. This was my benefactor. My protector and wish granter. The other half of my soul that I'd been forced to forget because together, we were simply too powerful. His gaze met mine and my brow furrowed.

Tyler.

I thought this moment would be a hell of a lot more dramatic.

"Hello, Darian."

My jaw hung slack. A thousand thoughts rushed through my mind but I couldn't articulate a single one. Levi beamed beside Camden who watched with mild amusement. Disappointment chased on the heels of my astonishment as I stared at the man I should know. The man I was told I loved and loved me too. The memories that I expected to fill my mind didn't come and I was left with nothing but the loneliness and frustration that had plagued me for months.

Why wasn't a kettle drum banging in my head right now? "I don't remember you." The words tumbled from my lips before I could stop them.

Something that resembled disappointment dulled Tyler's eyes for a moment but he quickly tucked the emotion away. He stepped over the threshold and closed the heavy door behind him, walking right in like he owed the place. Well, technically, I guess he did.

"I'm working on that."

He'd said something similar to me once. I wondered at the disconnect in his tone. I don't know what I'd expected this moment to be like, but it wasn't this. Maybe I'd envisioned a rush and return of the knowledge I'd lost and the memories I'd coveted —like when I'd walked into The Pit and instantly remembered Levi. And maybe I'd expected a tearful reunion with hugs and kisses and us saying how much we'd missed each other. It was silly, and romantic, and totally *not* me, but in the back of my mind, I'd hoped.

Standing before me was this perfect, gorgeous, god of a creature who was supposedly completely dedicated to me, and I felt *nothing*. Anger and resentment churned through my body like angry stormwater, and frustration burned the back of my throat. I wanted to hurt whoever was responsible for this feeling. Make them suffer, like I'd suffered for months. I couldn't control the downward spiral of my emotions, or the dark intent that blossomed like a black cloud in my mind. The daggers hummed at my sides, anticipating the need for violence that pumped through my veins and damn it, I was so far gone, I answered their call and drew them from their sheaths.

"Whoa, Darian." The nervous quaver of Levi's words barely penetrated my rage fogged mind. "Everything's okay. You're with friends."

Friends I could barely remember. And the only reason I had memories of Levi was because a selfish Jinn had deigned it necessary to serve his own agenda. The violation of my mind, body, and soul couldn't go unpunished. Someone needed to pay for what had happened to me. And I wouldn't rest until someone did.

I was a cornered animal operating on instinct. I crossed the distance that separated me from Tyler as nothing more than a wisp of shadow and I regained my corporeal form inches from him, one of the daggers poised at his throat. He was a Jinn. Who in the hell did these assholes think they were to trifle with people the way they did? What gave them the goddamn right to attach themselves to other creatures? To dictate the terms of their existence. To fuck with fate and help to curve the path of someone's life. To decide who lived and died because it suited them.

He didn't even flinch. Instead, Tyler's expression remained calm. A light of amusement sparked in his frighteningly beautiful eyes and a corner of his mouth twitched as though he wanted to smile. Tyler was either incredibly brave or incredibly stupid. He might have been omnipotent, but I'd learned in the course of my life that no creature on this earth was without a fatal flaw.

The dagger vibrated through my grip, thrumming with excitement. I held the weapon in check, but barely. Or maybe it held me in check. At this point, I was too worked up to tell. Quiet settled over the room and I swear, not a single one of us dared to breathe. Tyler swallowed and as the Adam's apple bobbed in his throat, the honed point of the dagger nicked the skin. A drop of blood bloomed on his skin. I watched as it traveled and forked, a rivulet of crimson on the column of his throat.

A sense of déjà vu sparked something akin to memory in my mind. I'd held a dagger to his throat before. He'd watched over me and I'd woken with him in my bed. His expression much like it was now. Calm and entertained, despite the sharp blade poised close to such a deadly spot. Either he had a death wish, or . . . .

My eyes went wide as I sucked in a sharp breath.

"Darian?"

I turned to Levi and exhaled. His expression was as nervous as his tone, and I slowly lowered the dagger to join its brother as my side. Anxious for battle, they continued to hum in my palms, and it took an almost physical effort to return them to their sheaths.

"I'm okay." Those words couldn't have been further from the truth. I wanted to scream and laugh and throw up. My emotions swung from one end of the spectrum to the other, and to be honest, I wanted to get off this damn wild ride. From the corner of my eye, Tyler watched me. Wary. It unnerved me that he could sense my emotions so clearly. A sudden chill drew my attention to the silver ring encircling my thumb and I looked down to study it. When I brought my eyes up to meet Tyler's, a furrow cut his brow.

It was his. This thing, this mystery, that was locked to my body was his.

I held my hand up, shoved it right into his gaze. "What is this thing?"

His calm demeanor didn't change. "Later," he said.

"Later?" Seriously. The audacity.

"Later," he said again. "Now isn't the time. We need to discuss the Délash."

Right. I gave myself a mental shake. I needed to focus on what we were all here for. We needed to kill the Délash and get it off Levi's—and my—back. Once I ticked that off my to-do list, I could tackle all that was left. And oh man, was there a lot.

"How do we kill a Délash?" Might as well get right to the point and not waste anymore of anyone's time.

"Let's all sit down."

Tyler motioned for the living room which I only just now realized was furnished. Jesus, had that stuff been here when I walked in, or had the genie conjured it out of thin air? I gave him a sidelong glance, but his expression gave nothing away. I swore I was losing my mind. I couldn't trust anything I saw anymore.

Could I trust Tyler?

The knot forming in the center of my gut left me feeling anything but reassured.

[19]

I should've felt . . . something.

An inkling. A spark. Some miniscule indication of the bond everyone—including Tyler—insisted that we had. It's not like I hadn't had encounters with him over the past year, though they'd been few and far between. Not to mention strange as hell. I'd been in a state of sensory deprivation, but I'd recognized something. A familiarity. A wholeness. Something my eyes and ears couldn't tell me. I'd been at ease. I didn't feel any of that now and it scared the shit out of me.

Maybe I should have told someone outside of my present company about tonight's meeting. It wouldn't have been a bad idea to have Raif or even Asher here. Stupid, Darian. Nervous energy pooled like mercury, heavy in my stomach. Nothing so far about tonight sat well with me.

The daggers hummed at my sides, ready to protect. And kill.

"Something's off." I wasn't about to pretend as though I was okay when I absolutely wasn't. "I don't like it."

Levi and Camden turned toward me, perplexed, while Tyler's expression remained one-hundred percent calm. My gaze narrowed as I studied him, wishing like hell I could get inside his mind and know what he was thinking. The gears were turning, no doubt about it, but in his expression, he gave nothing away.

Camden remained silent, but alert. The alpha predator, wary and ready. Levi shifted from where he'd settled on the new couch. He looked from me to Tyler and scooted to the edge of his seat, as though ready to burst into action as soon as the shit hit the fan.

Our eyes met. "What do you mean, Darian?"

Tyler's blank expression transformed into something dark as his lip curled into a sneer. The muscles in his arms flexed as he leaned into the balls of his feet as though to pounce. Instinct took over. I ran for the couch and plowed into it, tipping it backward and providing a barrier from Tyler just as the front door exploded into the house.

Damn it, I hated when my instincts were right.

"Darian, stay down!"

The command called out from the opposite direction of where it should have been. That voice vibrated through me as though someone had touched a tuning fork to the core of my soul. I sucked in a breath, dizzied by the effect. A sharp stab of pain speared through the center of my head and my vision blurred.

"I wish the pain was gone!"

With the command, the chill of frost snaked around my left arm. The pain vanished. My heart kicked against my ribcage and my stomach swirled with the beat of anxious wings. Chills danced down my spine and my heart beat a mad rhythm in my chest as I looked over the edge of the upturned couch at the vision of pure rage that had blown the door right off its hinges. Whoever had escorted Levi and Camden here tonight, it wasn't Tyler. I might not have remembered the mysterious genie everyone claimed I was bound to, but I'd recognize his power signature anywhere. It was the most intense thing I'd ever felt. Off the freaking charts. How could I have forgotten it? A second blast of artic cold flared from my ring, as though recognizing it too. He strode through the converted warehouse space, a vengeful god with violent intent.

Holy shit, he was magnificent.

I'd never been one to follow directions, though, and refused to simply cower in the face of danger. Levi needed protecting, and luckily, I had a formidable ally in Camden. He looked just as enraged as Tyler—the *real* Tyler—and his eyes glowed with a feral, golden light. We'd all been duped and this imposter was going to regret coming here tonight.

"Stay down."

I regurgitated Tyler's words to Levi who looked perfectly fine doing just that. Panic widened his bright blue eyes and paled his skin. We never should have taken him from the protection of The Pit.

"I'll get him out of here if it comes to it," Camden said before rolling from the protection of the couch and propelling himself to his feet. "You worry about yourself."

Wise words considering my predicament. Whoever the Tyler imposter was, he had to have been counting on finishing the job either Redmond, the Synod, or both had started. I rolled to my feet and the mystical daggers sang as I ripped them from their scabbards and readied myself for the fight.

As opposed to my initial reunion with the fake Tyler, this one —the real deal— was climactic as fuck. Not to mention familiar. I was struck with the notion Tyler had a habit of showing up at just the right time and in just the same manner to save my ass from impending danger. Rather than look at him, I focused my attention on the imposter and let my anger fuel the adrenaline that pumped through my veins.

"You're either very brave, or very stupid for coming here tonight." God, I loved a little shit-talk before a fight. "Why don't you do us all a favor and surrender now. I'd hate to have to clean your blood off my new floor."

The fake Tyler smiled and only now did I realize the differences—though miniscule—between the two. This one was a duller version of the real Tyler. Like cut glass next to a diamond. He lacked the one thing he couldn't replicate. Call it a soul, or some inner spark, it was what lit the real Tyler from within and shined like a beacon for me alone. And fate help me, I felt the enigmatic intensity of that pull.

I shook off my fascination and kept my attention focused on the asshole who'd tried to pull something over on me. His silence sent a shiver of trepidation down my arms and the daggers vibrated in response. It's the quiet ones you have to worry about. Raif once told me that fear is what keeps you alive during a fight. The posturing, shit-talk, etc., is nothing but a tool to bolster bravado. But what about someone who's so unafraid they don't care whether they live or die? Whoever stood before me now, their silence was a sign of fearlessness. Or at the very least over-confidence.

The lack of action on anyone's part made me twitch. I hated standoffs and this was no exception. I was more than ready to draw first blood, but both Tyler's and Camden's hesitancy gave me pause.

"Who are you, really?"

Beside me, Levi stayed hunkered down behind the back of the overturned couch. Camden crouched beside him, his right hand poised near a sheathed dagger at the small of his back. Tyler—the real Tyler—remained near the doorway, armed with nothing but his good looks. Perhaps that's what I truly should have been afraid of, because he looked one hundred percent at ease. Something his doppelganger couldn't hope to replicate.

The imposter's gaze met Tyler's. "Tylacharir Drásen ilndra, traitor of the Synod, heretic, and outcast. Adira sends her regards." His voice had changed. Dark and ominous. Grating. "You'll be seeing her soon."

A malignant smile curved his lips and his laughter sent a low vibration through the air that made my ears and head throb. I gritted my teeth against the sensation and pushed the heels of my feet into my boots. The urge to run away from that sound nearly sent me stumbling backward. Levi curled in on himself as he covered his own ears with his hands. Camden snarled. His keen senses no doubt reeling as intensely as mine. Who—no, *what*—in the hell was this thing?

The calm expression on Tyler's face turned into something so terrifyingly enraged that it changed him from awe inspiring to altogether deadly. His eyes sparked with an otherworldly light as he brought his right arm up and cut back down in a sweeping motion across his body. A rush of power unlike anything I'd ever felt sucked the air from the room and the resulting tidal rush as it burst back out from where he stood shook the building on its foundation.

Arctic cold frosted the windows and crystalized in the air as a flurry of snowflakes. The sub-zero chill vined from the ring encircling my thumb and wound its way around and through my body until I was completely numb and shaking. The shock wave rolled over me, through me, and the imposter's eyes rounded with shock as his mouth went wide, wider, stretching in a ghastly and unnatural way, the giant maw gaping as an agonizing shriek rent the air. No longer resembling Tyler, the thing that had entered my home in his guise became something twisted and ugly. Its limbs stretched too long and its arms came down to the floor as it launched itself at Tyler on all fours. Another shock wave pulled again, as though drawing on every atom in the room and then exploded, targeting the creature. It dropped to the floor mid-stride and with a sickening thud, it lay silent. Unmoving.

And it stayed that way.

Camden's eyes met mine. The unease between us was nearly tangible. I'd never seen any creature killed with such . . . ease. Tyler had dropped the thing with nothing more than a swipe of his arm. How was that even possible?

I gazed down at the ring on my thumb and fear shivered with the cold over my skin. Had I been afraid of Tyler before? I'd never seen such a raw display of power. I'd never felt it surge over me—

through me like that before. My breath quickened with my pulse and I swayed on my feet. I tore my gaze from Camden's to turn toward the source of cold that caused my breath to fog inside the building. A single word flashed a warning in my mind: *Dangerous.*

"What in the hell was that thing?" Levi's voice broke the silence, vibrating with his own fear. "It looked just like you. Talked like you. I never would have known . . . ."

"Ifrit." Tyler replied with disgust. "It's a demon sent by the Synod. They're getting more creative."

I'd never heard of an Ifrit before, but I sure as hell didn't want to encounter one again. With all I had to fear, I was beginning to realize the Synod might be the most dangerous of all my potential enemies.

"Can we be sure it was the Synod?" Camden asked. His posture straightened as he took several steps toward me. "Redmond's Arx has a few tricks up their sleeve as well. It could have just as easily been sent by them."

Tyler seemed to contemplate the possibility. "No. It knew my true name and it mentioned Adira. She's not Redmond's business."

Adira sends her regards.

The creature's words meant nothing to me, though I suspected from the dark expression clouding Tyler's face, it had meant something to him. If anyone else present had knowledge of Adira, they didn't let it show. At least, not to me.

"Am I the only one here more concerned about *how in the hell* he killed that thing than what it is?" Seriously. How? "I mean, he barely moved a muscle and dropped it to the ground."

Sadness, or maybe it was regret, clouded Tyler's bright hazel eyes for only a moment before he veiled his expression as though not to give anything away. He took a slow step toward me. And another. I stayed rooted in place, tense. Wary. And a little afraid. My fingers itched to touch the daggers now sheathed at my sides. He was supposed to be my protector. The missing piece to my heart and the other half of my soul.

My chest swelled with emotion as Tyler came toward me. His steps measured and purposeful as he closed the space between us. He was like a god bringing the first rays of the sun to a dark world. Or at the very least, *my* world. He was so beautiful it was almost too much to look at him. Softly curling hair run with streaks of copper, straight nose, expressive lips, perfect cheekbones. And his eyes . . . . I couldn't have imagined anything like them. Hazel, but not. Gold and bright green that formed a starburst pattern that fanned out from the pupil.

Why was I so goddamned scared?

I suddenly felt very vulnerable and I didn't like it one damn bit. I held my arm up, palm ready to stop him from getting any closer than I wanted him.

"That's far enough." A second wave of disappointment washed over me as the memories I'd hoped would be restored never came. "Just because you saved our asses doesn't mean I trust you."

A wide smile curved his full lips as he tested my boundary and took a step closer, forcing my palm to press onto his chest. A tingle of excitement shot through my bloodstream followed by a wave of heat that banished the cold still permeating the air. I didn't move as his eyes held mine for a beat too long. We weren't the only ones in the room and the intensity of his odd hazel gaze had nearly made me forget it.

"Some things never change." I shivered at the husky tenor of his words. Jesus. What in the hell was wrong with me? "Gods, I've missed you."

"I wish I could say the same." I was still a little on edge from being duped by the creature that still lay on the floor. We really needed to do something about that. "But I still don't remember you."

"Soon." The word held a promise that I didn't dare question. "Soon, everything will be as it should be."

The truth of his assurance vibrated through me. The doubt

and tension inside of me melted. Somehow, I knew he would never let me down.

"I hate to break up the reunion," Camden said as he came toward us. "But what would you like to do about that?" He jerked his chin toward the body on the floor.

"I'll be sending *that* back to the Synod," Tyler said, unconcerned. "As a message."

Ruthless. I liked it, sort of. "And what exactly is the message you're trying to convey?" I couldn't help myself. I needed to know exactly who, and what, I was dealing with. My memories were still gone, and I was cautious. Besides, Raif would kill me if I didn't do my due diligence.

"The message is pretty clear," Tyler replied. "Leave us alone, or share in the same fate."

Wow. Ruthless and then some. Camden was careful to keep his expression impassive, while Levi's openly showed concern, and that worried me more than anything. Tyler was like a brother to him. He trusted him implicitly. So why the worry?

"Does that 'us,' include Levi?"

Tyler glanced in Levi's direction as though just now noticing he was standing there. And even without my memories, I knew it must be a little out of character.

"Of course," he said. "The Synod has overreached their authority and I refuse to sit by while they threaten anyone I care about."

"I can't say what the Synod has or hasn't overreached." I really had no idea what the Synod was or wasn't capable of, nor did I give a shit about the parameters of their authority. "But I absolutely won't stand for anyone coming after me or mine." At least Tyler and I had that sentiment in common. "But how in the hell do you truly know the Synod sent that thing?" I jerked my head in the direction of the body sprawled out on the floor. "I'm not about to provoke them further by dumping some random dead body at their door if we don't have proof."

"It mentioned Adira." The sneer in Tyler's tone piqued my curiosity. "That's proof enough."

I had no idea who Adira was, but I intended to find out. I could find a way around my missing memories and fill in the blanks. "Okay, so I guess that brings us back to why we're here tonight. How do we kill a Délash? As far as I'm concerned, that black cloud of doom is infinitely more dangerous than whatever that is you managed to kill with a swipe of your arm. And by the way"—I shot an accusing glance his way—"you wanna tell me exactly how you managed to do that?"

Tyler responded with an enigmatic smile that burrowed into my skin like a tick. I didn't like games, or secrets. And my patience was running thin.

"Together, you and I can accomplish anything."

More cryptic bullshit. My patience wasn't thin, it was gone.

"I'm not going to beat around the bush. Frankly, I've had enough. I've been fucked with for over a year, hunted by every ambitious assassin in the city, and now a council of vengeful Jinn, and I'm sick of it. I want some goddamned answers and I want them now."

Tyler's smile brightened, and I swear to god it did traitorous things to my insides and threatened to banish the anger that boiled inside me.

"That's why we're here, isn't it?" He swept his hands toward the empty space just off the kitchen, and a square table and four chairs appeared. My jaw must have been on the damn floor, because his amusement sparkled in his eyes as he chuckled. He motioned for everyone to sit down and turned to me and winked. "That doesn't even scratch the surface of what I can do."

The cold confidence in his tone sent a wave of worry through me. Deep down, I knew in my heart that I could trust him. That he would never hurt me. And that the retribution would be swift and harsh against anyone who tried to harm me. But that niggling worry ate away at me. Something wasn't right. I just couldn't put my finger on what that was.

Everyone took a seat at the table, and I suddenly felt like a bad hostess. Was a charcuterie tray appropriate for a meeting to discuss how to kill a nearly omnipotent supernatural force? Maybe Tyler could whip us up something with that impressive power of his.

I banished the thought as I propped my elbows up on the table. Seriously, he conjured the damn thing out of thin air! How in the hell did something like that even happen? I figured I'd have plenty of time to grill him for answers later, but damn, I wanted them now. My priority had to be Levi, however, and how to keep him safe.

"I don't see any point in wasting any more of anyone's time." I tried not to think about the dead body that lay on the floor behind us. "We need to kill the Délash before it kills Levi." Not to mention myself. "And to that end, what happens when we do kill it? Will they send another one? We need a plan, and we need it fast. He can't stay a prisoner at The Pit forever."

"Not even Merrick knows how to kill a Délash," Levi said. His voice quavered, and I couldn't help but wonder if it had anything to do with the wary glances he continued to cast toward Tyler. "The magic used to protect me inside the building was hard enough to manifest. Merrick couldn't do it on his own, and he put himself in danger by getting it done."

"Okay, so we start there." If I'd learned anything in the course of my existence, it was that there was always a way around, even if you couldn't go straight through. "Who helped Merrick with the magic to protect the building? Maybe we can use it to our advantage and manipulate it somehow to kill the damn thing."

"Jinn magic is meant to protect," Levi replied.

Tyler shook his head. "Not necessarily."

I didn't like the sound of that.

"A Délash is tough to kill, but it can be done. And it's not something the Synod will be able to manifest again for at least a while. The rules have to be followed, after all."

"Says the guy who dropped a scary supernatural doppelganger with a flick of his wrist and then conjured furniture out of thin air." I had a feeling that Tyler had crossed some sort of line by killing the Ifrit tonight.

Tyler gave me a wry smile. "I've thrown off the shackles of the Synod. I no longer follow their rules."

I had no idea what that meant, but I was sure I'd find out. Tyler certainly didn't seem to be lacking in the ego department. "So does that mean you can kill it?"

"I can." His confidence was damn near frightening. "With your help."

Well, shit. Why wasn't I surprised.

[20]

"My help?" I couldn't squelch the incredulousness of my own tone. "Don't get me wrong, I've got skills." I mean, I could be confident too, when the situation warranted it. "But not against something like that."

I'd tangled with the Délash. It's energy signature rivaled, if not surpassed, Tyler's in power. It was incorporeal and at the same time, could pack a supernatural punch. I didn't stand a chance against it.

"You have no idea what you're capable of, Darian." All eyes turned to me and I flushed with embarrassment. I didn't like the scrutiny. At all.

"No offence, but I'm pretty sure I do." Tyler might have remembered our history, but I didn't. His confidence in me seemed more than a little displaced. "I get the job done with sharp, pointy objects and the last time I checked, they didn't work on ominous clouds of doom."

"She's right," Levi said. "I don't know what you've got planned Ty, but weapons aren't going to do shit."

"Then it's magic." Camden leaned back in his chair as he regarded the rest of us. No one seemed to buy Tyler's claim that together, he and I could kill the unkillable and for that, I was grateful. We needed to be realistic in our approach. Overconfidence wouldn't get us anywhere. "Who did Merrick enlist to help him protect your building?"

"A Fae sorceress," Levi replied. "Human magick is too weak."

I'd seen some damn powerful humans wield their particular witchcraft. Then again, I knew some scary-powerful Fae. I wouldn't put it past one to have the skills necessary to deter the Délash with its power.

"Who do we know?" I'd acquainted myself with a few Fae over the years who might fit the bill in the power department. Reaver, the Guardian of the gateway from Faerie to the Human Realm being one of them. But I planned on leaving him in my back pocket unless absolutely necessary. "What about the Fae that helped Merrick?"

Levi shook his head. "She barely managed to protect the building. She's powerful, but not enough."

"I know a few," Camden replied. "None more powerful than any other Fae creature, but they might know someone . . . ."

Tyler remained strangely quiet, an enigmatic smile curving his full lips. Though I should have found his calm comforting, all it managed to do was unsettle me. I threw a stern gaze in his direction. "You're supposed to be the all-knowing one. Care to add something useful to the discussion?"

"You and I will take care of the Délash," Tyler replied. "End of discussion."

Tension thickened the air and I leaned forward in my chair which was, by the way, the most comfortable dining room chair I'd ever parked my butt on. Tyler could have given Xander a run for his money in the arrogance department right now, and somehow, that seemed out of character for him.

"Okay, fine. Let's just say for a moment, that I believe you and somehow, the two of us can kill this thing." I mean, Tyler had just killed a demon with a literal flick of his wrist. Who was I to doubt him? "In the meantime, how do we protect Levi? In my experience, when a hitman gets waxed, the client just brings in more hitmen."

"That's why Camden is here," Tyler said.

"Okay, sure. But he's got other things on his plate." Redmond and the Arx for starters. "He can't just put everything on the back-burner to keep an eye on Levi until we can manage to come up with a viable plan."

Tyler smiled. I wished he'd stop, though. My abs hurt from all of the flips and twists the simple expression evoked. "I don't plan on wasting Camden's time. We end this tonight."

"Tonight?" The incredulous word burst from my lips. "Are you fucking kidding me?"

Only Camden had the nerve to not appear shocked. Thank god, Levi had the good sense to look appalled.

"You can't do this tonight," Levi said. "There's no way. Darian's right. We need a plan—"

"No." The word brooked no argument. "Tonight. I've waited over a year for Darian to be ready. We do this now."

Levi's eyes widened but he clamped his mouth shut. Damn it, I wished I had some scrap of a memory of Tyler, so I'd know for sure whether his behavior was truly off or if I should've disregarded the lump of dread that settled in my stomach. And ready for what? I didn't feel ready for shit right now.

"Look, I'm all for getting this taken care of as soon as possible. But the Délash isn't the only problem." My gaze slid to Levi and I sighed. "There's a contract out on Levi. I might not be the only professional it's been offered to. And how can you be so sure that killing the Délash will be the end of it?" Tyler needed to be more forthcoming if he wanted to win me over. "If the Synod wants him dead, simply killing off one assassin isn't going to deter them."

Sure, the Synod sent their sentient doom cloud out to kill Levi, but they'd contacted Misha as well. The crafty Fae had been afraid of whoever had contacted him. Afraid enough to push me into acting without vetting Levi first. Killing the Délash didn't necessarily guarantee Levi's safety.

"I know more than you think, Darian." Tyler leveled his strange hazel gaze on me and my breath caught at the power reflected in their depths. "You have to trust me. There are no other contracts. If we kill the Délash, Levi *will* be safe."

I let out the breath I'd been holding in a quick rush. I didn't like any of this one damn bit, but I'd lost control of the situation the second he'd knocked down the door tonight. I cast a quick glance at both Camden and Levi, unsure of what my next move should be. If I put my trust in Tyler, I might be dooming us all without the help of a big, black cloud.

"All right." I had no choice at this point but to take a leap of faith. If Tyler was to me all of things everyone assured me of, trust was my only option. "Let's do this."

Tyler pushed his chair out and stood. I don't know what I expected, but it wasn't to jump straight to action. I followed suit, still a little shell-shocked over the events of the night. My eyes found the dead body still littering my floor and my lip curled. Not exactly how I wanted to break in the new digs.

"I'm not doing anything until you take care of that," I said with a jerk of my chin. Tyler's eyes followed and landed on the grotesque form of the Ifrit.

His eyes drifted shut and when they opened again a rainbow of color flashed in his irises. My breath fogged in the resulting cold and before I could snap my astonished jaw shut, the damned thing simply disappeared.

Into thin air.

Gone.

Poof!

What the actual fu—

"Darian," Tyler's impatience interrupted my thoughts. "We need to go."

I didn't appreciate his tone any more than I appreciated being expected to blindly follow. I had a lot to process and the night wasn't even close to being over yet.

"Where?" I let my own annoyance sink into the single word.

"Away from here," Tyler replied. "It'll be safer for Levi and Camden."

Tyler wasn't worried about finding the Délash because he already knew it was tracking us. The thing was likely not far from the house and the realization didn't sit well with me.

"You threw us to the wolves." Deep down, I knew his actions tonight were completely out of character. I didn't need Levi's or Camden's concerned expressions as confirmation. "Why?"

"That's where you're wrong, Darian." Tyler leaned in close and my pulse skittered with a mixture of fear and excitement. "We're the wolves. Let's go."

God help me, I followed as he turned his back and headed for the doorway.

The crisp, freshwater scent air of Lake Union hit my nostrils and I took a cleansing breath. I stepped over the remnants of the threshold that littered the breezeway. Hopefully, Camden and Levi could piece together what was left of the door until I could get it fixed. Tyler raised his right hand and a commotion drew my attention. I turned to see the obliterated door repair itself, *Bewitched* style. Wow. Samantha Stevens didn't have shit on the all-powerful genie walking beside me.

"How did you do that?" I'd seen my share of magical creatures and I'd never encountered one with a scrap of power to match Tyler's.

He flashed me a sexy, wicked grin. "I can do anything you want."

I let out a snort. Tyler turned toward the waterfront and I followed. "Okay."

"You'll see."

Cryptic. The city sounds mingled with the gentle lap of water.

The city was never entirely dark, but the shadows that surrounded us seemed blacker and bigger than usual. The shadows usually gave me comfort, but tonight they seemed ominous. Threatening. And I couldn't shake the fear that I might just leave this world for good tonight.

"Why haven't I been able to see or hear you until tonight?" It seemed too simple that I could wish my headaches away and suddenly Tyler and I could occupy the same space. "I mean, if I could wish for anything I wanted, why not tell me to do that a long time ago? It would have saved all of us a lot of trouble."

"You weren't ready," Tyler said. "You wouldn't have believed me, and the magic wouldn't have obeyed your command."

"What makes you think I believe you now? And what makes you think I'm ready?"

"That we're together right now, answers both of those questions."

He had me there.

"Did you make my headaches go away? And when am I going to get my memories back?"

Tyler chuckled. "You made your headaches go away. And you'll get your memories back when you're ready to have them."

Seemed like a lot depended on my "being ready."

"Seriously? I've been ready for over a year." I couldn't help but poke a hole in his seemingly waterproof ego. "I thought you said you could do anything I wanted."

A frown marred his gorgeous face. "Maybe I needed to be ready, too."

We continued to walk in relative silence for a tense twenty or so minutes. I waited for an ambush, but nothing came out of the shadows to obliterate us. We'd put a safe distance between us and Levi and soon, Pier 57 and the wheel came into view. With each step, the anxiety that pulled my muscles taut began to loosen. Despite my misgivings, Tyler's presence comforted me. I knew I was safe as long as he was close.

"Really, though, how did you get rid of my headaches?"

"You got rid of your headaches."

Yeah, he'd already said as much. I didn't buy it. "Somehow, I doubt that. If it had been within my power to get rid of them, I wouldn't have suffered through a year of my head feeling like it was splitting in two."

"I'm sorry about that." His voice went low and dangerous. "I never expected it to be so long. I'd thought you'd figure it out sooner."

"Figure what out?"

He smiled. "The magic words."

If only all of life's problems could be solved with a couple of magic words. "Abracadabra?" I asked, hoping to lighten the mood.

Tyler stopped and turned toward me. "I wish."

Guess he wasn't interested in levity.

I can do anything you want. Could it really be that simple? Tyler's eyes delved into mine and I lost myself in the mysterious hazel depths. Delicious heat flooded me and my mouth parted on a breath. Tyler reached out, his thumb brushed my cheek and traced the outline of my jaw before settling on my bottom lip. The yearning in his expression squeezed my heart in a fist. I'd felt that same yearning so many times over the past year, though I hadn't known exactly what it was I needed to make me whole.

I knew now. And the emotion surging through me was damn near overwhelming.

"I'm yours, Darian," Tyler said, low. "Forever."

Mine? What did that even mean? I was struck with another strange sense of déjà vu, as though we'd had this exact conversation before.

"Some of my friends don't trust you," I remarked. I needed to deflect and not think about the heat that swamped me. "Why is that?"

"Xander," Tyler scoffed. "I'd really hoped he'd stay in Banff where he belongs."

So the animosity went both ways. I wasn't surprised. Tyler seemed just as arrogant and possessive as the Shaede King. Though again, I was struck by the feeling that his current behavior was out of character for Tyler. I couldn't see myself caring for him in the way everyone I claimed I did if he was simply another high-handed, overprotective blowhard.

"Stop."

Tyler's command cemented me in my tracks. The fine hairs at the back of my neck stood on end and a nervous tingle ran the length of my spine. We were being watched.

"Okay." I dropped my voice to barely a whisper. "What now?"

The giant Ferris wheel on Pier 57 loomed above us, its colorful lights flashing and undulating over the heads of the usual throngs of people out for the evening. This was a terrible idea, luring the Délash out into public where we could possibly get some innocent human hurt, or worse, killed. The supernatural world existed alongside—but apart—from humanity. I was already in deep shit with Redmond and his Arx. A battle royale in the middle of one of the busiest areas of the city wasn't going to score me any brownie points with anyone.

Tyler turned toward me. My heart slithered into my throat and my stomach twisted into a pretzel. He reached out and my body tensed. Electricity sparked in the air between us and I sucked in a sharp breath. This was my other half. The missing piece to my puzzle, and the person who filled the empty hole in my heart. And yet, that worrying thought wouldn't let go of the space it occupied in the back of my mind.

Beware.

He leaned in close, and I inhaled the warm cinnamon-sugar scent of him. His mouth brushed the outer shell of my ear and I shivered.

"Trust, Darian," he whispered. "Together, we can accomplish anything."

I pulled sharply back. "Trust?" I was supposed to kill a nearly unkillable being with trust? "That's it?"

I was so focused on Tyler that I'd dedicated all of my senses to him. Stupid to let my guard down. And when the dark cloud of the Délash struck me, sending me a good fifty feet from where I'd stood, I landed with the crack of broken bones that I one hundred percent deserved for my foolishness.

We were as good as dead.

[21]

As my femur, arm, and hip bones began to knit back together, my only thought was getting to my feet and luring the Délash far from the crowds of people. Tyler had chosen the worst possible location for a fight and he wanted me to trust him? Right now, I was having a hard time not charging toward him and laying a solid right hook to his gorgeous face.

There'd be time for that later, though. At the moment, I had an omnipotent cloud of doom to deal with.

Everything hurt, but I willed myself to stand. The magical daggers hummed at my sides, and my katana waited to be drawn from the sheath at my back. But they'd be useless against the Délash, and likewise, I couldn't hide from it in my incorporeal form. The creature hovered over me, the glowing red orbs of its eyes sizing me up before it swirled in a dark whirlwind and ascended into the night sky.

I was helpless. Dead in the water.

Oh, but there was always that *trust* Tyler had mentioned.

Wonderful.

The Délash created its own whirlwind, and my hair whipped at my face. Through the strands, I caught sight of Tyler striding toward me, murder written in the hard lines of his face. I held out a staying hand and shouted over the wind, "We have to protect the people on the pier!"

Tyler kept his laser focus on me and raised his left hand. An iridescent bubble surrounded us, effectively closing us in with the very thing that was trying to kill us. Well, at least the innocent bystanders were protected. Now I could focus on my impending death, rather than worry about who I might inadvertently take down with me.

Yay!

I thought about Raif. About Asher and Misha. About Brakae, Guardian of the Faerie Realm and my responsibility to protect. I thought about Xander and even Anya. I was about to die and I wouldn't be able to say goodbye to those I held dear. I wouldn't be able to apologize to those under my care. The Délash let out an enraged shriek as it hit the top of the dome Tyler created and changed its trajectory, diving straight toward me.

I thought about Tyler. And my heart sank with the regret that I'd never regain the memories of him that I'd lost.

I'd never know what he'd meant to me.

Trust, Darian. Together we can accomplish anything.

Even if I could get myself to take that fall, how could we possibly win?

The swirling mass of black increased in velocity as the Délash whooshed back to earth, toward me. Tyler's gaze went skyward and his form blurred as he moved faster than my eye could track. One second he was fifty yards away, and the next—five feet from me.

He wasn't fast enough for the Délash, however. The boiling black cloud placed itself between us, its obvious goal to keep us separated. Maybe there was more to that whole trust thing than I was willing to admit.

I couldn't see around it, past it, or through it. For something ethereal, the damned thing was remarkably solid. It ballooned in size, no longer as big as a sedan. The inky blackness spread, consuming every inch of space in the sphere that contained us until I couldn't see my own hand in front of my face.

Tyler's voice intruded into my mind as though he spoke against my ear. *Trust.*

If he knew me in the way that he claimed, inside and out, he'd know that trust wasn't something that came easily to me. Especially when I was preoccupied trying not to die.

Trust what? He'd managed to plant his thought in my head, was it so farfetched to think that he could, in turn, hear mine?

The Délash burst into hundreds of seeking tendrils before I could form another coherent thought. Tyler was somewhere close. Perhaps right next to me. But the darkness permeated everything. Stole the breath from my lungs, the sound from my ears. My limbs went numb and I couldn't trust my own eyes as I stared at the black tentacles that writhed against an even blacker backdrop to squeeze me tight.

"Ty-ler." My voice rasped through my constricted throat.

The Délash let loose a venomous hiss that pierced my ears like a thousand needles. A strangled scream lodged in my chest and I squirmed in its wraithlike grip as I fought to reach my daggers, desperate for something—anything—that might lend me some measure of strength.

Stars swam in my vision as my chest grew tighter still. The empty red slashes of the Délash's eyes swam in and out of focus as my arms dropped to my sides, useless. We didn't stand a chance. Or at least, I didn't.

Looked like the Synod would get its way. And the Arx, too.

For all his arrogant optimism, Tyler was wrong. We were going to die.

Light burst through the darkness. White and blinding. My eyes squeezed shut against its brilliance and the black tendrils of the Délash released their grip on me. I dropped to the ground, gasping for air as a broken rib popped back into place. The light radiated from Tyler in beams that cut through the diaphanous mass of the Délash, severing its twining limbs and leaving pools of glistening black on the pavement.

He walked through the darkness, and it cowered in his presence.

I drew another ragged breath in through my nostrils and it shuddered on the way out. My entire body ached. I needed to rest. To let my body heal. But the fight was far from over. I braced a palm on the pavement, cold as ice. My breath fogged the air and the chill sent a shiver over my skin. Tyler noticed none of it. His focus was on me and the evil black cloud still intent on my death.

I was starting to believe that if anyone could kill this thing, Tyler could.

Where he passed, the dark moved back in to occupy the space that contained us. For every wisp of darkness Tyler severed, two grew from the Délash's massive form. I pushed myself to stand, willed myself to ignore the cold that caused my body to quake and my teeth to chatter.

I stumbled and Tyler reached out to steady me. His skin was nearly blue from the cold but he showed no other sign that it affected him. He pulled me tight against him and his mouth settled at my ear.

"I need you. I can't do this on my own."

My heart wrenched at the plea, but how in the hell could I possibly help? The usual tricks at my disposal were useless against the Délash.

"I don't know what to do."

"You do." His voice was a warm caress that banished the chill "Just let go."

How? Did he even know me? I was a total control freak. Letting go was practically impossible.

Tyler had disrupted the Délash's overwhelming presence, but he hadn't banished it. And the creature wasn't going to give up without a fight. Darkness billowed once again to swallow Tyler's light. Focusing on letting go took a back seat to survival as the creature's nearly corporeal form shoved into me to separate me from Tyler. I flew backward and landed with a bone jarring impact that forced the air from my lungs. The Délash didn't let up, but charged at me. It seemed to concentrate its efforts on the weakest of its opponents: me. Not gonna lie, it bruised my ego a little.

I hate not having the upper hand.

Before I could get my ass up off the ground, the Délash charged again. I instinctively raised my hands to shield my face and the cloud of sentient energy stopped short before making contact again. I peeked through one eye to find it studying me, or more to the point, my hand. It leaned in close as though sniffing, and reared back as though shocked before letting out an enraged shriek that made my eardrums pop. Cold pulsed from the ring that encircled my right thumb and a fragment of memory flashed in my mind. *Nys'Asdar*. A gift from Tyler that I'd been unable to remove since the day I'd put in on.

"You don't like this?" I shouted over the din of the Délash's screams as I shook my fist at it. I had no idea what the ring was or what it could do, but I was sure as hell going to bluff until I figured it out. I brandished the ring like it was a weapon, part of me expecting a laser beam to shoot out of it. I mean, it worked for Green Lantern, right?

Nothing.

My confidence deflated, but I wasn't giving up yet. Somewhere within the total blackout, I heard Tyler's shouts, though I couldn't make out what he said. Boiling black surrounded me, filling my nostrils with a sulfuric burn and stealing the air from my lungs. I left my corporeal form, joining with the darkness that threatened me, but it didn't faze the Délash. Its inky tendrils wrapped around me once again, lifting me up, up, up, until my concentration flagged and I came back to my solid self. I couldn't see the ground through the darkness, but I had to be dangling at least fifty feet in the air. At the moment I regained my corporeal body, the Délash released its grip on me. My stomach launched into my throat as I fell. Even with supernatural healing, this was going to hurt like a bitch.

I tried to return to shadow, but fear shut me down. Instead, I squeezed my eyes shut and waited for impact. *Stop, stop, stop, stop, stop, stop, stop.*

My prayers were answered as a force reached out and halted me in midair, inches from the pavement. My body bounced from the abrupt standstill, as though I was attached to an invisible bungee. The sensory deprivation was starting to get to me. I couldn't see, couldn't hear, couldn't fight, and now, I was barely in charge of myself. Cold flared from the ring on my thumb, veining outward until it pulsed throughout my body. Usually, I hated being cold, but this was different. Almost comforting. Like a cold cloth on a fevered forehead. Had Tyler saved me from hitting the ground?

Or . . . had I done it myself?

I dropped face first to the asphalt with a painful groan. Keeping myself from splatting on the pavement had happened almost effortlessly, but as soon as I put some thought into how it had happened, I'd apparently broken the spell.

Maybe I shouldn't have been so quick to discount Tyler's blind belief that we could accomplish anything. Well, with the help of a magic ring, anyway. I gave myself over to the fight, not allowing myself to overthink or dwell on the hows, whys, and whatifs.

Speaking of . . . where was the mysterious genie? The dome that contained us wasn't too big—fifty yards or so in diameter— but the Délash must've been one hell of a multitasker to keep us apart. Which meant if I was fighting for my life, chances were, so was he.

If the Délash could be in two places at once, I needed to keep it occupied and disrupt its concentration to keep most of its attention on me. It was the only way we'd stand a chance. I drew the enchanted daggers from the sheaths at my sides. They might be useless, but they'd keep me on the offensive and it was time for the momentum to shift.

Both my katana and the daggers were gifts from Xander and among my most prized possessions. The grips fit perfectly to my palms and hummed with magic and bloodlust. They were an extension of me, bonded to me, and could never be used against me. And they yearned to kill.

I charged the Délash, focusing on the part of it that was the darkest. I crossed my forearms high over my head and slashed downward at the most opaque part of its roiling form. The daggers vibrated with hunger, as though they'd tasted its magic and wanted more. The Délash let out an angry growl and retreated a few feet from where it hovered.

The damn thing couldn't bleed, but that didn't mean it couldn't sustain damage. My confidence bolstered and I charged again, no longer testing the waters but ready to dive headfirst into the depths. I slashed and stabbed, spun, and switched the daggers' grips as I brought my arms down and jabbed behind me before dropping to my knees, dragging the blades through the seemingly incorporeal darkness. The Délash's shout of pain was like the roll of thunder, and I felt its force in the center of my chest. Cold chased up my arm and whether my ring, or the daggers, or both had anything to do with the damage I inflicted, I held on to the advantage, refusing to give the creature a reprieve.

"Darian!" Tyler's shout sounded miles, rather than yards, away. "Keep it on the defensive!"

I rolled my eyes. What in the hell did he think I was doing? The Délash didn't seem to understand verbal communication which gave us an advantage. It was nothing more than magic given a purpose, and that purpose was to kill.

It was hell-bent on putting an end to me and came at me again with more force. It knocked me off my feet and sent me thirty or so yards into the air. I had my wits about me now, though. I was laser focused and let my body turn to shadow, swooping through the air and regaining my body as my booted feet hit the ground.

I spun the daggers in my grip, almost disappointed the Délash wouldn't appreciate the show. Shit talk, impressive maneuvers, not even my own Shaede magic affected the mindless creature. It honestly took a lot of the fun out of the fight. But at the same time, it kept me from worrying about anything other than charging forward and doing whatever damage I could.

I cut, slashed, spun, and stabbed. The dark cloud whirled and boiled, the red glowing orbs that served as eyes the only thing in its gossamer form that never moved. Cold chilled my skin and my breath fogged the air, but it no longer affected me. Ice crystals webbed along the blades of my daggers, glistening like threads of diamonds in the dark that surrounded me. Tyler's voice called out again, almost inaudible and even farther away. I shut him out completely. Couldn't allow myself to worry about anything but the weapons in my hands and the enemy before me.

I would no longer allow this creature—or anyone else—to meddle in my life. It was time to take back control.

The daggers guided me, their instincts in battle nearly infalli-ble. I gave myself over to the magic that lived within them and let fire fight fire. Twining tendrils of black reached out for me, and my daggers sliced through them before they could wrap them-selves around me, severing the magic before it could make contact. A scream of frustration rent the darkness and it fueled me to fight even harder.

My mind went almost blank as I gave myself completely over to battle. The Délash tried like hell to get its snakelike limbs around me, but my daggers were faster. They sliced through the darkness and the various appendages exploded in clouds of char-coal dust. The Délash raged and growled. It expanded and contracted, its mass boiled, and its red eyes glowed like menacing rubies. The cold that chilled my skin frosted the air and formed into ice crystals that fell like snow from the sky. My limbs ached with fatigue and a sharp pain tugged at my chest from my labored breaths. I didn't let up. I couldn't. This ended now.

"Die you son of a bitch!"

The ice turned to snow. Fat, wet flakes clung to the Délash's form, muting its overwhelming darkness and clearing some of the sootiness from the air. The demon cloud lurched and wound itself around my ankles as it pulled my feet out from under me and jerked me up into the air once again. Below me, Tyler's form emerged from the now gray fog.

He didn't need weapons to be deadly, just a wave of that magical arm of his. The snow turned to a blizzard and the Délash let go of its grip on me as it whirled in confusion. I floated to the ground, nothing but shadow. We had it completely on the defensive, but would our efforts kill the damn thing?

No longer separated, we fought side by side. We divided the Délash's attention, never giving it a clear target. It tried to surround us with its darkness, but the blizzard we created kept it confined to a compact mass. Our unrelenting assault contained the creature, shrunk it, until the darkness that had given way to gray turned into a blinding white-out with only a small sphere of black to mar the pristine wintry backdrop. Outside of our little world, the rest of Seattle went about its business. Had Tyler somehow hidden us from their view or did they watch, rapt at the real-life snow globe beyond the pier.

The fight seemed never ending. Tyler and I stood back-to-back, guarding each other between attacks. Despite its seemingly weakened state, the Délash refused to give up and there didn't appear to be any way to kill it. My frustration mounted until it became a physical thing. Every muscle in my body tightened. My stomach curled into an angry knot. I visualized the Délash exploding into dark sand, and I shouted my anger and helplessness at its empty red eyes.

"I want you to die! Right. Fucking. Now!"

A shockwave of cold burst from where Tyler and I stood. It hit the Délash and the creature exploded into millions of tiny particles that fell like ash from the sky. My entire body went numb from the cold, and I dropped to my knees as a wave of power washed over me. A slow throbbing began from where the ring encircled my thumb. I couldn't catch my breath. I had to be hypothermic and my eyes drifted shut as the exhaustion finally took its toll. Tyler grabbed me under the arms before I fell over and hauled me up against him.

"S-s-so c-c-c-cold," I said through chattering teeth.

"It'll pass," he said close to my ear.

"Not fast enough."

Our surroundings blurred and swam in and out of focus as cold and exhaustion overtook me. I tried to hold on to consciousness, but it was a battle I was going to lose.

[22]

I woke to the glorious warmth of a down comforter. It enclosed me in a cozy cocoon that I never wanted to leave. Back in my bed. Home. In the only place I'd ever felt truly safe. My teeth no longer chattered, and I flexed my hands and wiggled my toes, glad I could once again feel my limbs. If I could, I'd stay in bed forever, warm and safe, with no worries whatsoever. Light filtered in from a high window, not my familiar skylight. My brow furrowed as I took in my surroundings and cleared the haze of confusion that clung to my mind. Not my treasured loft. I was at my new place. The place that Tyler had created for me.

The home I'd known, my sanctuary, was gone. Blown to bits. By the Arx and Mitchell Redmond.

I planned to hold him accountable for it, too.

Moments passed and more of the fog cleared as the events of the past hour or so—or could it have been longer ago—became clear in my memory. Tyler. The Délash. And the creature's death that I still didn't understand.

I stared up at the exposed metal beams of the rafters. Dust motes swam in the light that filtered in through the skylights. When we'd left to fight the Délash, the loft bedroom hadn't been completed yet. Had I been knocked out for days? Or, had Tyler simply whipped up a finished bedroom, like he'd done with the dining room table. Neither thought comforted me.

I pushed myself up in bed. God, everything hurt. No way had I been out for days. This was fresh-from-the-fight pain. Muscles I didn't even know I had ached. I wanted to sit in a boiling hot shower for at least a couple of hours. And then, head straight back to bed. Exhaustion didn't even begin to explain the soul-deep weariness that blanketed me.

I should have bounced back by now. What in the hell had happened to me during the fight?

I eased out of bed, wobbly as newborn fawn. I steadied myself on the bed—remarkably similar to the one from my old place— and made my way to the railing that overlooked the rest of the house. Tyler sat at the kitchen bar, a cup of coffee in his right hand, his cell on the counter in front of him. He studied something on the screen, his attention undivided.

"How are you feeling?"

Well, maybe not entirely undivided. "Like someone ran over me with a semitruck."

He kept his attention focused on his screen. "It'll pass."

Wow. So much concern for my wellbeing. How could I not have fallen head over heels in love with him? Was I missing something here?

"Great." I held onto the railing and inched my way toward the metal stairs, taking each one at a time. No way was I going to risk my legs giving out and rolling my way down. Tyler cast a brief glance my way before turning his attention back to the phone screen. I guess romance wasn't dead after all. His concern for me was truly touching.

The house was entirely finished. Like, *Better Homes and Gardens* photoshoot ready. And fit my style to a tee. "Why bother with the construction crew?" I asked as I rounded the bar into the kitchen. "I mean, seems like a waste of time and money when you just took the ball and ran with it. Can you seriously whip up anything you want?"

"They were working too slow," Tyler replied. "I'd been trying to keep up appearances, as well as a safe distance, but I got impatient, and distance isn't an issue anymore."

Impatient was an understatement. And seriously, someone who cared about "keeping up appearances" didn't instigate a melee in the middle of a busy city street. "How's Levi? And where is he?" I'd missed all of the aftermath and hated being out of the loop.

"He's home," Tyler said. "And safe. I have some things to discuss with Merrick but he's no longer in danger from the Synod."

I let out a slow breath. "How can you be sure? I was contracted to kill Levi. Who knows how many other professionals were offered the same contract?"

"There aren't any others," he assured me. "I took care of everything." The hard edge to Tyler's voice raised my hackles. Somehow it didn't suit him. "And I took care of Misha as well."

"What in the hell is that supposed to mean?" I let my annoyance seep through my tone. Whatever our history—or my feelings for him—was, I didn't like people meddling in my personal life. No exceptions. "How do you know about Misha? And took care of him how? I didn't ask you to butt into my business."

Tyler finally looked up from his phone and set it on the table. "You are my business, Darian. And you shouldn't have been so quick to trust Misha. His loyalties follow money and nothing else."

"I have no reason not to trust him." Aside from this recent job involving Levi, he'd never steered me wrong. Misha had taken good care of me. I'd begun to consider him a friend. Sort of. "And besides, Xander trusts him." No way would the Shaede King set me up with someone who intended to harm me.

Tyler let out a derisive snort. "All the more reason *not* to trust him."

The animosity between Tyler and Xander was real. They were both high-handed pains in the ass as far as I could tell. I was surprised they weren't thick as thieves.

"What did you tell him?"

His gaze met mine. The hazel depths hardened. "That the Synod's contract was null and void and anyone who even tried to lay a finger on Levi would answer to me." The screen lit up on his phone and he flipped it over, face down, on the counter. "Oh, and I told him you would no longer require his services as a handler."

Son of a bitch. Hot anger washed away the dregs of weariness that had clung to my limbs. "You'll have to forgive me, since I don't remember anything about how our relationship worked, but no one decides what's in my best interest except for *me*. Understood?"

A corner of Tyler's mouth hitched with amusement while my eyebrows arched at the audacity.

"You think I'm kidding?"

"Not at all," Tyler said through suppressed laughter. His smile grew, transforming his face and banishing the guardedness that had me so on edge. "Gods, I've missed you, Darian."

"I want to remember." I'd come into the kitchen to pour a bowl of Honey Nut Cheerios and slowly ease myself into this conversation with him. But since Tyler wasn't the only one with the patience of a toddler, I jumped right in. "And I'm tired of waiting."

"You're the only one standing in the way of it now," Tyler said. "You can remember any time you want."

I scoffed. I've had the power all along, huh? "Like Dorothy trying to leave Oz?"

Tyler laughed. "Sort of. But you don't need ruby slippers to get it done."

I was so tired of vague explanations. "How?"

"The same way you killed the Délash," Tyler said. "Manifest it."

"Manifest it," I deadpanned. What was this, some sort of meditative, progressive therapy session? "Just like that?"

"Yup." Tyler leveled his gaze, no longer smiling. "I told you, everything is different now. There are no more rules to restrict us. Our bond is unbreakable and together, we can do *anything*."

An unpleasant shiver traveled the length of my body with that last ominous word. I'd told the Délash I wanted it to die and . . . . Poof! It had exploded into dust. An unkillable entity, gone, because I'd willed it so.

"Anything?" The concept of omnipotence was dangerous, not to mention hard to grasp.

Tyler nodded. "The rules no longer apply."

"What rules?"

"Take your memories back, Darian," Tyler said. "You have everything you need to do it."

"I'm going to take a shower." I no longer had an appetite, and the conversation had become more disconcerting than comforting. I needed to clear my head and put a little distance between me and Tyler.

"I think you'll like it," Tyler replied as he scooped his phone up and swiped his thumb across the screen. "Unlimited hot water."

"Great." I didn't want to know by what means he'd acquired unlimited hot water. The unease that something wasn't right with Tyler wouldn't go away. Unlike with the Ifrit, I knew in my heart that this wasn't an imposter, but something had changed. And I wouldn't know what it was until I got my damned memories back.

The bathroom was better than I could have imagined. Spacious, with a heated tile floor, and a floor-to-ceiling glass enclosed steam shower big enough for two. Multiple shower heads poked out from the walls and ceiling. Luxurious. I turned on the water and set the steam setting to eighty-five degrees before closing the door and undressing. When the glass rectangle filled with a glorious white fog, I stepped inside.

And let out a long, pleasured sigh.

My god. I could consider overlooking the danger of omnipotence for this shower. The heat enveloped me, soaked into my pores, and banished the cold that still clung to my skin from the fight with the Délash. My muscles relaxed, and I lowered myself to the tiled bench seat. If the hot water was unlimited, might as well take advantage of it.

My mind wandered and I let it go where it wanted. I thought of Raif and Xander, the loneliness I'd felt before they found me and took me from the shadows. Of my life before Azriel had made me into what I now was. The many battles I'd fought since. Adversities and enemies overcome. And of Tyler.

Somehow, I knew Tyler had taught me how to trust. How to let down my guard and open up. How to love.

"I want to remember."

The words slipped from my lips and a cold rush of power spread over me. I slumped against the shower wall as the chilly vortex of power sucked me down a swirling dark drain. I reached out blindly, desperate for a handhold as the sensation of falling overwhelmed me. My mind's eye filled with images. My first interaction with Tyler, the moment he slid the mysterious silver ring on my thumb, our many jobs together, our blossoming relationship and the love that I'd pushed away for so long. I thought of the large bear that protected me when Azriel wanted to kill me, the reassurance of his presence when he took me from Padma's dungeon, and the unconditional love and protection that Tyler always offered me. All of it rushed back in a tidal wave that stole my breath and caused my temples to throb. As the pain ebbed, so did the cold, and once again the steamy heat of the shower soothed my skin and aching head. My hands slid from the shower wall and the bench to cradle my face as I began to sob. The rush of memories and the emotions attached to them were too much. The influx too sudden and instant. I cried until I could no longer catch my breath as I slid from the bench onto

213

the shower floor and drew my knees up tight to my body. I hugged myself as though I could somehow hold in the emotion that burst from me like water from a broken dam. I drew in ragged, stuttering breaths to calm my racing heart as I swept away tears that sluiced down my face with the hot water that cascaded over me.

I'd regained everything I'd lost. I was complete.

And yet, I felt more fractured than ever.

Minutes passed and I didn't move. I soaked it all in, every memory I'd lost, reliving each as though they'd just happened. I reexperienced the pain, the pleasure, and the joy. The void in my heart was full, but with my reclaimed memories came confirmation of all my current fears.

Something was very wrong with Tyler.

When I finally felt strong enough to stand, I reached for the faucet and turned off the water. I breathed in the steam for a few more minutes before turning that off as well, and even then, I lingered in the enclosure for another half hour or so before finally leaving the shower and wrapping myself in an oversized, fluffy white towel. I padded from the bathroom and shivered as the cooler temperature of the house kissed my still damp skin.

Tyler looked up from his phone. A wry smile curved his handsome lips. He knew. Without me saying a word, he knew what had happened in the shower.

The rules no longer apply.

Cold dread congealed in my chest. The Jinn/Charge bond came with a very strict set of rules, one of which that wishes based on wants couldn't be granted. I *wanted* the Délash dead, and it disintegrated into dust. I *wanted* my memories back, and they flooded my mind and heart. I didn't have to wish, and likewise, Tyler no longer had to grant or deny those wishes. Was it really possible that any frivolous thing I wanted, I could have? I gazed down at the ring that encircled my thumb and shivered. *Nys'Asdar.* A piece of Tyler's soul. His being. And his power. Somehow, through our bond and the ring on my thumb, we had broken all of the rules and I had no doubt, we would be made to pay for it.

Tyler abandoned his perch on the barstool and rushed toward me. He seized me in an unyielding embrace but it was me who closed the last small distance between us, putting my mouth to his, desperate, searching, and hungry. My arms wound around his neck and my lips parted. Emotion swelled in my chest as I held him tight, reveled in his taste, his homey smell, the firm pressure of his lips and the silky glide of his tongue.

He reached for the towel and tugged it away before cupping my breasts in his cool palms. My nipples hardened and goose-bumps dotted my flesh. Tyler had always been the cold to my heat. But as my left palm came to rest on his chest, the chill vanished and I no longer felt that contrast. I had always thought of myself as the Yin to his Yang, but what now? Before I could contemplate the complexities of such a seemingly small thing, Tyler lifted me in his arms and crossed the kitchen to the iron staircase that climbed the west wall to the loft.

I lost myself in his kisses, only vaguely aware when he laid me down on the bed. I drank him in, enjoying every inch of Tyler as he peeled off his shirt, kicked off his shoes and socks, and shucked his pants and underwear. His urgency matched mine as he covered my body with his, skin-to-skin, our hearts beating in time.

Nothing else mattered. We were together again and the empti-ness in my soul was now filled. I didn't need to tell Tyler how I felt, and I didn't need him to tell me. There was no need for words. We were inextricably bound, two halves of a whole. The many problems and worries that scratched at the back of my mind quieted as Tyler's hands searched my body, reawakening passions that twined like wildfire through me. He took my lower lip between his teeth as he settled himself between my thighs. Our bodies moved in synchronicity and Tyler's mouth left mine to find the hollow of my throat as I arched into his thrusts. He braced an arm beside me and the other gripped the back of my neck. Our gazes locked and held as something powerful arced between us. My breath fogged the air as snowflakes formed above us and fell gently around the bed. Tyler murmured unintelligible words against my ear, a language so old it was all but forgotten. Magic saturated every particle of the air until its electric spark tingled on my skin to heighten my pleasure. My nails dug into his back and Tyler let loose a primal groan that sent me over the edge of my control. I gasped and cried out as sensation flooded me and Tyler followed right behind me, his own breath ragged as he finally came to rest on top of me.

Tears escaped from the corners of my eyes and ran in hot rivulets down the sides of my face. So overcome with emotion, I didn't know if I should be ecstatic or angry or maybe a little of both. So much time stolen from us. And at what cost?

No matter Tyler's confidence, I knew our business with the Synod wasn't over. Especially if they'd caught wind of the Arx and their concerns that I was somehow dangerous to the world.

Tyler buried his face in my hair and breathed deep. "I've missed your smell," he said, low. "And your taste. The way you feel, the sound of your voice." He let out a breath. "I felt dead without you."

"I know." And god, did I know. "I was empty without you."

"No one will ever separate us again," he whispered. "I promise you."

An anxious shiver traveled the length of my body. I ran my fingers through the silky soft strands of Tyler's coppery hair and willed myself to ignore the terrifying sense of foreboding. I kissed his forehead, the bridge of his nose, and his mouth, pulling away only after I was once again intoxicated by him. His hand wandered the length of my body and settled between my legs, replacing my anxiety with a shiver of delight.

"I'm not letting you out of this bed for at least twenty-four hours." His husky tone sent a rush of heat through my center. "We have a lot of lost time to make up for."

"Yes." I smiled through the words as I arched into his touch. "We do."

Redmond, the Synod, Xander, Raif, and the rest of the world could wait. Tomorrow. When the roar of memories and emotions finally dulled, and the tempest of our lovemaking quieted, I'd tackle the obstacles that lay before me. Tomorrow, I'd dissect and assess the change in Tyler that sent a flutter of fear through me.

Tomorrow was uncertain. Tomorrow would bring reality crashing down on me once again. Tomorrow, everything could and likely would change.

But for today, for these few and fleeting hours, my life was going to belong to *me*.

ACKNOWLEDGMENTS

First and foremost, I want to thank my amazing agent, Natanya Wheeler. I've had more than a few ups and downs since my writing journey started, and she's been by my side and supported me through it all. Her faith in me has kept me going and I couldn't ask for a better partner in my writing journey. Thanks also to everyone at Nancy Yost Literary Agency for all of their hard work. It's a group effort and I love our team!

This book wouldn't have been finished without the support of Sarah Johnson and Cassidy Winter. Sarah, thank you for reigniting my spark and my love for the craft, for being my cheerleader, and crit partner, friend, and writer support system. You're amazing! Cassidy, thank you so much for being you and being my friend, and making sure my butt was in the chair and giving me the time I needed to get back on the horse. I wouldn't have finished without you giving me the opportunity and encouragement to write. Thanks also go out to Susan Harris and Zhalia Moon for beta reading and giving me your feedback. I appreciate you so much! I also owe a huge thank you to Niki Baxter for her keen eye and proofreading skills. I hope you continue to crack the whip over me and make sure I stay the course!

As always, I take full ownership of any and all mistakes. The buck stops here, but in my defense, sometimes it's tough to type with a cat on my lap.

ALSO BY AMANDA BONILLA

The Shaede Assassin Series

urban fantasy

Shaedes of Gray

Blood Before Sunrise

Crave the Darkness

Against the Dawn

Shadows at Midnight

Lost to the Gray (novella)

When Shadows Call (novella)

Comfort In Darkness (short story)

Secrets at Nightfall

The Last True Vampire Series (writing as Kate Baxter)

paranormal romance

The Last True Vampire

The Warrior Vampire

The Dark Vampire

The Untamed Vampire

The Lost Vampire

The Wicked Vampire

Shapeshifter novellas (writing as Kate Baxter)

paranormal romance

Stripped Bear

The Big Alpha in Town

In the Mood Fur Love

Thanks Fur Last Night

US Marshals Series (writing as Mandy Baxter)

contemporary romantic suspense

One Night More

One Kiss More

One Touch More

At Any Cost

Locked and Loaded

Texas Billionaire Series (writing as Mandy Baxter)

steamy contemporary romance

Tall, Dark, Billionaire Texan

The Billionaire Cowboy

The Billion Dollar Player

Rocked by the Billionaire

Christmas with the Billionaire Rancher

The Billionaire Single Dad

The Billionaire Heartbreaker

ABOUT THE AUTHOR

Amanda Bonilla lives in rural Idaho. She's a part-time pet wrangler, a full-time sun worshipper, and only goes out into the cold when coerced. When she's not writing, she's either reading or talking about her favorite books. For more about Amanda, visit www.amandabonilla.com.

Mandy Baxter (Amanda Bonilla pseudonym)
http://www.mandy-baxter.com
http://www.facebook.com/AuthorMandyBaxter
https://twitter.com/MandyJBaxter